At Chr
leave yo.
Spring. you came into my
life in our 11th year and I
have loved you every moment
since.

SIX

OF

ONE

VENDETTA

DeAna Cristina
2018

a novel by

DEANNA C. ZANKICH

For more information or to contact the copyright owner visit:

www.deannaczankich.com

ISBN: 978-0-9992935-3-9

"Sooner or later, everyone sits down to a banquet of consequences."

—Robert Louis Stevenson

Continued immediately from Volume One: *Blackwing*

CHAPTER ONE

THE VILLAGE IN Mammoth Lakes teemed with visitors moseying through the shops or dining at the many restaurants. Kathryn and Evan were tucked into a booth in their favorite Mexican place working on their second round of drinks. On the back of a paper placemat next to the remains of their nacho appetizer, Evan drew a crude map of Mount Iolite.

Kathryn watched him gnaw his plump bottom lip in concentration as he marked off the general store and the big pine tree behind it. That towering old conifer had dutifully held their succubus hag for nearly a quarter century, until it was weakened last summer by bark beetles. He drew the roads winding through the village to the lakefronts of Bonny and Robbin, using stars to place Henry's and his own houses between the two lakes.

Around the bend, he denoted the fork of Sylvan Road and Parker Drive, then indicated Jewel's house and the Parker Compound with more stars. A shaded triangle marked the spot inside the fork where the Brochs' cabin stood.

"While we're working on a plan to dispatch this old bitch," he said, "Henry and I were thinking about doing a widespread thatching of all our properties."

Kath raised a brow at his map. "You're planning to thatch the whole town?"

"I wish." He sipped his cold beer. "As we know, we can't do anything about public roads or land not privately owned, but a good solid thatch resonates quite a ways from its point of origin. Henry and I think that if we ramp it up around our respective plots of land, it might radiate wide enough between them to link together." He nodded to the map. "Henry's lot and mine are close enough to link, and all three of yours certainly are."

She squinted doubtfully. "You and HH are close, but there would still be a gap between you. You're three streets apart and separated by at least fifteen buildings."

"Hopefully the gap will be short enough to get across quickly. Besides, I'm less concerned about Henry and me than I am about our vessel and outcaster." Evan tapped his pen on the map over the compound. "All of our land has been thatched at some point, but Sonya's place never has. We've only done a sage clearing up there, which wouldn't be strong enough to keep out an old one like this. We should see to that first since she and Kellan are circling the runway for landing."

Thinking of all the tools of seduction her brother might currently be applying to Sonya's crumbling wall of restraint made Kathryn smile. "He asked her over for dinner tonight since I'd be out of his hair."

Evan scoffed playfully. "You're being awfully presumptuous, young lady—thinking you're spending the night with me."

She nudged his leg under the table, then slid her foot up the inside of his thigh where he caught it. He slipped his fingers underneath her pant leg in search of the bare skin above her ankle boot; he marveled at how smooth she felt.

"Oh, sugar, I'm all waxed and polished for you tonight." She batted her lashes, so relieved to be back on track with him. Since they'd reconnected, the months of turmoil inside her had finally settled. Kath had slept well for the first time since last fall.

Evan leaned across the table and kissed her, lingering to nibble her bottom lip. His blond whiskers tickled her as he whispered, "I've been waiting nine months to put bite marks all over your thighs, little lady."

Kath narrowed her eyes, but couldn't keep from smiling. "That's Blackwing to you, soldier."

"That's right." He sat back down, then raised his glass to her. "Our outcaster earned her spirit name from the great shaman. Congratulations."

"Thank you." She touched her Jack and Coke to his beer. "Now all I have to do is live up to it."

"He wouldn't have given it to you if you hadn't already done so. Just be proud and let it give you strength. That's the point."

"Our Gray Wolf should know."

Evan's full lips tilted in his signature lopsided grin, then he returned his attention to the map he'd drawn. "Does Kellan know he's supposed to stay inside Ginny's walls for the time being?"

"I didn't make a big thing of it, but your Peach knows he needs to wear a talisman if he leaves the property."

"Good. I'm mostly concerned about that road between your place and Sonya's. It's public land. If he walks her home, he'll be vulnerable—and in the dark. I'd rather he didn't do that."

Kath took out her phone. "I'll text him that he needs to drive her home instead. All our vehicles are protected."

"Including Sonya's?"

"Kell and I did a blessing on the Rover the other day. I hung a cat's eye and black onyx around her rearview." She tapped the message and sent it to her brother. "I don't want to freak Sonya out unnecessarily, though. For now, she's not in any danger."

Evan frowned. "Think about it, babe; if you were this hag, wouldn't you interfere with everyone close to your enemy? She's already come at me once."

Kath didn't want to consider the myriad ways this spirit could meddle with her unassuming new friend. She sighed, trying to stay positive. "Well, if my brother's charms are as potent as I think they are, he won't need to take Sonya home tonight at all."

Evan laughed. "You really think he's got her on the ropes?"

"If I were a betting person, I'd lay odds he bags that prize tonight. And if he wants to keep his limbs, he'd better be a goddamned gentleman about it."

Their meal arrived and they ordered another round. Evan said he and Henry were thinking of doing the thatching at Sonya's place in the morning.

"She'll need to be there for the blessing," he said. "It's her land; her intention sets the magic."

"I'll make sure she knows." As Kath worked on her bubbling hot enchiladas, she thought of the time she and a young Henry Hunter devised the ritual of thatching.

She and Kellan had just returned from college in the UK and were in Mount Iolite for the first time in five years. It was also the first time they'd ever stayed at the cabin without their father. So much had changed while they were away. They'd all grown into adults and that maturity informed their new ways of interacting with each other. But some things couldn't be altered by any amount of time.

✍

Kath still wasn't accustomed to overseeing things. She'd had to remind herself to lock up every night, to take the trash to the dumpster regularly, and that she and Kellan had to manage all the household duties by themselves.

Kellan, on the other hand, had taken to the new arrangement with aplomb. He'd already sorted out the leak under the bathroom sink, nailed down the loose floor boards in the kitchen, and patched the hole in the shed roof left by the heavy winter snowfall. He seemed in his element as caretaker of the cabin; he'd even commandeered Big Jackson's favorite chair.

But after being there for a week, they still hadn't found their footing with Evan. He'd come home from Afghanistan on a medical discharge from the Marines. His combat wounds had healed physically, but the experience had disturbed the topsoil of his good nature and turned him broody. Kath and her brother felt they no longer knew him. Their most precious Evan had become a mystery.

Henry had spent the most time with Evan since his return. She'd asked Henry over that day to continue a conversation they'd started about strengthening the protective wall Grandma Ginny already had around the cabin. Kath was also hoping he might enlighten her a bit on this stranger now walking in her sweetheart's skin.

Henry hauled a fully-loaded trash bag across the Brochs' backyard, depositing it near the picnic table. "I want to run an idea by you." He wiped his dusty hands on his jeans.

Kathryn brought two glasses of iced tea out from the kitchen and set them on the table. She eyed the trash bag. "What's all that?"

Henry grinned under the brim of his well-worn black cowboy hat. "That, my dear outcaster, is the raw materials to make a magical wall. At least that's the theory."

"*Cool.* Show me."

It was late August and he paused for a deep drink of the cold tea, then he opened the trash bag wide and tilted it so she could see the contents. To Kath, it appeared to be the remains of an overzealous garden clean-up.

"Yes, it's a bag of pine branches," Henry confirmed. "Needles and cones, too. I cut these at the back of my uncle's garden where they were scraping the rabbit fence, but I think it would be best to include trees growing on the property itself." He scanned their backyard then pointed to a young Jeffrey pine standing close to the shed. Its lowest branches reached all the way across the narrow path leading to the wood storage door. "That one right there could use a shave."

"I'll get Kell to do it. He'll be thrilled."

Henry smirked. "Is he bored already? You guys have only been here a week."

"No, he's just excited about being the man of the house for the first time. He's become Tim the Tool Man looking for things to fix."

Taking one of the branches out of the bag, Henry placed it on the picnic table then dug around for a pine cone and a handful of needles. "I'm thinking if we use a mixture of natural materials and magical elements, combined with an incantation we'll compose together, we can boost the strength of Ginny's boundary significantly. Maybe even make it impenetrable to spooks."

Kath had frowned at that. "It wouldn't interfere with Grandma, would it?"

Henry removed his hat and ran his forearm over his damp brow. "Virginia's not a visitor here, she is this place. But we'll get her blessing before we implement anything."

"Okay." She was already getting ideas for amalgamations of herbs and oils. "Let me get my kit." As she passed through the kitchen on her way to the living room, Kath heard Kellan talking on the phone upstairs in Big Jackson's room. She could tell by the purring tone of his voice that he was talking to Evan. Even though they were still finding their way in this new configuration, the core connection between her brother and Evan vibrated on the same frequency it always had. She wished the same were true for her.

Kath collected her kit from the breakfast nook and started back outside. As she passed under the stairs, she heard her brother say her name. She paused to listen.

"Kath misses you, man. She just wants to be close to you again." He'd listened to Evan respond and then, "she loves you; she's not gonna care about the scars."

Kath hadn't been so sure about that. Not because of any superficial issue, but simply because some monster had damaged Evan's beautiful body. The scars wouldn't bother her, they would enrage her. But as yet, Evan hadn't let her see them.

Back outside, she placed her kit on the table and sat down to open it. Henry had the branch, the cone and the needles in a neat pile and was carefully winding a length of twine around to keep it all together.

"If we do this right, I believe we can turn up the intensity of the protection whenever we want—or need to," he said.

"How do we make it stick, though? We can't leave a big ring of branches around the house all the time. Big Jackson'll lose his mind."

Henry gave her a knowing smile. "That's where the magic comes in. What oils do you use for protection spells?"

Kath reached into the apothecary drawer in her kit and took out the bottle ribboned with blue yarn. "Grandma swore by a combination of betony and lilac combined with sage smoke." She removed the tight cork and sniffed the bottle's contents for efficacy.

"Okay, how about a few drops of that, the sage smoke and a birch twig. We combine those in a bunch and place them end to end, then we say the words over the entire line."

"Starting at the directional corners," Kath said.

Henry nodded agreement. "That should set the magic into the earth under the thatch—then we can reuse these bundles until they get too dry."

"I like it."

Henry stood and headed for the shed. "Can I grab a clipper to get some birch twigs?"

"Sure, but be warned: I saw a spider the size of a Buick next to the dryer about an hour ago."

"I'll knock first."

While he attended to twig gathering, Kath took a small leather-bound journal and a charcoal pencil out of her kit. The spine of the journal had a thin sprig of periwinkle Lupine affixed to it. This had been Ginny's way of identifying her grimoires, which she'd dutifully kept since she began practicing at age fourteen. She had one for every year of her life, each identified by a different botanical element, and each entry denoted by the day and month it was written.

When she died, there were fifty-eight volumes—the last, of course, was incomplete. That journal and all the others had been willed to Kathryn with the instruction that she begin her own entries immediately after Ginny's last. It was Ginny's wish that the grimoires of the Broch Witches would link them across time.

Kathryn cleared her mind and focused her energy on words of protection. She jotted a few things, crossed one out, jotted another. By the time Henry returned with an armload of thin birch branches, she had a rough draft.

"How's this: The light runs deep below these branches. From sky to ground, this wall is sound. Evil halts at this gate and cannot pass."

Henry squinted in thought. "The sky to ground part's good, but we need to establish the land boundary clearly. We're protecting a specific area of owned property."

"Right, okay ..." Kath scribbled then read again. "From cornerstone to farthest fence, this land declared is armored. From sky to ground, this wall is sound, and evil cannot cross."

"*Now* we're cookin' with gas," Henry grinned. "Let's include the power of intention which we can adjust as needed to each situation. 'With smoke and light, we cast a shield that can't be worn by time. Our strength creates a concrete bond of body, soul and mind'."

She felt a little chill in her belly. "That's *it*, my friend." They read the full incantation aloud then high-fived each other across the table. Together, they said, "So mote it be."

Beneath the scribbles of her drafts, Kath wrote down the finished version carefully, making sure her handwriting was legible. Grandma told her to always leave her scribbles in the grimoire as they established the progress of the magic. In the top corner of the page, just as Ginny had done, she wrote the month and day to identify the spell. "Lupine 8/20," she said and then frowned slightly. "It's almost September. Ev's been back for a year."

Still wrapping twine around the foliage, Henry said, "And he's doing better every day. He'll get there."

"I know." She tucked the pencil between the pages of the journal then folded her hands over it. A breeze flirted with the lush, summer-green aspen leaves around their backyard, the soft whisper-slap dying away as the wind moved off toward the lake.

"He's so different, though. It's hard to talk to him now."

"He's changed, but he's still Evan. He just needs time to get his feet back under him."

Kath had scrutinized Henry's face. "Has he told you what happened over there?"

Where Henry always met her eyes in conversation, he hadn't looked up then. "You know how he was wounded."

"Yes, but that's not why he's in mandatory therapy twice a week. He did something, or something was done to him, that he's struggling with." She was quiet until Henry finally met her eyes. "Has he told you what that was?"

His expression was cautious. "He's told me only vague things, but I'm sworn to secrecy about them, Lady Kathryn. More from the Golden than you, but Evan was very clear that he didn't want either of you to know." He put the tied bundle on the table between them with a sigh. "I'd appreciate if you didn't press me on that. I gave him my word as a brother."

To acquiesce pained her, but Kath knew how serious an oath that was to Henry. It held equal weight for them all. "Will he ever tell me?"

"Maybe. But it won't be soon. Right now, his demons are still in control."

She hated the sound of that, but knew all too well Evan wouldn't be budged until he was ready. Pushing him would bring no reward. Kathryn wanted to be there for him, to help him through the healing process. She just wished she'd known where to start.

❧

"Do you have room for dessert?" Evan held Kathryn's hands across the table, gently caressing them. "They have those balsamic strawberries on the menu."

Kath brought his hand to her lips and kissed his fingers. "I'm in. Order them while I run to the ladies'?"

"You got it."

She gave his thick blond hair a sensual stroke as she passed him on her way to the restrooms. She couldn't wait to make love to him again and wanted him to know it.

The night she gave Evan her virginity, he'd arranged a romantic picnic in front of the fireplace in Jewel's guest house near Robbin Lake. He had dark chocolate and white grapes, and the little honey pretzels Kath was obsessed with at the time; he also had strawberries in a sweet balsamic glaze that they fed each other with their fingers. To that day, every time they saw strawberries of any kind on a restaurant menu, Evan insisted on ordering them.

Kath smiled politely at two women she passed in the doorway of the ladies' room, then slipped into a stall. She heard someone else still in the room, but her mind was on Evan. The strawberries had reminded her of how beautiful he was the summer he and Kellan were sixteen, and how sweet and considerate he'd been the first time they made love. He'd been no virgin by then, but she'd waited for him. That was the last summer they spent together in Mount Iolite before she and Kellan left for college.

There had been many female rivals for the attention of the hunky blond local boy in those days—the most aggressive had been Lisa Tucker. She was the older of two sisters close to their age whose parents rented a large house on Robbin Lake every summer. Sleazy and loose, Lisa once told Kath she had no hope of keeping Evan MacTavish; she wasn't hot enough. Kath had been scalded by that and had fired back that Evan would only touch Lisa if he'd decided to die of syphilis. The girls' feud had been a virulent subplot of that last summer, making many of Kathryn's memories bittersweet.

The hag had appeared to Evan a few days ago in the guise of teenage Lisa Tucker. Somehow reading the dark corners of his mind, the succubus was able to manifest itself in such a close likeness, that Evan had doubted his own senses.

He had a theory as to why the hag chose that particular image of Lisa—she'd had the leading role in the pornographic fantasies teenage Evan and Kellan shared together. With Lisa Tucker as the catalyst, the boys explored each other's responses to her and thoroughly enjoyed the shared release. That memory was erotic to Evan, not because of any attraction to Lisa—but because of his resulting experiences with Kellan. The hag knew that somehow and had used it to show what she was capable of.

Kath tried to put that out of her mind as she went to wash her hands at the ladies' room sink. She primped a bit in the mirror, making sure she didn't have anything between her teeth. The stall door behind her opened and a bleach blonde came out, going to the sink beside her. Kath glanced at her briefly as she dried her hands on a paper towel.

The woman was staring hard at her in the reflection of the large mirror. Her low cut red polyester wrap dress was a size too small for her pudgy frame, and the black lace of her bra peeked out around her bulging cleavage. Her hair was too blonde—fake and brassy; her lipstick a cheap drugstore coral. Her expression was a grimace of smug recognition. When Kathryn saw the caked-on sparky blue eyeshadow the woman wore, her breath stopped in her throat.

Lisa Tucker. Grown, but still working the exact same slutty presentation she'd been known for as a teen. Kathryn's teeth connected in her mouth. Every hateful emotion she'd ever had toward this person came rushing back in a wave; her knees went wobbly.

With an icy sneer, Lisa said, "Why, Kathryn Broch. I thought that was you." Her heavily-painted blue eyes took contemptuous inventory of Kath's entire body. "You haven't changed a bit; still scrawny and tit-less."

Tossing her crumpled hand towel into the bin, Kath's heart raced with bitter adrenaline. "Neither have you, Lisa." She quirked an eyebrow at that tacky red dress. "Still a white-trash skank." Not wanting her great evening with Evan to be ruined, Kath pulled open the ladies' room door and started out. But Lisa wasn't about to let her get away so easily.

"Saw MacTavish out there—dude's still hot as *shit*."

Kath glared back over her shoulder, level and cold. It wasn't a challenge, just discordant agreement.

Undaunted, Lisa snorted. "Bony little bitch. He'll never marry you. You're too much of a cunt. No man wants to spend his life with a harpy."

That was it. "Fuck *off*, you bloated cow." Kath was pissed at herself for responding at all, but that Tucker bitch had worked her last nerve for a quarter century. What were the freakin' odds she'd be right there, just then, *that night*? Kathryn marched down the hallway back to the dining room telling herself to just walk it off.

Halfway to their table she heard the clacking of Lisa's cut-rate high heels on the tile. Kath couldn't stop herself from turning back. When Lisa entered the dining room, the women locked eyes. Kath wished she possessed some superpower that would smite that bitch down with a lightning bolt, but all she could do was glower. She made sure to do it well.

"Babe?" Evan called to her from their table. "What's up?"

Kath pointed to where Lisa had started toward the bar. "It's like I conjured her just from thinking about her. That sleaze in the red dress is Lisa *fucking* Tucker—all grown-up and lumpy."

Evan stared in the direction Kathryn pointed, but his brow creased in confusion. "Where?"

When Kath turned back, Lisa stood just inside the entrance to the bar staring right at her with that same seething grin. She wasn't more than twenty feet away and there were no obstructions to block Evan's view. To him, Kath said, "there's only the one whore in a red dress standing in the bar. You can't possibly miss her. She just ambushed me in the loo and told me you'd never marry me because I'm too much of a cunt."

Evan slowly stood and placed his strong hands on Kathryn's shoulders. He spoke as though she were clinging to the ledge of high-rise building threatening to let go. "Babe, there's no one in the bar but those three dudes in flannels."

Kath blinked at him. His blue eyes were stormy with concern. She gaped back toward the bar and saw the three flannel-clad men on the barstools conversing noisily over their beers, but there was also Lisa, big as day, standing there, facing her and Evan. Kathryn's skin went cold as she realized what was happening. "You're telling me you don't see her?"

Evan checked the bar area again, even scanned the rest of the patrons in the dining room. "No one in here is wearing a red dress. Are you seeing her now?"

Swallowing audibly, Kathryn turned to the bar again. Lisa was there, but when Kath's gaze landed on her, the fleshy, overly made-up face melted away to reveal the withered, mottled countenance of a wretched old woman. Her grimace peeled back over blackened, broken teeth as she began a grating laugh. To make sure she'd been properly recognized, the entity turned its head to the side to show the deep gash of a scar in the shape of a jagged 'W'. Shrill and chiding, the hag cackled.

To the outcaster, the sound of it was like icy fingers scraping her bones.

CHAPTER TWO

Earlier the same day

SONYA'S BAKING TIMER startled her from her thoughts. She'd spent the day in her large commercial kitchen in the common building experimenting with vegan cookie recipes she'd collected over the years. She planned to place a basket of baked goods in her guest cottages every afternoon, but she was still searching for a signature treat.

Kellan had texted her around 2:30. He was still in bed after his active early morning providing spiritual energy to his grandmother. Sonya had found him standing in his pajamas in the frigid backyard, unresponsive and dazed. A moment later, she had her first physical encounter with the ghost of Virginia Broch when she tried to go into their cabin to wake Kathryn.

Ginny had been right there in the back doorway, making sure this busybody neighbor didn't meddle in her magic. She'd been friendly enough about it, but Sonya was deeply shaken. It wasn't every day one had a conversation with a ghost.

Hey, pretty lady. Kellan sent an emoji with hearts in its eyes. *Still speaking to me after this morning's fright fest?*

Wiping her rice flour-covered hands on her apron, Sonya took her phone outside to get a better signal. For some reason, electronics never worked properly in the compound's common building. She sat on the stairs in the late afternoon sun and tapped a reply.

Of course, silly. Are you all right? I was very worried about you.

I know, I'm sorry. We did mention that you'd see crazy stuff living so close to us.

Sonya smiled, thinking again of Ginny's fragmented ghost telling her to leave Kellan alone—they weren't done yet. *You weren't kidding. Did you get some rest after all that?*

Rejuvenated and bushy-tailed, thanks. Ev is taking big sis out to play tonight so I'll have the house to myself. Have plans for dinner?

Glancing down Parker Drive toward the Brochs' cabin, Sonya took a deep breath before answering. She knew this would be a bona fide date that would likely end in some sort of romantic encounter, but she wasn't entirely sure she was ready. Breathing through it, she replied. *I'm free and happy to do the cooking. I've been baking all day so my kitchen's already messed up.*

Let me cook, Kellan wrote. *I can dazzle you with my skills on the wood burner. Six-ish?*

Sounds good. What can I bring?

Whatever you were baking all day for dessert.

She laughed. *You don't want that—it's all healthy junk. Jewel says my vegan cookies taste like socks a la mode.*

He sent back an emoji with an exaggerated grin. *If it's sweet, I'll love it. See you soon.*

Sonya sent a wink.

Jittery with fresh excitement, she went back to her recipe box in the pantry. She knew she had a few things in there that would make Kellan happy. While she searched, she thought about what she should wear for this occasion. Kathryn had told her that Kellan 'melted for nice boobies bouncing loose under a t-shirt,' so she thought she'd play that card. Hers might not be much on size, but she was proud of their shape and fullness. And she wanted him to know he was invited to touch her.

While she puttered and baked the rest of the afternoon, she'd seen him a few times moving around their cabin. It seemed he was spending the extra boost of energy he'd received from their grandmother by cleaning house. She'd watched him going in and out of the shed with baskets of laundry, sweeping leaves and pine needles off the back porch, and cleaning the rain gutters. Sonya didn't believe he knew how good her vantage point was from her property and she wasn't going to tell him. It was too much fun observing him unguarded.

As 6:00 approached, she showered off the flour and sticky sweeteners she'd been elbow-deep in all day and got dressed in jeans rolled up a bit to show her lean ankles. Sonya chose an over-sized teal t-shirt with a plunging V-neck that she tied in a loose knot at her waist. She went bravely braless.

Strolling down Parker Drive, she tugged her jacket in close. The nights were crisp as October marched on, turning the aspen leaves yellow and gold. Papery brown leaves that had already died floated on the gusty breezes and littered the ground. Pine cones heavy with seed were dropping like bombs all over town; they'd even cracked a few windshields.

Busy hiding food for the winter, chipmunks scurried in the understory as she passed. The Iolite Twilight gave an eerie but beautiful glow to the landscape as Sonya made her way down into the Brochs' backyard. She glanced warily at the big pine tree where she'd found Kellan in his pajamas that morning. Kathryn had explained what was happening well enough, but everything about the Brochs was still an unnerving mystery.

The welcoming glow from the kitchen windows spilled across the back porch. Something thumped in the dryer in the shed as she lightly knocked on the storm glass. No one responded, but she was expected; Sonya went inside.

"Hello?"

At first there was no sound other than the crackle of the fire in the stove. The kitchen was warm from it and deliciously fragrant with their cooking meal. As she hung her jacket on a hook by the bathroom door, Sonya spoke quietly into the empty room.

"Mrs. Broch? I'm back. I hope you don't mind that I'm here alone with your grandson." She smiled a bit impishly. "I brought him cookies." She walked her container of goodies over to the counter and then heard footsteps overhead in Kellan's bedroom.

At the living room doorway, she called out again, turning toward the stairs. "Kellan, are you up there? It's Sonya."

He came in suddenly through the front door, startling her, and lit up when he saw her. "Hey, there! Sorry if you were looking for me; I left my smokes in the car." He set the pack on the small table by the door, then came toward her.

"No worries at all." Sonya's heart fluttered at the sight of him. "Is Kathryn home?"

"No, Ev picked her up an hour ago." He grinned mischievously as he pressed a soft kiss to her cheek. "I'm afraid you're alone with the big bad wolf."

Sonya laughed shyly, then glanced at the stairs again. "I heard someone walking up there a moment ago. I'm sure of it."

"I have no doubt you did." His amber eyes twinkled. "Grandma's probably checking her work from earlier, making sure we're buttoned up tight before full dark."

Eyeing the stairs uneasily, Sonya folded her arms across her chest. Kellan saw this and stopped in the kitchen doorway.

"You don't need to worry about my grandmother. She's always here but usually only manifests if she needs to warn us about something. Everything's quiet tonight."

"She made sure of that this morning with her wall?"

"Exactly. Grandma Ginny's a guardian, not a frightener."

Frightener. Sonya turned that word over in her mind. "You mentioned that ghosts are human spirits and have the same feelings and motivations they had in life."

"That's been our experience."

"Then are frighteners humans who did bad things in life?"

"No." Kellan leaned in the doorway. "Usually, they're spirit entities that mimic a human in order to interfere with the living. Their reason for doing this is a mystery, but they cross into our dimension and learn how to imitate us for some purpose. They're not always easy to identify. Getting rid of them can be challenging."

"The thing that was inside you a few days ago—was that a frightener?"

"That was a vampire; a succubus. They're energy feeders, which is something different yet again."

"My god." Sonya shivered and rubbed the backs of her arms. "So many monsters."

"Indeed." He reached out to take her hand. "But you're safe here with me, little lady. Well, safe from monsters, at least." He brushed his warm, silky lips over her forehead, making her shiver in a far nicer way. He smelled of lemons in the summer sun mingling with his delicious natural scent. "Let me get you something to drink. I want you to relax."

"Yes, please. I'd love some wine."

"Coming up."

He'd showered and changed clothes, his chestnut hair gleamed in its loose layers. Kellan's dark brown t-shirt was thin cotton but nicely cut and showed off his lovely arms and collar bones. As she followed him into the kitchen, Sonya guessed that faded Levi's might have been invented specifically to adorn his attractive lower half.

She sat at the island, glancing once more toward the room overhead. She tried not to think about Ginny's ghost wandering around up there. Concentrating on the moment at hand, she said, "What is that delectable smell?"

He poured her some cold white then got himself a fresh beer out of the fridge. "Me, I hope. I got all coiffed and pretty for you."

She blushed. "And you look lovely, young man, but I was referring to the food. It smells so good, I'm famished."

He went to the stove and wiggled open the iron oven door handle with a pot holder, showing her the casserole bubbling away on the rack. "Our friend Mae is a personal chef in EDI—this is her Chicken Divan recipe. *Absolutely* incredible."

"I can't wait. Can I help with anything?"

"All under control. I'm just finishing up our salad."

The stereo in the living room was tuned to a mellow classic rock station playing an old Linda Ronstadt song Sonya loved. She sang softly as she sipped her wine, watching Kellan chop cucumber at the counter. She knew he was listening to her and hoped she didn't sound too terrible. She was on key at least. After a moment, he smiled.

"It's nice hearing someone else sing in this house for a change."

Her cheeks burned but she couldn't stop smiling. "You should hear me in the front seat of my car—I can make dogs howl for twenty miles."

He laughed brightly as he scooped the cucumber into a salad bowl, then he spotted the container she'd brought sitting on the counter. "Ooh, are those your vegan goodies?"

"Some," she said. "I was hoping to convince you to taste-test a few of the healthy samples, but I brought you something special, too."

This pleased him. "Evan brought me sweets yesterday, too." He munched a bit of tomato from the salad bowl. "I must look like I need sugar."

She was far more curious about this than she wanted to reveal. "Oh? What did he bring you?

He rinsed his hands, then sat across from her. "There's a bakery down in Bishop that makes these amazing cinnamon crullers. Ev knows I love them. They only do them on certain days of the week. He was down there getting some supplies for work, so he grabbed me some. I was so excited, I ate all of them at once standing over the sink. It was heaven."

Imagining Evan making the 90-mile round trip from Mount Iolite to Bishop, she grinned. "He said he went for supplies, but I bet he drove down there just to bring you those crullers."

"Evan doesn't need to woo me." Kellan's voice was buffed and low. "He meets no resistance here."

A little tingle raced through Sonya's belly and she leaned forward on the island. "I'm learning a little bit about your relationship with Evan. The ... more mysterious particulars of it."

"There's nothing particularly mysterious." He reached over to a low shelf in the kitchen wall and handed her a small stack of instant camera photographs.

Sonya was delighted. "Wow, I haven't seen these in forever. They still make instant cameras?"

"Oh, yeah; very popular with the young folk. Ev and I took these at Harris Lake last week out on Rattlesnake's Cove."

Sonya recognized the area from the sharp curve of the shoreline. During the severe drought conditions California had endured over the last several years, this section of the manmade reservoir Harris Lake had dried out so completely it became a wildflower meadow. Now full again, Jewel told her Harris was one of the best trout fishing spots in the Sierras—especially if you were tucked down into the shady depths of Rattlesnake's Cove.

The first photo was of Evan with his pole in the water, dressed in jeans and a tight black t-shirt. Those stark aviator sunglasses rested on his nose. His blond hair and stubble gleamed gold in a band of autumn sun. Kellan had framed his friend artfully with the lake behind him.

"He is terribly handsome, your Evan."

"Always was."

Next was a close-up selfie of the two of them lying on the rocky lake beach in their flannels with their cheeks pressed tight; whiskers rubbing, golden blond on dark auburn. Their pupils were huge from whatever they were drinking or smoking, and they both looked alluringly sleepy. Under that was a shot of Kellan tying a fly on his line, the waning sun behind him catching the many shades of chestnut in his messy hair. He was looking right at the camera with distinct longing in his amber eyes. It was so palpable, Sonya quivered.

"Phew." She sipped her wine, fanning the photos out on the table between them. "Look at this expression on you. What were you thinking then?"

Kellan held up the photo to examine it. "I was thinking about eating the fish we caught with some lima beans and nice Chianti," he grinned.

She rolled her eyes. "It looks like you were thinking about eating him."

He picked up the photo of him and Evan together and turned it around to face her. "Tell me what you see here."

Her eyes moved over the two subjects, noting their easy posture together, the affectionate press of their cheeks. She could almost see them rubbing their whiskers together just before they snapped the photo. "You look a little stoned," she said with a smirk. "And you look like you know each other better than anyone else in the whole world."

Kellan smiled at that. "Evan knows all my secrets."

"And you know all of his?"

He shrugged. "He tells me I do, but our Evvy-Ev is an expert evader."

"Evvy-Ev?" she laughed. "How did that happen?"

"Kath's doing. She called him that when he was a kid and hopelessly obsessed with Mark Wahlberg's 90s boy band. She hoped such ruthless ridicule would make him see the error of his ways."

Sonya shook her head. "It's so girly; I bet he hates it."

"He's never said so." Kellan went to the stove to take out the casserole.

She looked again at the photo of them together. "You two can do no wrong in his eyes."

After setting the casserole on the counter to cool, he rejoined her. For a moment, he just sat there watching her, a trace of misbehavior gleaming in his dark eyes. "Would you like me to explain the nature of my relationship with Evan?"

"Only if you want to. I don't want to pry."

"I have no reason to hide anything from you, Sonya." Kellan extended his hand across the table and ran his fingertip slowly along the outside of her forearm, gently sifting the fine blonde hairs on her skin. She felt the tingling chill of this tiny touch in every cell.

"Do you feel that?" He held her gaze.

"Yes." Sonya reached across to tickle her fingertips through the springy dark hairs on his tanned forearm. "It feels lovely."

Kellan blinked, slow and sultry. "It does. Imagine being twelve years old, boiling with sexual energy and hormones, and feeling that for the first time. Then imagine that the one doing it is the person you love most in the whole world."

Sonya struggled to envision such a scenario. "I can't even remember who I loved most in the whole world when I was twelve. Maybe Matt Dillon—I had a horrible crush on him."

Kellan chuckled. "I don't mean a teen idol, I mean your best friend—the person you trusted and admired more than anyone else. The person you wanted to be if you could."

The mixture of emotions in his soulful eyes was almost heartbreaking. She saw passionate love there and the agony of longing, all wrapped in the glow of veneration. Evan had embodied all those things for Kellan then. From what Kathryn had shared about the depth of their relationship, Sonya believed he still did.

"I've never had anyone like that in my life," she said softly. "I had close girlfriends in school, but we didn't bond in such a way."

His brows drew together. "Then how did you bond?"

Sonya shrugged, her fingertips still gliding over the silken skin of his arm. She couldn't tell which she was enjoying more, his light caresses or the pleasure of caressing him. "I don't know, we bonded like teenage girls from affluent, conservative families. We had lots in common; we went to the same school, liked the same music, wore the same clothes, crushed on the same boys."

"I see," he said. "So, no deep, soul-searching talks where you laid bare your deepest feelings?"

Thinking of the superficial, colorless girls she'd known in her childhood, Sonya had to laugh. "No. I don't think there was a single deep feeling circulating among the lot. They were nice enough, not catty bitches or anything, but they were shallow suburban rich girls. They wanted for nothing, so they had no drive to achieve anything other than getting good grades so they could brag about going to a posh college."

He'd been watching her closely while she spoke, his expression keen and pensive. "How did this woman sitting across from me happen, then? If all your friends were surface relationships, how did Sonya become this kind, inquisitive, sweet-spirited caretaker?"

"That's very nice to hear," she said, truly flattered. "But it's not quite the whole story of me. I have my bad traits, just like anyone else."

He shook his head with a little grin. "I'm not buyin' that. Name one."

Steadying herself for an act of boldness, Sonya's heart began to race. She slipped her fingers into the warm cup of Kellan's hand, then lowered her voice to a whisper. "For starters, I've significantly reconsidered my position on becoming the Cougar of Mount Iolite."

Laughing low in his throat, Kellan slid off his stool and stepped right up to her. The warmth and sweetness of his skin surrounded her just before he closed the space between them. His lips covered hers with satiny heat.

Sonya had imagined their first real kiss would be soft and tender, but as she opened to his assertiveness and finally tasted him, she realized what a foolish fantasy that had been. That simply wasn't Kellan's way. He was animal desire; a creature in constant pursuit of pleasure. This freedom of spirit made him irresistible—and not only to her. But he was hers at that moment. Sonya breathed in deep to take in as much of him as she could.

His whiskers were dense and luxurious with just the lightest bit of virile prickle. Her fingers dove into them, cradling his fine jaw. Kellan sighed into her touch, his hands tucking around her hips.

He tasted her bottom lip, sending sparks through her whole body. She felt the graze of his teeth and then his tongue teased hers inside her mouth. It wasn't invasive, just the gentlest tickle. He was holding back to make her want it. Sonya shivered. Kellan pressed his body flush to hers, letting her feel his heavy, swelling response through his jeans. She knew he'd just learned she was naked under her t-shirt and lifted her breasts against him.

The dizziness came on in a flash. Pulling away for a second, Sonya tried to catch her breath. She held onto his face, her eyes closed, lips burning to feel his again. She noted everywhere Kellan touched her: his hands resting low on her hips; his warm, taut belly aligned with hers; his full erection urgent against her pubic bone. He sighed, nuzzling for more kisses.

"Don't be afraid," he whispered. "Nothing will happen that you don't want." He nipped her lips then slid his tongue between, skimming it over hers until she whimpered.

Encouraged, Kellan's strong right arm looped behind her and hauled her to him. Sonya had a flash of his intense wet dream in her bed the night of Kathryn's vision quest. His need had been a living thing then, as it was now: pulsing and insistent with a primal velocity of its own. He'd obviously had no control of it in his sleep, but was he in control now?

Her heart pounded so hard and fast she was barely aware of drawing her thighs around his hips. He responded to her invitation, rubbing himself between her legs. Sweet and salty, he was delicious. Sonya gently bit his scrumptious lips. Everything about him and this molten moment was perfect except that she was about to pass out from panic.

Pulling for breath, Sonya pressed her trembling fingertips against his hot lips. "Wait, Kellan … please. I'm sorry."

He panted, so tense and aroused. He stilled immediately but didn't move away. Kellan waited for her where she could feel his desire. She was hyper-aware of the quick pulse in his lips and against her left thigh. Sonya took a long, slow breath and looked in his eyes; all pupil with lust, rimmed in a corona of gold.

"Dial it back?" he murmured.

She touched her forehead to his, sighing miserably. "I honestly thought I was okay. I'm so sorry. I think this is just too fast."

He kissed her cheek softly. "No, I came in too hot; my fault." He took her hands away from his face and held them gently. "Did I misread you?"

Sonya groaned. "Not at all! I thought I was ready for you, I really did."

Kellan's amber eyes twinkled knowingly. "You are; that much I know for sure. I just need to learn a little more of your language."

"You didn't read me wrong," she insisted.

He drew her into a soft hug and put a kiss on top of her head. "We'll just hit the pause button for now and enjoy our meal." Lifting her chin on his finger, he smiled gently. "We've got all the time in the world. Okay?"

"Okay," she said, but her heart still pounded from the flashfire they'd started. Sonya had never felt such sexual intensity in her entire life.

Leaving her to catch her breath, he refreshed her wine, then went about putting dinner on the table out in the breakfast nook. When her legs stopped shaking, she helped him carry things out and then they sat across from each other just inside the window that overlooked the starlit surface of Bonny Lake. He'd set the table with fresh flowers and a heavy cotton cloth. Candlelight flickered on the pretty china plates.

"This is all so fancy," she marveled.

"Well, I'm trying to impress a special lady." Kellan was also having wine with dinner and he raised his glass to her.

"She is quite thoroughly impressed." Sonya remembered watching him that afternoon as he bounced around doing chores. There were times when the forest was so quiet, she could even hear him humming as he worked. She pictured him taking his time ironing that tablecloth and cleaning the cabin to make everything nice for her. As they tucked into the delicious meal he'd prepared, she tried not to get distracted by the memory of his hot kisses and the burning rod of him pressed against her.

They were laughing about how much they'd both hated high school when the footsteps upstairs came again, light and quick with purpose that time. Sonya had forgotten all about the ghost of Virginia Broch up there. She flinched at the sound and looked fearfully toward the stairs.

Kellan rested his hand on hers, firm and reassuring. "Sonya, it's okay. I promise. Remember, she's just a lady. There's nothing to be afraid of. And this is her house."

Heart pounding anew, she forced a smile. "Do people really get used to this?"

"Eventually," he said. "The more you experience her, the less she'll upset you. Just be open to it. She's one of the good guys."

As though in response, the footsteps moved over their heads again, slower that time like Ginny might be dusting knickknacks. Sonya could easily tell those were high heels clicking on the wood floor. This made her laugh, albeit uncomfortably.

"She's wearing heels in a cabin in the mountains."

With a grin, Kellan reached for his wine. "She wore pearls with her fishing waders, too. That's how Grammy rolled."

Sonya loved that image and it calmed her a bit. At least for the moment.

CHAPTER THREE

I-395 WAS A gloomy band of asphalt in front of the Jeep's headlights. Stars pinpricked the velvet black of the cold mountain night, broken only by the silhouette of tall pines.

The radio played "Bell Bottom Blues" as Evan drove them back to Mount Iolite from Mammoth. That song always reminded Kathryn of her dad. He had played it a lot right after the divorce. She sat close enough to rest her head on Evan's broad shoulder, needing to feel him against her. His height and physical strength comforted her, even though she knew neither of them was entirely safe.

His right hand gently eased along her thigh as he drove. "My girl doin' okay?"

"Why couldn't you see her?"

They'd left the restaurant in a hurry after the hag posing as grown-up Lisa Tucker vanished into nothing inside the bar. Kathryn had long outgrown the need to scream when monsters did terrifying things like that, but all the elements of the encounter had shaken her. How had the hag suddenly appeared in the adult guise of her teenage nemesis just after Kath had been thinking of her? How had she known just what to say to cut right to Kathryn's quick? And why could Evan not see or hear the entity at all?

"She was vibrating on your frequency, I guess," he offered. "Ginny can only fully manifest to one of us at a time because of that, so maybe it's also an issue for succubae. We don't have a lot of information on them, other than what they eat and how to bounce them. That's all we've needed so far."

Kath went over the chain of events in her mind for the tenth time. "Maybe the talisman you're wearing does more than just protect you from being touched. Maybe it protects you from seeing her, too."

"I saw her fine when she was outside my gate the other day. I had the talisman on then."

Frustrated, Kath sighed. "I shouldn't have such basic questions at this point. What kind of fuckin' outcaster am I?"

"A rattled one at the moment." Evan's deep voice vibrated in her bones as she leaned on him. She put a little kiss on his warm neck, breathing in his scent.

"I'm more pissed off than rattled. Is she trying to scare us into submission by appearing in ways that freak each of us out personally? What is she waiting for? Get on with the attack, already! *That* I know how to deal with."

Evan laughed darkly. "Careful what you wish for, witchy-poo. This one is old and strong. We have no idea how quickly it could drain Kellan. I, for one, do not want to play with that."

"I would never." She pressed her fingers to the throbbing point between her eyebrows. "There has to be some purpose to these side shows, though. Why bother?"

"Saber rattling," he said. "'Look what I can do, pussies! I can read your stupid little human minds! Fear me!'"

"But why does she *care* about scaring us? Just attack! That's what succubae do—they SUCK! She hasn't even tried that yet!"

"We know that evil things prefer the taste of frightened victims. *And* there's that pesky little revenge thing." Evan looked at her sidelong. "You did lock her in a tree for twenty-three years—something with which I'm sure she takes umbrage."

"She's a monster," Kath grumbled. "She should just do monster shit. This is human shit."

"Old and strong," he repeated. "This one's ingested the life force of thousands of humans over its existence. Imagine what it's learned about us."

Kath decided she'd rather not. Resting her head on the seat back, she stared up at the stars through the dusty glass of the sunroof. "At least I know Kell's okay tonight."

Evan gently squeezed her knee. "And probably enjoying himself immensely by this time."

"*If* Sonya hasn't slapped his face yet," she said with a grin.

"She hasn't. She doesn't mind him at all."

Evan took the turn off the interstate slowly and started for town. The peak of Mount Iolite was invisible in the moonless dark, but the mountain's mass had a palpable presence. In daylight, the iconic summit was hidden until one crested the hill that opened to the stunning view of Bonny Lake below. Kathryn often wondered what it was like for the first people to find this remote group of lakes. Beneath the sawblade granite of the Sierra range there was nothing but sage-covered desert for hundreds of miles. This place must have seemed like an alpine mirage to the original visitors.

"This brooding quiet is making me nervous." Evan stretched his right arm around her shoulders, pulling her closer.

Kath breathed a laugh. "Now you know what it's like to hang out with you."

"I'm not quiet," he playfully defended.

"But you *are* the perpetual king of brood." Kath leaned in and nipped his silky earlobe.

Keeping one eye on the road, he kissed her; his lips were soft and inviting. She tried to put the hag out of her mind for the moment. Evan's house was as well-protected as their own cabin—they would be safe there until morning.

There was a little time to breathe before she had to don her battle gear, so she let her warrior's wheels turn in the background.

⁓

When she came out of the bathroom, Evan had a merry blaze going on the hearth. She'd changed into one of his old, soft flannel shirts she'd found hanging on the back of the door. It smelled gloriously of him. She held it to her face a moment before slipping it on.

As teenagers, the boys began translating Grandma Ginny's magical push toward each other into various expressions of carnal pleasure. One result was that both Kathryn and her brother shared a passionate response to Evan's scent. They both liked to wear his shirts, especially after they'd seen a day's work on his body. Evan's response to their worn garments was similar, except he stole Kathryn's knickers and kept them in his pocket. She was fairly certain he didn't try them on, but she'd never actually asked.

Kath grabbed a pair of his cuddly winter socks out of the bedroom drawer and sat on the bed to slip them on. In the full-length mirror in the corner, she caught her reflection—long bare legs under the oversized shirt, the curve of her calves accentuated by the socks bunched at her ankles. The flash of pink lace from her skimpy panties would make him crazy. Evan loved the contrast of his willowy tomboy in ultra-feminine lingerie.

He was busy with something at the kitchen counter, so she stepped up behind him, winding her arms around his solid torso. Kath kissed the back of his neck then peeked over his shoulder to see what he was up to.

A small platter held plump red strawberries that he'd carefully sliced in half and arranged around a ramekin of steaming chocolate sauce. He smiled and kissed her lips.

"I'm not letting that monster jack up our dessert," he said.

Emotion washed over her so suddenly, Kathryn almost started to cry. She didn't want him to see that, so she let him hear her laugh as she made her way to the pile of pillows in front of the fireplace. "You are hopelessly romantic, Evvy-Ev."

"And you love it." He brought the platter into the living room and set it on the coffee table. Kath felt him watching her as she positioned the pillows in front of the fire. She made sure to bend over nice and deep so he could see the pink lace.

"I can get you a clean shirt." She heard the grin in his voice as his strong hands curled possessively around her hips. "I chopped wood in that one."

"Which is why I'll keep it." She turned in his arms and made sure he could see she only had one button done—way down near her waist.

Ogling the curve of her bare breasts peeking out from the flannel, he drew her close enough to feel his appreciation of the view. "Uh huh," he grinned. "You have bite marks in your future, little lady. Just so ya know."

"I bloody well hope so." She covered his voluptuous mouth with a kiss, but before she could pull him down into the pillows he stepped away.

"One more thing—hold that thought." Back in the kitchen, he got a bottle of something sparkling out of the fridge and popped the cork over the sink. He took two flute glasses out of the cupboard and brought everything back to her. "Strawberries go great with prosecco."

Kath chuckled. "I'm gonna start calling you Martha Stewart."

"Yeah, don't." Evan filled their glasses and handed one to her. "To my beautiful, formidable Blackwing. May she vanquish this hag as easily as swatting a mosquito."

Kath tapped her glass to his. "Thank you, sir. I need all the confidence I can get." The sparkling wine was delicious and light; she savored two sips before raising a glass to him. "And to my fierce and loyal Gray Wolf. May his passion for his woman get the better of him until the sun comes up."

Evan laughed, took a drink, then put both their glasses on the coffee table. "It would appear *someone* needs some attention. Mount up, woman."

The one button Kath had fastened on his flannel shirt did nothing to deter him. Evan had her naked and on her back on the pillows in a flash, those lacy pink panties tucked safely in the pocket of his jeans. After being lovers nearly their whole lives, he'd amassed quite the collection of her undergarments—what he called 'spoils of war.' She loved imagining what he did with them during their long months apart.

Unlike their highly emotional reunion the other night, Kath and Evan were back in their natural habitat. Laughter, rough kisses, hard, messy, intercourse and repeated orgasms allowed her to forget about the hag altogether until they lay breathless and weary on his bed in the wee hours.

Pulling the covers over them, he grinned down at her. "Better?"

Kath smirked. "For now. Your efforts are much appreciated, soldier, but I've had a very long drought."

He settled in beside her, tucking her in next to him. Kathryn ran her fingers over his well-muscled chest and belly, trailing lightly over the web of scars from his wounds in Afghanistan. As she always did, she put a little kiss on her fingertips and touched them to the spot.

Lacing his fingers with hers, he nuzzled her forehead. "Peach does that, too—every time he sees them."

"I know. It makes us angry that we can't take them away."

"They're just scars, babe. The wounds are long gone."

She didn't want to bring up the fact that Evan had never told her or her brother what actually happened to him in the war, but she felt like she had to. They knew he was both shot and stabbed in some sort of ambush—he bore the dramatic scars of each—but he'd never shared the details of *how* he got wounded. Henry Hunter was the only person he'd revealed any of that information to, and Henry was sworn to the secrecy of brotherhood.

Evan saw her fretting and kissed her, trying to distract her. She knew he knew what she'd been thinking, and she took his handsome face in her hands gently.

"Just tell me. It's been 15 years."

He lowered his head onto the pillows. "I can turn that around on you just as easily—it's been 15 years, let it fucking *go*."

"Evan, what the hell? You're my man, aren't you?"

"You know I am."

"Then why can't you share that with me? I tell you *everything*."

"I don't demand that of you." His blond brows drew tightly together like they always did when she pressed him on this topic.

Kathryn knew she was starting a fight she'd lost every time prior, but she had some potent new ammunition. She pushed up on her elbow to see his face clearer. "Listen, this is a memory you'd rather not have brought into the light, which makes it fair game for our clever hag. She's proven she can read our minds and she obviously favors our locked rooms. Do you want *her* telling me that story in some hideous monster way, or do you want to tell me yourself and take it off the table?"

Evan threw the covers back, going to the chair in the corner for his sweats. His square jaw was set stubbornly as he pulled them on, then marched out of the bedroom muttering about going for a smoke. She heard him put on his slippers, then the front door opened; the metallic snick of his Zippo lighter rang hollow in the entry hall. Kathryn buried her face in the pillows and groaned. It didn't help much.

She knew it was impossible to get Evan to talk if he didn't want to. He'd just shut down and get sullen, say stupid shit and make her want to smack him. She figured it was safer to drop the subject for now and just spend the evening playing together. She'd missed doing that so much. Kath had missed everything about him, even his sulky silence. But she also knew she had a solid point this time.

The bedroom window over the bed faced the front porch and Kath could see him out there puffing irascibly on his cigarette. She rolled into the pillows, breathing in the warm scent of him in the bedclothes. Kath watched him standing there against the railing, bathed in the orangey light from a nearby street lamp. Evan felt her gaze and turned to look at her through the window. The smile she gave him offered a truce.

He came to the glass and tapped on it, his lips tilted in grin. Kath was relieved to see his shift in mood. She reached up and slid the window open just a crack, batting her lashes at him.

"Are you the big bad wolf?"

Evan blew smoke into the air. "Not at all; I'm the best of all the wolves. Let me in, cute little piggy."

"No, no, no," she grinned. "You're a *bad* wolf. I can tell by those big teeth. You mean to do me harm."

Evan leaned in close to the screen. "All I want is to cook you up and eat your sweet meat. It won't hurt or anything."

Kath rolled onto her back, showing him her naked breasts. She knew it turned him on to see her touch herself; she ran her fingers over her nipples. "You don't want to sniff and lick me first? I thought all puppies loved to sniff and lick. You want to go straight to cooking and eating?"

Evan lowered his chin. "I'll sniff and lick if it'll make your meat more tender."

"Ooh," she murmured. "I'm not tender enough now?"

Growling playfully, he pressed up against the window. "So now you *want* me to eat you?"

"Always," Kath purred. "But do it slowly so I can feel every bite." Gliding her right hand down her belly, she dipped her fingers between her legs. She was a little sore from his deliciously rough attentions, but her desire was very resilient. Kath knew from long experience that she could take a lot more of him that night. She let him see her fingers moving; she moaned softly. "I feel *very* tender to me."

His focus locked on her ministrations. She saw his breathing speed up. Evan licked his full lips, taking another pull on his cigarette.

Kath opened her thighs wider, lifting her hips to give him a better view. She gazed up at him, her long, shiny hair tumbling over his pillows. She knew he loved her hair. Her fingers moved a little faster as she grew aroused watching him watching her.

In a rough voice, Evan said, "Little piggy, turn around and put your sweet meat right up to the window where I can see it."

His direct command enflamed her. Kath kept her eyes on him, scooting around on the bed until her knees were touching the window pane. She gave him a good view.

"That's it." Evan leaned into the window, his breath a puff on the glass. "Titties up, now."

Kath arched her back, displaying her breasts for him. Sometimes he would text her telling her to take various sexy photos of herself and send them to him. His most common request was images of her breasts spilling out of her bra, or peeking out bare from an unbuttoned shirt, as she'd presented herself earlier. He said it reminded him of making out with her when they were kids when the mere sight of her plump breasts would make him leak. Through the window, she could see Evan's cock straining in his sweats from her posing. Kath knew she had him.

He took one more hit from his smoke, then crushed it out against the wall. He reached up to the edges of the screen and unhooked it, setting it aside on the porch. Grinning like the wolf in a fairy tale, Evan stuck his fingers into the opening of the window and slid it just wide enough for him to crawl through.

Kath giggled as he climbed on top of her, clumsy in his puffy coat and sweats. On his knees on the bed, he pulled the coat off and tossed it aside, then hooked her under her arms with his hands. He slid her to the middle of the bed. Evan opened his mouth over the flesh of her left thigh and bit down hard.

She squealed, laughing, knowing she'd have a deep purple mouth mark there tomorrow. He lifted her up by her hips and buried his face between her legs, lapping right up the center of her. Kath fell back on the bed and screamed through a deep orgasm, pulling at his arms with her fingers. Her whole body burned to have him inside her.

Lifting her effortlessly, Evan slid her body down on him. He groaned and thrust himself hard into her. Kath held onto his strong shoulders and bit his earlobe. She squeezed him inside her and he trembled. Looking up, his gray-blue eyes suddenly went cloudy with an incoming storm.

"Evvy-Ev …" She moved up and down slowly, stroking him inside her. "Stay with me, baby—don't get all moody. I'm going to hypnotize you."

He smiled but those clouds were still there. "You think you can make me bark like a dog? Mmm … Kathryn …"

"Oh, no baby. I'm going to make you understand that I'm right. Because I'm always right."

He chuckled, his hips tensing. "My ass. Now hush, woman. Let me get off in peace."

She covered his mouth with hers and felt him swell inside her. Evan moaned, his strokes shortening and intensifying. She held on and tightened around him, speeding up to bring him closer.

She'd been having sex with this man for seventeen years; she knew every possible way to please him. They were bonded so deep that separating was no longer an option. But Kathryn needed him to hear her on this point—she needed him to agree with her.

After his climax, he panted in her arms; she stroked his back in long, slow caresses. She felt him getting heavier as he relaxed, sleep stealing in to claim him. Before he drifted off, she tried again.

"Evan, you know I'm right."

"Shh," was all he offered.

Kath sighed under him, feeling her own eyelids growing heavy. It was just after 3:15—deep in the devil's hour. She moved the curtains aside to look out at the street in front of Evan's little house. Everything was still and quiet, not even a whisper of wind. She pulled the covers around them and slipped into an uneasy sleep.

CHAPTER FOUR

SONYA COULDN'T BELIEVE how long they'd been talking; the conversation had been so effortless and engaging. She'd learned many things about Kellan Broch, most notably that wool socks made him itchy, he found animals talking in movies hilarious, and he hated eggplant—another thing they had in common.

At nearly midnight, they finally cleaned up the kitchen and settled on the plush sofa. Pine logs softly snapped in the pot belly and the radio played some vintage Eagles. The Brochs' cabin was warm and cheerful and there had been no more footsteps upstairs.

Kellan waited until she'd arranged the throw pillows to her liking and then he drew her legs over his lap. His fingers curled around her bare ankles where she'd rolled up her jeans. Sonya gently moved his soft hair off his forehead. Relaxed, affectionate and tipsy, he was impossibly alluring. She basked in his attention.

"You were telling me about the day you first met Evan. Your sister filled me in on her experience, but she said I should get yours directly."

"Definitely," he said with a grin. Kellan had, in fact, started that story several times over the evening but kept getting sidetracked to tell her something he found more entertaining. A buoyant storyteller, he had her in stitches half the time, but she was anxious for him to fill in those details.

She reminded him of his progress. "You got as far as not knowing what to make of him as he rolled up to you on his bike in front of the candy store. You mentioned that he frightened you. How so?"

He let his head fall back on the sofa cushion. "All I knew was that he was coming at me with a ton of velocity. And I'd never seen a boy like him in LA. He was just so untamed and natural, you know? This creature of the mountains with his blond hair, tanned skin and bare feet. But the way Ev tells it, he could see the golden and he didn't know what the hell it was. It was freaking him out."

"Right. Kath mentioned that."

"I remember being totally mesmerized by his blue eyes," Kellan went on. "Like the lakes before a storm. They were the most beautiful things I'd ever seen." He turned to her in earnest. "It was love at first sight. There's no other explanation."

With a gentle smile, she said, "You were only eight, Kellan. You couldn't have understood those feelings yet."

"I did, though. It was pure and bright as day. And it has never gone away. I feel that every single time I see him."

Her fingers still wandered in his silky hair, which he seemed to enjoy. His eyes fluttered when she ruffled the strands close to his ears. He was intent on her expression, trying to read her reaction to what he was saying. Sonya wasn't sure how she felt. She still had lots of questions.

"Are these feelings mutual?"

Without hesitation, Kellan said yes. "And he's got all this other stuff rolled in, too—the protector, warrior, caretaker thing. Grandma Ginny chose him very well."

Sonya recalled Henry sharing a quote from his uncle, Shaman Fred Hunter, the night of Kathryn's vision quest ceremony. "Beyond the three, the six are fluid," she said aloud. "Henry told me his uncle believes you three will all die close together, too."

Kellan nodded thoughtfully. "We've always felt that way, even when we were kids. There's a sort of tether between us. We're only whole, fully functioning individuals when we're all together."

"But you're apart for most of the year."

"For now." Kellan grinned and waggled his brow. "I have it on good authority that will all be changing soon."

Sonya smiled at that. "I have heard rumblings of an expected proposal."

He was clearly pleased by the idea of Evan marrying his sister. "That's the rumor."

"But, won't that complicate things?" she said.

"How so?"

Sonya shifted in her seat, carefully selecting her words. "You still haven't really told me the nature of your relationship with Evan, but I've heard enough from your sister and Jewel to deduce that it's sexual."

"*Sensual* is more accurate." He winked. "We don't actually engage in any man-on-man plowin'."

Her heart began to race, but she proceeded casually. "No?"

"No. We have our own variation of snuggling that we both find *very* satisfying, but we've never felt the need to cross that particular line."

"I'm curious as to why not," she said. "It seems like something you carnal little beasts would enjoy."

"Does it?" Kellan said with amused interest. He shifted toward her, almost close enough to kiss her, but he didn't yet.

"Yes. What, is it too gay?"

"Well, two men having intercourse would indeed be defined that way, but that's not the issue." He shook his head and corrected himself. "There isn't an issue at all; we just don't feel moved in that direction. Never have."

"How far does this particular brand of snuggling go, then? Do you enjoy this activity naked?"

Kellan lightly tickled her belly. "The lady is *very* curious about this."

"Yes." Sonya blushed furiously but laughed it off. "She is. But she doesn't want to offend you by prying, so don't let her."

"You couldn't offend me. If you come too close, I'll let you know—but I'm curious about what you'll ask."

"You think my questions will reveal my own desire?" She said this playfully, but his expression went dead serious.

"I *know* it will. And that information will be very helpful to me."

Her anxiety returned suddenly, frustrating her. Thinking of how she lost her grip when he'd kissed her earlier, she said, "I'm not trying to be difficult, Kellan. I'm just out of practice."

His warm fingers gently caressed her bare ankle. "You're not difficult; you're tentative. And that's absolutely to be expected. But I don't want to frighten you, so I need to learn how to safely proceed. Tell me what you're most curious about with Evan and me."

There were so many things, Sonya didn't know where to start. She took a sip of the ice water she'd switched to after a few glasses of wine, then settled into the pillows with him again. "Your sister told me you shared your ice cream cone with Evan that first day you met. She said I should ask you why you did that."

He wriggled a bit closer to her. His scrumptious scent flooded her senses making her swallow involuntarily. It was vaguely intoxicating like breathing in nitrous oxide. She assumed Evan had a similarly intense experience because he'd based his nickname for Kellan on his scent.

"He was so close to me, inspecting me trying to figure out why I was glowing. But I couldn't stop looking at his mouth. I'd never seen lips like that; so juicy and full, like they'd *pop* if you bit them. I wanted to kiss him so bad, but I didn't even know his name yet." Kellan laughed. "I think Kath might have tried to introduce us, but we were too busy investigating each other to notice." His eyes got a bit misty with the memory. "When Kath handed me my cone, all I could think to do was ask if he wanted to share it. That way I'd get his mouth in the same place as mine, sort of like a kiss." He grinned. "Made really good sense to my eight-year-old mind."

"I'm sorry," she laughed. "That's just too adorable."

"Ev still teases me about it. But that's how it started."

"And how long was it before you actually got that kiss?"

"Roughly four years."

"Wow, you were patient!"

He laughed, shaking his head. "It had to be *his* idea; that took a minute." Kellan pointed toward a group of old photographs tacked directly to the wooden wall above the sofa. "See the one of the two boys in swim trunks with that huge stringer of fish?"

Without moving too far from him, Sonya tilted back enough to get a good look. Among many timeworn black and white photos of Ginny and Jackson Broch, Sr. displaying colossal catches of the local trout, were more recent color images of Jackson, Jr. and his children at various activities on the lakes. There was even a photo of Jewel in her small skiff with a very young Kellan as her passenger. Sonya thought of the photo albums in Jewel's collection and wondered if a copy of this was also among them.

"That's sweet of you and our neighbor."

"She used to take me on rides all around the shore because I don't like the deep water."

"You can swim, right?"

"Sure, but spirits ride water far easier than land; makes me too vulnerable."

"Oh, I see." Sonya squinted at the photo he'd pointed to; an image of a sunny day in mid-summer, judging by the color of the daylight. He and an uber-blond young Evan were holding up a stringer with four massive brown trout hanging on it. The fish were almost the length of the boys' legs. Kellan was in a red life vest and blue trunks, his dark hair summer-long and clinging to his small neck. Evan was shirtless and in red trunks, his lean chest just beginning to fill out. Both boys displayed huge, proud grins.

"Look at those fish; that's quite a haul you've got there."

"We caught all those right off the dock with wet flies."

In the photo, Sonya could see a saddle of sunburnt skin over Evan's nose and a spray of dark freckles on Kellan's bronzed little cheeks. The alluring plumpness of Evan's lips was undeniable. She imagined inquisitive, affectionate young Kellan would have craved to taste them.

"You were both ridiculously cute."

"And still are," he grinned.

"No argument." She settled back down with him on the sofa. "So, how did he do it? What was sly young Evan's first move?"

Kellan told a wistful story of the two boys hiking to their favorite summertime shady spot in an aspen grove high above Robbin Lake. There was a small meadow in a clearing that attracted the local fauna for afternoon nibbles. The boys would lie on their backs in the tall grass and let the deer amble around them, munching tender leaves and rose hips. Wild hares bounced among the wildflowers, while butterflies and bugs floated in the hot air. Dressed in shorts and t-shirts, Kellan and Evan would talk for hours in soft voices so as not to disturb the animals.

"They weren't afraid of you?" Sonya asked.

"Critters love me. They can see the golden, too—it attracts them."

She recalled the photograph in Jewel's collection of Kellan and the swallowtails out on their dock—a picture his whole family was unaware their neighbor possessed. Sonya had no intention of spilling those beans.

In a soft voice, she said, "You're the critter whisperer, then?"

With that Kellan shifted, stretching out alongside her on the sofa. Sonya fluffed the pillows, her legs resting easily against his. He rested his arm lightly over her waist.

"I can get most animals to come to me by tuning in to them and sending them a sort of broadcast of welcome. It's a sound frequency but very faint."

"You do this with your voice or your mind?"

"Both," he said. "It's the same sound joining from two different sources. It works almost every time."

Gently grazing his silky whiskers with her fingertips, she asked if he was using that superpower on her at the moment. She did indeed feel bewitched. Kellan just laughed.

"I'm afraid it only works on animals. I've never figured out how to apply it to women."

"You don't seem to be having any trouble attracting them, though."

"That's just me flirting. If I find someone attractive, I'm frank about it. People respond to that honesty. Plus, I'm irresistibly cute. Or so my grandmother used to say."

Sonya laughed. "She may have been the tiniest bit biased."

"Maybe." He went on with his story of that sunny afternoon the summer he and Evan turned twelve.

The heat had them sleepy in the long grass, turned toward each other and only talking occasionally. Kellan had been transfixed by the way the sunlight filtered through Evan's blond eyelashes and found all the flaxen honey in his unkempt hair. They'd both started getting facial hair and had spent a good amount of time comparing the differences in their progress. Evan's baby blond fluff didn't show as much as Kellan's dark auburn peach fuzz, even though Evan had more growth at that point.

Sonya whispered, her fingers playing along Kellan's jaw. "You both have lovely full beards now. Don't you give each other whisker burn when you snuggle?"

Amber eyes dancing, he said, "We've made a little game out of that, actually. Whenever he wants to make me laugh to the point of peeing my pants, he'll give me a scratch of his whiskers across my belly. It tickles *so* bad! I scream like a little girl."

That intimate image came so completely alive in Sonya's mind that she drew in a sudden breath. Instantly embarrassed, she covered her face and laughed.

"You like that idea?" Kellan purred. He nuzzled her hand away to get to her mouth and kissed her, nice and soft. "Don't be shy about it. I love that you think it's sexy."

"I'm just not at all sure why I do," she said, wishing she could control her flaming cheeks.

"My sister loves it, too—if that helps. She's been spying on us for years."

Hearing that did make her feel better. "Maybe I'm not that much of a pervert then."

"You're about as far from a pervert as I can imagine."

"You don't know that." Despite her embarrassment, Sonya didn't want him to think of her as a retiring, prudish widow. "I've had some *very* impure thoughts about you, young man. I've even made myself blush a few times."

He raised his eyebrows in approval. "That makes me happy."

"Of course it does," she laughed. "I'm sure that's at the root of my interest in your physical relationship with your best friend. The idea of you experiencing sensual pleasure is ... exciting to me, no matter the source. I even got butterflies thinking of you devouring those donuts he brought you." Her heart pounded, she was so surprised she'd told him that. But she had—and there it was.

Kellan found this very interesting. "Really?"

"Really. God." She covered her face again.

"Stop doing that," he said quietly. "There's no reason to be ashamed of your sensuality, Sonya. You're a beautiful woman who's full of life. Be alive. Enjoy it." He kissed her again as he moved to get off the sofa.

"Where do you think you're going?" she said, playfully indignant. She was, however, truly disappointed that he'd moved.

"You reminded me we haven't had dessert." He went to the kitchen to collect her container of cookies, swinging by the fridge for a carton of milk on his return. He climbed back in beside her, handing her the milk while he popped the lid off the container.

Kellan inspected her offerings, asking what to expect from each different morsel. He tried two of her vegan cookies first—one of which was salty and sweet from molasses and she thought he might like it despite it being good for him. She was pleased when he licked his fingers after finishing it off.

"Yummy. Wait, did I just eat something healthy?"

"You did—and look at you: still breathing." She took one of those for herself and munched it while he chose a different sample.

"How about this one?" He held up a delicate sandwich cookie made with lemons, cornmeal and rice flour. "It looks reasonably bad for me with the creamy stuff in between."

She laughed. "Just try it. I'll tell you what it is afterward."

He popped the whole cookie in his mouth and grinned while he chewed. "That's nice," he said with lemon cream sticking to his lips. She ran the pad of her thumb over his neatly trimmed mustache to clear the crumbs.

"You're a perfect glutton," she said.

"You have no idea." Kellan plucked another lemon cream from the container and devoured it.

This was the batch she'd made special for him—full of decadent butter and sugar. Seeing him enjoy them so made her tingle. Sonya imagined Evan felt a similar triumph from seeing Kellan voraciously consume the treats he brought. She put a light kiss between Kellan's brows. "Back to those two sweet boys in the summer grass."

Crunching, he continued. "Ev was lying on his back and I was on my side facing him. He had his hands folded behind his head— we were both in tank tops. I tended to obsess over his blond body hair because it was so different from mine; used to crack him up. 'Yes, Kell—the hairs on my arms and legs are blond because I have *blond hair*.'"

Sonya laughed, picturing the mild cantankerousness Evan exhibited as an adult coming from the cherub in the photographs.

"I was watching the fluffy hairs under his arms moving in the breeze and I reached over to touch them," Kellan said. "Ev laughed at me and called me a weirdo, then rolled toward me to tickle me."

"Uh oh," Sonya grinned. "Here it comes."

Kellan munched on the raspberry almond cookie that was likely the healthiest of the bunch. He didn't seem to mind or even notice.

"He pinned me, and we were both laughing and then we just froze for a second, watching each other. I can see him right now just like he was: backlit by the sun making his hair look like floating gold, just a tiny frown in his blue eyes. His expression was a mix of uncertainty and determination, two things we rarely see on his face at the same time—even when he was a kid."

"I'm sure he was wondering if he might get punched," she said.

"Maybe," Kellan grinned. "His hips were on top of mine and I could feel all of him. I'd seen him naked before when we were swimming out on Swamp Rock, but that had been a few years earlier. We'd both grown up a lot since then."

"Had you already kissed a girl at this point?" Sonya had rested her hand on the pillow between them, her fingers gently brushing the warm cotton of his t-shirt. He was still nibbling her cookies.

"We both had, but he was a lot more experienced than me. I mean think about it: he's here in this tiny little town in the mountains, and he looks like *that*."

She laughed. "I'm sure they were lined up all the way out to the Interstate."

"You know it. There weren't many girls close to our age who lived here year-round, but the summer locals and the skiers brought in a constant stream of fresh blood—and all of them found Evan at some point. He lost his virginity at thirteen."

"Some wily older girl, I bet."

Kellan smiled as he took a sip of milk straight from the carton. "Why would you think that?"

"I assume he would have tried for older girls who were more developed. He was tall and very confident, from what your sister shared with me. I'd guess he lied about his age and was able to make considerable headway. "

This made Kellan laugh. "You are quite right. He always liked older girls—not a ton older, but a few years—and for that very reason."

"That's why he was drawn to Kathryn, I'm sure."

"Well, that and Kath has always been smokin'. Plus, she was having about none of his shit, which he secretly loved. Ev responds to a challenge."

"He's certainly found one with her," Sonya smiled. "She told me they've always had a lot of thrust and parry."

"Which they both need," Kellan said. "My sister has men falling all over her, but the few times she's stood still long enough to give one of them a chance, they've run squealing into the hills. Evan is the only man who's never been afraid of her. He's like this fortress she keeps throwing herself against, but he never crumbles. He just stands there asking if that's all she's got."

With a little frown, Sonya said, "Your sister said there was a problem last year, though. An unexpected crumbling?"

Kellan's amber eyes darkened briefly. "That was just a bump in the road. It's over now." He set the remaining cookies on the coffee table, then relaxed next to her in the pillows. "That day when we were twelve, the uncertainty in his eyes overruled him at first and he didn't kiss me right then."

"Oh?"

"He waited until we were walking back to the cabin to get some lunch. We were making our way through the new-growth trees at the trailhead when he asked me to wait a minute. He said he'd wanted to tell me something but was afraid of how I might react. I told him, whatever it was, spill it; he could tell me anything."

"What was the secret?" she said.

"Ev hesitated for just a second, then he hooked his fingers in the waistband of my shorts. He pulled me to him." Kellan shook his head with a smile. "I remember it like it just happened. I could taste the Dr. Pepper we'd been sharing out in the meadow. His lips were so soft and hot and the peach fuzz on his upper lip tickled. I closed my eyes out of instinct and then shot them open again because I didn't want to miss anything."

Sonya's cheeks hurt from smiling. "Had you been expecting it on some level?"

"Not even!" he laughed. "I had a *horrible* crush on him, but figured I'd just have to wait to grow out of it. I was completely blown away by this. I remember just standing there letting him kiss me. He pressed his lips to mine once, then when he didn't get punched, he did it again and lingered. No tongue yet, just those amazing lips. I felt a spark low in my belly that spread out across my torso and down my legs. It was the most *delicious* tingling."

Sonya's body mirrored his description and she had to take a quick breath. Kellan leaned in and brushed his lips against her neck, his silky whiskers raising all the tiny hairs on her skin.

He murmured in her ear; she felt his little smile against the bend of her neck. "I want to express my appreciation of your outfit this evening, especially your lack of undergarments up top. I've found it very inspiring."

She couldn't help laughing, even though her heart was racing a mile a minute. "Your sister's suggestion, actually. She knew something as simple as going braless would be a massive step for me, but encouraged it nonetheless."

His right hand curled around her waist, then slipped underneath her shirt, taking time to caress her lean belly with tender reverence before his fingertips found her nipples, tight and eager. Another sensual kiss and he focused on her, his eyes heavy-lidded.

"I want to make sure I'm reading you right," he whispered. "Just so I don't make you feel cornered again."

She shook her head. "No, you didn't, I just—"

Kellan's lips stopped what she was saying as he shifted to tuck his hips between her legs. Once he'd settled there, he smiled down at her. "Do you feel my heartbeat?"

"Yes." Sonya's voice was barely audible. His pulse throbbed against her in several places, and hers throbbed much faster against him. She knew he could feel her excitement and tension; she hoped he could also feel that she was ready for him. She caressed the warm silk of his back under his t-shirt, boldly easing her fingers between his jeans and his waist. Sonya smiled, waiting.

He said, "You understand I'm vulnerable to you. I'm at your mercy. I'm not going to do anything that I don't instinctively know you want." His hand under her shirt cupped her right breast and gave it a slightly possessive squeeze. He was testing to see how much control she wanted to give him. Sonya lifted into his touch in answer, her thighs hugging his lean hips. With a smile, he lowered down to place a kiss at the V of her collar and then pushed the cotton fabric out of his way to cover her nipple with his mouth.

Her eyes drifted closed, enhancing her other senses. Of course, Kellan was beautiful and sexy to behold, but this moment was about their primal connection as a man and woman. This moment was meant to be experienced through touch, scent, sound and taste.

When he kissed her next, his pulse had quickened and his voice was rough. "My instinct is telling me to take you, Sonya. Not to gently coax you and ease you along, but to dominate you. Is the message I'm receiving correct?"

Trembling with desire, she whispered into his kiss. "Zero distortion, sir."

He paused to meet her eyes. "Would you like me to use a condom?"

She breathed a nervous laugh, but was grateful he'd asked. "I had my tubes tied years ago. A condom is only necessary if you have rock star cooties."

"This is a cootie-free zone, I promise." Kellan's eyes danced with a playful smile. "I'd never have invited a true lady into my sandbox otherwise."

She knew he was lightening the mood a little to keep her calm and she appreciated it, but when he sat up on his knees to peel off his shirt, she grasped his belt with both hands and undid it quickly. Sonya wanted him to know she was through demurring.

He had both their clothing removed in no time. In fact, she didn't even remember him doing it.

When she thought about it later, all Sonya really remembered was the second Kellan entered her and how she came right away like a starving child, and then again and again before he shuddered in her arms and moaned like he was in pain. His orgasm tore through him. Toward the end, he was whimpering against her and then just collapsed.

Sonya held him close, breathing with him. Her body had conformed to his ample size the more he aroused her, so she knew she'd feel empty when he pulled out. She wanted him to stay for a little while. Maybe longer than that.

Kellan wrapped them in a handmade quilt on the couch. They slept easily in each other's arms without moving for the rest of the night.

CHAPTER FIVE

IN THE MORNING, Sonya quietly searched for her underwear. The panties in question had found their way behind the flat screen, dangling from the cable wire where he'd triumphantly flung them the night before. While Kellan lay snoozing on the couch, she laughed to herself as she tiptoed through the kitchen with her clothes and ducked into the bathroom.

It was just after nine and all she could think of was telling Jewel about her most interesting evening—ghostly footsteps and all. She freshened up a bit, then quietly started a fire in the kitchen stove to keep Kellan warm. She gave him a soft kiss on his forehead before slipping out the back door and making her way across the Broch's side yard.

At the foot of Jewel's cascading stone stairs, Sonya's text notification rang. She stopped to read the message when she saw it was from Evan.

If you're free, HH and I would like to do a thatching at your property this morning. Let me know.

She read the message twice but still couldn't make heads or tails of its meaning. Sonya trotted up the stairs to Jewel's back door. Through the storm door glass, she saw her friend inside at the kitchen counter pouring herself a mug of coffee. She let herself in.

Jewel greeted her with a playful smile. "Well, good morning! I was worried that boy ate you alive, but I see you're no worse for the wear."

Sonya rolled her eyes as she came inside. Monty circled her excitedly. "More on that in a moment. What on earth is a thatching, and why do I need one?" She held out her phone to show Evan's message.

In a rust-brown flannel shirt and jeans, Jewel held up her reading glasses and squinted at the screen. "Yup. I got a text about that, too. Could be any number of things—not to worry. Have you had breakfast? I was just going to make some bacon and eggs."

"That sounds great. I'm starving."

"I bet," she said with a good-natured grin. "Did he take good care of you?"

Sonya set her bag on one of the kitchen chairs, then took the two steps down into Jewel's sitting room. She looked across at the Brochs' cabin, radiant in the bright morning sun. "You know how heroin users get hooked after the first dose?"

"Uh huh," Jewel grinned.

"I might need an intervention soon." Sonya peeked over her shoulder to catch her friend's look of surprise.

"My gravy! Look what's got into my bashful little Sonya." Leaning on the wall at the top of the stairs, Jewel was clearly pleased. "The boy's as good as all his swaggering, then?"

"Well, between his swaggering and my own imagination, my expectations were pretty high. I'm pleased to report that he left them all in the dust." Sonya gazed at the little green house where Kellan was sleeping the morning away. "In all seriousness, it was hard to leave him just now."

"Then why did you?"

Two kids on bicycles flew over the bend of Sylvan Road below Jewel's window, spinning spokes whining like a swarm of insects. Sonya watched them until they disappeared. "I don't want him to know *quite* how much I enjoyed him. If he knew, he'd stop courting me. I love his courtship."

Jewel handed her a cup of coffee. "I getcha. But I'm guessing he's tickled pink to have crossed that bridge with you. From where I'm sitting, his interest appears genuine."

Sonya blew on the steaming brew before taking a sip. "He has so many women, Jewel. This inexperienced widow can't be all that interesting to him. I'm practically a virgin."

She waved her hand as she leaned on the wall at the top of the stairs. "You're talking about the gig skanks that only want to use him. Those girls get what they ask for: grabby quickies against a wall or in the backseat of a car."

Sonya let that image come into her mind, then drift right back out. She had no right to be possessive of him and didn't want to wind herself up. "Isn't he using them, too?"

With a shrug, Jewel said, "He certainly enjoys them—eager sluts are always fun. But I've never heard him talk about them in a derisive way, believe it or not. He's just taking them up on their offer. But you are most definitely different." She turned and went to the fridge for the breakfast fixings.

Sonya pulled out a chair at the kitchen table and Monty parked himself at her side waiting for pets. "We'll see how it goes, but I need to keep my perspective as much as possible. I've already gone plenty bonkers over him."

Jewel snorted. "Good luck with that."

"I know. Back to the morning's other mystery: what's a thatching and why does Evan think I need one?"

Jewel went about preparing their breakfast as she enlightened Sonya on the details of the mystical procedure Kathryn and Henry devised when they were young. "It's a damned effective mix of Wiccan and native magic," she said as she dropped two pieces of the local sheepherder's bread into the toaster. "The kids did it to my place about ten years ago and they refresh it every so often, as needed."

"As needed." Sonya blinked pointedly. "You mean, whenever there's some sort of spiritual danger afoot?"

"Danger that might directly affect *me*." Jewel brought their well-loaded plates to the table then went back to butter the toast. She'd made fluffy scrambled eggs, delightfully crispy fried potatoes with slivers of onion and bell pepper, and lean, crunchy bacon.

Sonya's belly rumbled at the sight of the feast. "Thank you. This looks amazing."

"Dig in, darlin'. I'll be right there." Jewel dropped a piece of toast on both their plates, then refilled their coffee before sitting down.

Sonya took four delicious bites before she even looked up again. She couldn't believe how hungry she was. Laughing self-consciously, she apologized for wolfing her food.

Jewel just grinned. "No greater compliment to a cook. Glad you're enjoying it."

Dabbing at her mouth with a napkin, Sonya said, "Ginny made herself known to me last night."

"Oh?" Jewel's eyes went round. "Did you finally see her full apparition?"

"No, just some very noisy footsteps upstairs on multiple occasions. Scared the crap out of me at first, but Kellan kept assuring me there was nothing to worry about."

"She just wanted you to know she was on guard keeping you safe."

"Safe from *what*, Jewel? Why do I suddenly need all this protection?"

Reaching across, Jewel patted Sonya's hand. "The kids will tell you everything; just be patient. It might be nothing more than them battening down the hatches and wanting to include you in the sweep. That's a good thing."

She sighed into her coffee cup. "If you say so." Sonya took her phone out of her bag and sent a reply to Evan that she was free all day. "I just wish I knew what Ginny was thinking about me. Is she glad she brought me close to them? Does she regret it? Is she ever going to tell me why she chose me?" Sonya met her friend's eyes. "Have you spoken to her lately?"

"No. It's hard when the kids are here because the cabin is usually occupied. Ginny needs her conference room to be empty for her to arrange a meeting with me."

Sonya found it difficult to imagine remaining calm during a live, in-person conversation with the ghost of Virginia Broch. "Last night, I couldn't help thinking she was watching me molesting her grandson," she smirked. "I hope she doesn't disapprove."

"I can't imagine why she would. Anything or anyone that makes those two happy is all right by Ginny—in general, of course. And, just to put your mind at ease, the way Ginny explained it to me was that she *can* see us in our flesh and blood form, but her perception of people is primarily their energy. She sees colors and light and movement more than she sees skin, hair and eyes. If she did happen to look in on you and the kid, she would have just been checking on the wellbeing of the vessel—*not* being a supernatural Peeping Tom."

Unable to keep herself from smiling, Sonya stacked another bite of potatoes and eggs. "In that case, she would have found his being quite well."

Jewel chuckled. "What'd did he make for dinner?"

"The most incredible Chicken Divan. I could've eaten three plates of it. He said the recipe belonged to one of their friends in Edinburgh—I think he told me she was a personal chef."

"That would be Mae," Jewel said. "Lovely girl. She's been here before—a few years ago. Her Scots accent is so strong she sounds like she's gargling marbles, but she's a good egg." With a wry grin, she added, "a snarky one like me, so we got along fine."

"That's nice that they've shared this place with their Scottish friends."

"Just Mae, as far as I know. She's a key figure in their Edinburgh tribe—a lifelong practicing Druid. She's sort of their UK version of Henry. The kids are closest to her, but they're also tight with Mae's wife, Lily, and a guy named Brodie who was Kellan's college roommate."

Sonya had heard the Brochs mention all of those names when they shared stories of their lives in Scotland. She'd known that Mae was married and that she and her wife had two small boys. She'd heard less about Brodie, but knew that he ran their website and handled the majority of the social media for KKB.

"But that's only five," Sonya said around a mouthful of heavenly bacon. "Don't they need a tribe of six?"

Jewel lifted an eyebrow. "Evan might not be there physically, but he is *always* their third. I assume you know a little more about the three of them now?"

"A little." Sonya recalled their long conversation the night before. "Kellan told me a lot last night, but it was all parceled out because he kept going off on tangents. Sometimes he'd come back and finish the story he started, but not always. It feels like I'm still missing a lot."

"Well," Jewel sipped her coffee, "you know that he and Evan have a physical relationship that goes beyond the parameters of friendship. Kath and I told you that much."

"Yes, but Kellan was reserved on the details. He probably thought I couldn't handle specifics. He was reading me very well; he may have been right."

"I'm not even sure it's all that big of a thing anymore." Jewel shook her head with a grin. "They were horny little shits when they were young, but things have likely mellowed out in their thirties."

"I don't know. It didn't seem so from Kellan's expression when he talked about it. My gut tells me they're still plenty active."

Jewel shrugged. "Ever since that bear ate their hammock all those years ago, my voyeur days have been over. I have no idea what they get up to anymore."

Sonya laughed.

"Does it bother you at all—stir up jealousy or anything?"

"God, no; it doesn't have much to do with me, does it?" Sonya said. "I worry more that Evan might be feeling encroached upon by me. I want to ask him."

"I doubt it's an issue. He's protective to a fault, but I've never seen him flinch over any of Kellan's girls."

Hearing it phrased in such a way made Sonya cringe inwardly. "I'm another one of his girls now; a notch on his bedpost."

With a twinkle in her hazel eyes, Jewel asked if that was such a bad thing.

"No, it's just … new. I've never been anyone's notch before."

"Enjoy the ride, my friend. Kellan Broch doesn't have the heart to be a heartbreaker—you'll be all right." She sipped her coffee. "Evan asked me if I was available to help with the thatching ritual, and I am. He'll probably walk you through it first then the whole gang will get together to do the deed. It's a little clunky, so the more bodies, the faster it goes."

Monty had been well-trained not to beg and had waited politely for Sonya to finish eating, but now that her plate was clean he slipped his big head back in her lap.

"It sounds fascinating, actually. But I hope the reason they think I need it isn't as bad as I'm imagining."

"What are you imagining?" Jewel took their plates to the sink. Outside the kitchen window, a gust of autumn wind snatched some dead leaves and skittered them against the glass. The daylight reflecting off the shimmying trees turned everything golden, even the very air.

"Oh, the typical horror movie stuff," Sonya said. "Demons, ghouls, dark shadow figures with huge red eyes and razor-sharp teeth. The usual."

Before Jewel could reply, Evan's Jeep rumbled around the bend of Sylvan Road and pulled into the Brochs' driveway. They watched him and Kathryn get out and go up into the house, then Sonya heard her phone chirp in her bag. Jewel's phone, perched on the rail of the sitting room, went off seconds later.

"Sounds like we've got our marching orders." Jewel went to get her phone as Sonya took hers out and read the message from Evan. It was the same for them both.

We'd like to start the thatch at the compound at 10:00, if that time works for all.

Frowning across to Jewel, Sonya said, "You promise they'll eventually tell me what the hell is going on?"

"I think they'll have to."

With a little sigh, Sonya tapped her response. "I want to grab a shower before they get there." She brought her cup over to the sink where Jewel had started the dishes. She pressed a kiss into Jewel's softly creased cheek and thanked her for the delicious repast.

"My pleasure, sweetie. See you up top in a bit."

Sonya grabbed her bag and trotted down the cascading stones, heading up the hill on Parker Drive.

She glanced at the back of the Brochs' cabin as she passed, but all the curtains were still drawn on that side. Even though she was crawling with anxiety about what was going on, she couldn't help smiling as she recalled the sweet, erotic moments of her evening with Kellan. If nothing more were to ever happen between them, she could live on those memories forever.

CHAPTER SIX

KATHRYN OPENED THE front door slowly. She didn't care about seeing her brother naked, but didn't want to embarrass Sonya by catching her unawares. When she saw only Kellan's clothes in various heaps around the room and him alone on the sofa snoring, she assumed the coast was clear. She grinned behind her to Evan.

"Sex coma." She nodded to her brother.

He chuckled as he followed her inside, closing the door after them.

A fire was going in the kitchen stove, but the pot belly had long since gone out. She went to light it while Evan headed for the coffee maker. While Kath built the fire, her brother stirred and stretched under the quilt.

With a groan, he rubbed his eyes and smiled at his sister. "Hey."

"Hey. Where's my girl?"

"I put her in Grammy's old cauldron with some onions and carrots. Good flavor, but she was a little chewy—no fat on her." He sat up, pulling the quilt around himself. He craned his neck toward the sounds in the kitchen and gave Evan a sleepy smile. Kellan tried to smooth down his poking hair to no avail. "I heard Sonya sneak out about an hour ago."

"Undamaged?" Kath teased, sitting on the end of the sofa.

"Mostly. She wanted to be roughed up a little."

Evan sat himself in Big Jackson's chair. He grinned at the disheveled Kellen on the sofa. "You behaved like a good boy, Peach?"

Kellan nodded and gave him a wink. "You'd have been proud."

Evan reached over and patted Kellan's knee through the quilt. "Good lad. So, Henry's on his way. We're thatching Sonya's place in about an hour. We need to crank up protection around the tribe."

Concerned, Kellan looked at his sister. "Why? What happened?"

"I had a nasty encounter with the hag last night at the restaurant. She's hovering way too close."

"Direct contact?"

"Very," Kath muttered, disgusted. She filled him in on the details of her exchange with the image of adult Lisa Tucker, and how Evan was unable to see the hag in any form whatsoever.

"But I saw her a few days ago in front of my house," Evan said.

This information did not please Kellan. "What? Why didn't you tell me?"

With a shrug, Evan recounted his experience with the teenage version of Lisa Tucker in his driveway. Scrubbing at his messy hair, Kellan flopped back into the sofa cushions.

"Why is she so fixated on that Tucker bitch?"

"Well, I know why she's using that for me," Kath said. "And Ev thinks he knows why she's using it for him, too. Wait'll you hear this." She went into the kitchen to pour them all coffee while Evan explained their theory on the hag's ability to access all their most private memories.

With a shiver, Kellan simply said, "Ew."

"Right?" Evan took the cup Kathryn handed him. "Thanks, babe. I mean, imagine what might be available."

"Yeah, no thanks." Kellan took his mug and blew on the contents.

Kath sat on the arm of the chair beside Evan. "I knew the old bitch would be pissed at me, but I had no idea how she might manifest that. Looks like she's planning to mess with anyone close to me in this creepy-ass way—hence, the need to thatch Sonya's property post haste. She's there by herself; she needs to be safe."

"But," Evan said. "Your sister doesn't want to spook her out too badly, so she's thinking we might sugarcoat the reason we're doing it—just for now."

Holding his mug in both hands to warm his fingers, Kellan shook his head hard. "I disagree. She should know the truth. And as long as we're thatching, we should rev up Jewel's place, too."

"Way ahead of you," Evan said. "We're all meeting up at Sonya's at 10:00. We'll do hers, then Jewel's, then you guys again. Tomorrow we can do Henry's and mine."

Kellan stood up, pulling the quilt around him. "Excellent. I'm gonna grab a shower." He shuffled around the coffee table, stopping a moment to warm himself in front of the pot belly before he headed to the bathroom.

Kathryn could see the distress in his eyes. "It'll be okay, Kell. We'll make everyone safe."

He nodded, forcing a smile. When they heard the water start to run, Kath slipped down into Evan's lap in the chair. He grinned, wrapping his arm around her legs.

"Hello."

"Hello." She kissed his beautiful lips, brushing the tip of her nose over his. But then her expression went sober again. "He's right about Sonya knowing what's up. I think it might be easier if it came from me, though. Less freaky, at least."

"Whatever you think."

"I'm going up there now. I'm weirded out about her being alone without the thatch, anyway." She gave him another lingering kiss, then slid off his lap. She nodded to the closed door of the bathroom. "You'll get him to the Greek?"

"Right behind you." Evan smiled at her as she grabbed her jacket and went out the back door.

❧

At the halfway point of Parker Drive between their property and the compound, Kathryn stopped. She turned toward Bonny Lake and scanned the sapphire sparkle in the morning sun. The aspens that got the most sunlight were already shedding their leaves, the translucent golden discs floating in the chill autumn breeze. She closed her eyes and raised her arms high above her head, fingertips reaching into the daylight.

Her prayer for strength went out to the elements and to the ancestors, to the sun and moon and the encompassing presence of the white light. She felt the granite gravel beneath her feet as leaves floated around her dark hair blowing in the wind, reminders of the constant cradle of nature. Behind her eyelids, Kathryn saw the eyes of her crow; gleaming black, focused and steely. It returned her gaze directly, squarely, ever vigilant. The crow awaited her summons as it anticipated her needs. After weeks of communing and learning, she and it were finally in harmony.

The outcaster smiled and opened her eyes on the sunny morning.

Part of her expected to find some hideous version of Lisa Tucker standing right in front of her on that unprotected road, but she was alone. It was only a short stretch, but utterly exposed public land that couldn't be sheltered by their magic. Until the hag had been dispatched, this road was a problem they could not solve, they could only fortify themselves as they traversed it. Determined that their victory wouldn't take long, Kathryn walked up the road to Sonya's house.

The front door opened as Kath stepped onto the porch. Sonya beamed at her with open arms.

"I saw you coming up the road," she said as they embraced. Her hair was up in a loose bun and damp from her recent shower. Kathryn smelled the lavender soap and light floral lotion Sonya used on her skin.

"Good morning. I hope you don't mind me just popping in." Kath shut the door behind her as an adamant breeze whirled leaves around the courtyard.

"Not at all—I'm thrilled to see you." Sonya's cheeks were prettily flushed, and she couldn't seem to stop smiling. "I'm assuming you know that your brother and I spent the night together."

"Well, it *was* on the front page of the Mount Iolite Gazette."

Sonya's laughter tinkled like bells. "Not that it's any surprise, of course."

"No, but I'm hoping you had a lovely experience together."

"We did." Sonya led her into the living room and offered her a seat on the pretty white sofa. She knelt to start a fire in the fireplace. "I just got here so I haven't had time to make coffee or tea for everyone. Evan didn't give me any specific instructions or…explanation, actually." Crumpling some newspaper, she sat on her knees and looked a bit helplessly at her guest. "You'll tell me what's going on, right? Before they get here?"

"That's why I came up." Kath reached for her friend's delicate hand. "But not before you tell me about your evening with Kellan. As your friend and his big sis, I need to make sure he was good to you."

Sonya's lovely green eyes welled up a bit as she described her experience, at times giddy as a school girl. From her recollection, Kellan had been a perfect gentleman. He'd made her laugh and feel safe, even with their grandmother's ghost making her presence known upstairs. He'd shared things about himself that allowed him to be vulnerable to her, and he'd made her feel comfortable opening up to him. All in all, he'd done exceptionally well. This made Kathryn happy.

"Good boy," she said, and then with a playful smile, "but are you sure you were with my brother and not some other, far more mature man?"

Sonya cracked up. "It was definitely him. He did his diligent instructor proud."

Smiling, Kathryn asked if Kellan sang to her.

"I'd hoped he might, but we were talking so much I don't think there was time."

"That'll come later." She knew this because she'd heard Kellan working on a new love song as he sat on the back porch at sunset. He hadn't asked his sister's input on the tune, which meant it wasn't being created for their band—it was a gift for someone. All she'd heard of the lyric were the words 'emerald' and 'blue'.

The fire on her hearth was going nicely and Sonya had made them cups of delicious green tea. Sitting beside Kath on the sofa, her expression went solemn.

"What's going on, Kathryn? No hedging."

She took a deep breath. "Okay. Twenty-three years ago, I did something bad to a negative entity—a succubus. It was attacking Kellan inside our cabin, but I wasn't strong enough to send it on yet, so I bound it to that old tree behind the general store. The bark beetle infestation last year weakened the tree to the point where it couldn't hold the entity any longer. I'm afraid it's out now."

"Oh my god." Sonya drew her knees up on the sofa. "Are you sure it's the same thing?"

"Positive I.D. has been made."

Sonya shivered. "And now it's after you?"

"It appears it's going to toy with me first—me and my loved ones." Kathryn did her best to describe the events that had so far transpired without any unnecessary drama or fanfare. She just wanted to share the facts, not terrify her inexperienced friend. "Our concern is that the hag is able to read our thoughts—in particular, the ones we'd rather not share with others."

"I see." Sonya let out a tense breath, turning her focus to the burning logs in the fireplace. Her strawberry-blond eyebrows knit. "I think I may have seen this thing, Kathryn."

A tight, hot lump formed in her belly. This was the last thing she wanted to hear. "When?"

Sonya gave a tentative description of seeing a decrepit old woman amongst the forest shadows right outside her property on the same morning she'd found Kellan standing in his pajamas in their backyard.

"I convinced myself it was just a trick of the light," she said. "But it pointed at me. I saw it do that just before the sun crested the mountain and washed out the shadows. If there was a scar on her cheek, I couldn't tell from where I was standing. But the expression of malice was unmistakable. It seemed to want me to know it knew me." Sonya set her tea cup on the coffee table. "I told myself I was imagining things since I'd just seen the ghost of your grandmother for the first time."

"Unfortunately," Kathryn said, "when you see something strange in Mount Iolite, nine times out of ten it's real. And that's why we need to thatch your place."

"But that won't keep out positive energies, will it?"

Kath smiled. "I asked Henry the same question when we were first devising this method. He assures me that this magic only effects outside visitors, not positive spirits of place who are there to protect it. Think of this as bug spray for bad juju."

Sonya seemed to understand as the low thunder of Evan's Jeep started up Parker Drive. Leaning forward on the sofa, she said, "This Lisa Tucker—how bad were things between you and her? Was it more than just rivalry over Evan? Why would this entity use such a specific tool to manipulate you?"

Kathryn sifted through her cornucopia of unpleasant memories, looking for anything she might have missed all these years. Lisa's contention had been ever-present since Kathryn and Evan began to date when he was thirteen. "She was just always there, you know? Chiding me and rocking my confidence with Evan at every turn—like she could make me hate myself so much that I'd believe I wasn't good enough for him."

Sonya's green eyes fixed hers, but she spoke softly. "Were Evan and Lisa ever intimate that you know of?"

"Ev would've told me." The words came out reflexively, but weren't even convincing to herself. Kathryn smirked ruefully. "Then again, maybe he wouldn't have. Now that you mention it, I've never asked him flat out. I'm not sure I want to."

"Understood," Sonya said. "But it might be beneficial to know. This spirit is striking your soft underbelly—it must believe there's a wound it can get to."

"Then why appear to him in that form first—or, at all?" Kath said.

Sonya bit her lip in thought. "Evan saw her as a teenager, right? The way Lisa looked when she was sixteen or so?"

"That's right. That was when she was most actively stalking my boyfriend; her and those big, sloppy tits. Her gawky little sister, Carrie, kept trying to devour Kellan around that time, too. Carrie

Tucker is probably the only girl in this town Kellan never made out with. She had great tits, like her sister, but he *hated* her."

"Interesting." Sonya's wheels were clearly turning as she went to open the door for the others piling out of the Jeep in her driveway. Turning back to Kath, she said, "Do you know where they are now—the real, living Tucker sisters? They're your age, right?"

"Same exact ages as Kell and me. Last I heard, Lisa married some construction worker down in San Diego and popped out two of his kids. Carrie went to school back east, but I don't know where she landed after that." Kath brought their cups to the sink and watched Evan through the window as he gathered gear from the Jeep's cargo bed. His blond hair seemed to be on fire in the golden sunlight.

Leaving the door open for them, Sonya came to stand beside Kathryn and followed her gaze through the window. "He's a perfect beauty," she said. "But he's *all* yours, young lady. Have no question of that."

Kathryn gave her a smile, but Sonya's keen perception had started her mental hamster wheel spinning. Kath and Evan had been apart most of the year for their whole lives; he could've got up to anything without telling her. His secretive nature was no help there, either. He'd been successfully hiding what happened to him in the war for fifteen years—a teenage indiscretion would have given him no trouble.

As she watched him come inside Sonya's house with Henry, Jewel and her brother, Kathryn wondered if knowing the truth might do more harm than good. For the time being, she decided to shelve that inquiry. Her focus was needed elsewhere.

CHAPTER SEVEN

HENRY PASSED THE nearly empty decanter of wine across the farmhouse table as they all chatted in the Brochs' breakfast nook. They'd just finished a wonderful pot luck meal after spending the day completing the thatching of all three of their properties on Bonny Lake.

"That's almost a dead soldier," he said in his deep, rumbling voice as Kath returned from the kitchen with a fresh pitcher of water for the table.

"That's because you lushes drink too much," she teased, refilling his water glass. Sonya saw them exchange an affectionate wink.

Evan sat beside Kellan who was at the head of the table on the living room side. They leaned forward over their glasses, talking in earnest about the hag's possible next move.

Concerned about the volume of their conversation, Sonya turned to Kath as she resumed her place at the head of the table on the lake side. "What we're saying can't be heard by the spirits in here, can it?"

"None other than Grandma," Kath said. Her flowing chestnut hair was framed through the window by the fluttering aspens silhouetted against the expanse of moonlit lake beyond them. "Her wall is a barrier for outbound sound and inbound invaders. We can be seen through it, but not touched or heard."

That was some relief, at least. Sonya sipped her fresh glass of red, her belly full of Jewel's delicious slow cooker roast beef, Kellan's potato gratin, Evan's sautéed Brussels sprouts with prosciutto and shallots, and the most flavorful cornbread she'd ever eaten made by Henry's Aunt Tilly. Her own basket of cookies for dessert waited in the kitchen. She smiled down the candlelit table at their happy gathering.

Jewel was beside her, intently listening to the boys' conversation. She turned to Sonya and leaned in close, sotto voce. "You look good in this room, my dear. You belong here."

Sonya kissed the old girl's forehead. "I have Ginny to thank for that, I assume."

Shaking her head, Jewel glanced back at Kellan, so animated in his conversation with his best friend. "You have *you* to thank for that. These two don't let anyone get close unless they know they can trust you. Look at the roses on that boy's cheeks."

Sonya *was* looking, but she interpreted that flush as a result of Evan's attention. She smiled for Jewel, but was still inwardly uncertain what to make of this strange dynamic.

Kellan suddenly stopped in mid-sentence, sitting bolt upright in his chair. He turned his head toward the kitchen. A second later, Kath sat forward and turned her head in the same direction. For a moment, they both remained stock still and breathless, and then appeared to hear something that Sonya did not. From the way the others were frowning, she guessed they didn't hear it, either.

Quietly, Evan asked, "Our succubus?"

Kellan shook his head, looking to his sister. "Do you hear—?"

"I do." They were both up and heading for the kitchen.

A moment later, they stood in their coats out on the back porch in the cold, dark mountain night. The porch light was on but only shed a small pool of illumination across their yard. Their breath puffed in the air. Sonya and Evan crept into the doorway behind them leaning out into the cold, while Henry and Jewel hung back a bit. Henry's bulk behind her made Sonya feel safer from whatever might be out there in the dark.

The Brochs were staring at the road in the direction of Jewel's house. The lights were on in her sitting room, but Sonya didn't think they were hearing anything that had to do with Jewel. Squinting in the direction of the Brochs' attention, she saw nothing but the inky night. Sonya turned to Evan standing beside her with confusion in her eyes; he shrugged.

Suddenly, Kath and Kellan both flinched and turned toward the road just above their yard.

"Someone's there," Kath said softly. "Do you see anything?"

"I hear … I think it's a boy." Kellan took one step off the porch and into the yard. Kath was right behind him. "Hello?" he called into the darkness. "Is someone there?"

He and Kath both took a breath at the same time reacting to a sound that, once again, Sonya and the others did not hear. All she heard was the soft cooing of night birds and the creaky chirping of crickets. She'd been listening so intently that when Kellan next spoke, she jumped.

"Can you see me?" He walked out a few more feet into the yard.

"Careful, Kell," Evan said under his breath.

Sonya wrapped her arms around herself against the frigid air and her growing anxiety.

Kath turned back to them in the doorway. "Ev, I need you to help shift the thatch."

"Roger that." He grabbed his coat from behind the door and slipped it on, going quietly out into the yard. As he passed, he whispered to the others, "Stay here. It's okay. It's not a monster."

Relieved, Sonya nodded and squinted into the darkness as the three of them approached the edge of their yard where the thatching lay in a thick line near the road.

Earlier, they'd marked lines around all three of their properties using bundles of fresh pine branches, birch twigs, pine cones and needles all tied neatly with hemp twine, then sprinkled with oils and wafted through pluming sage smoke. They taught Sonya the words for the ritual and she joined them in their blessing as they moved the branches from the compound, to Jewel's house and back to the Brochs'. When they'd completed the ritual there, they left the branches out around the entire cabin, laid end to end like a wild fence.

Sonya felt safer after they'd finished, believing wholeheartedly in the magic set by their intention. But as the Brochs got closer to the road and it became harder to see them beyond the reach of the porch light, she became frightened again. What were they about to encounter? Kellan was almost at the thatch barrier.

Evan reached for the back of his coat and grabbed it, holding him. In a low, commanding rumble, he said, "No further."

Kellan sighed, but stopped about five feet from the thatch. He called into the darkness again. "Can you see me?"

Sonya heard a tiny, frail voice say, 'yes'.

It came from somewhere near the rocks that flanked the backside of Parker Drive just above Jewel's property line. Frozen, she stared in that direction, but she still didn't see a thing.

Kath spoke into the darkness next. "Can you tell us your name?"

Faint and breathy, the tiny voice said, 'Jeffrey'.

"Hello, Jeffrey." Kath's tone was kind and maternal. "My name is Kathryn. Do you see the light beside me?"

'Yes.'

"That light is coming from my brother, Kellan. He's here with me. Can you come toward us?"

There was a stretch of silence and then Kellan reached his hands out toward the road.

"That's it, Jeffrey," he said. "I can see you now. Come closer to my light so you can see us better. Are you lost?"

The tiny voice said, 'I was sure I knew the way.'

"That's okay," Kath reassured him. "You probably just made a wrong turn. We'll help you get where you're going. Come toward the sound of our voices. It's okay."

Just beyond the thatching near the road, a faint bluish-white glow appeared in the shape of little boy. Sonya was sure her heart had just stopped. He moved toward Kellan and Kath as though he were a cloud crossing the sky, slow but seeming to follow a sort of track. Kellan kept his hands held out in welcome.

Kathryn looked around them in all directions and so did Evan; they were looking for the succubus lurking in the dense blackness. Sonya cringed, pressing back against Henry for safety.

His big hand fell gently on her shoulder and he whispered. "It's all right, Lady Sonya. This duty is what the vessel and outcaster were made for."

She nodded unsteadily, knowing she was about to witness something extraordinary. Jewel had moved in beside her in the doorway and gave Sonya a comforting smile. They all peered into the yard.

Still scanning the immediate vicinity, Kath whispered to Evan. "I've got nothing but the boy. You?"

"Nope." Evan moved toward the thatching in front of Kellan. Kath went with him, standing close.

She said, "Wait to open it until he's right up on it."

"Yep." He knelt at the ready with his hand hovering over the thatch.

The little voice called out, plaintive and scared. 'Are you still there? I can't see you now. Where'd you go?'

Kath spoke quick and soft. "We're right here, Jeffrey. Come toward my voice."

The small reply was full of trepidation. 'I see the light again, but, there's a big white dog next to it. Will it bite me?'

Sonya frowned, confused. When she'd seen Kellan's wolf in her yoga studio, it was glowing red and gold. What was this little spirit seeing?

Kathryn's tone was calming, gentle. "No, honey—that's a nice dog. He's protecting my brother and he'll protect you, too. Don't be afraid of him. Come forward."

'But …" Jeffrey said. 'There's a wall.'

"Yes, and we're going to open a gate in the wall right now so you can come inside." She turned to her brother and whispered. "Stand close to me so he can see where to go."

Kellan moved behind her, hands still outstretched. "I'm right here, Jeffrey. See? Come toward me."

The boy's image floated to where the three of them waited and hovered there just beyond the thatch. His tiny voice wafted on the air. 'I can see you now.'

"Good," Kellan smiled. "My sister is going to open the gate right now. As soon as you see it open, come right through really fast, okay?"

The boy said he would.

Kath and Evan looked around warily again and then each took hold of a portion of the thatch branches. She nodded to him once and they shifted the branches together, just enough to make a tiny opening in the line.

"Now, Jeffrey," Kellan said.

The filmy boy slid right through the opening and into the Brochs' backyard. Kath and Evan immediately closed the line of branches again. With a collective deep breath, they moved around Kellan and the image of the little boy, Jeffrey, who drifted in front of him at about four feet high. Kellan held his arms open with a little smile.

"Do you see that lighted room right there?" he said to the boy.

'Yes. There's a big chair and I smell hot cocoa.'

"That's right. It's all for you, Jeffrey. Come on in."

'But, I have to find my grandpa. He won't know to look for me there.'

Now that the little spirit was inside their barrier, Kath appeared much calmer. She put her hand on her brother's shoulder which must have created an illumination of her so the boy could see her, as well. Sonya gathered the spirit was only able to hear Kath's voice before.

"Can you see me now?" She smiled sweetly.

'Yes. Hi.'

"Hi, there." Kathryn's big brown eyes danced with kindness. "Are you okay?"

'Yes, but I died, though.'

She nodded. "I know, honey. It's all right. Just another part of the journey. You're safe now."

The boy accepted that well enough, as though this information wasn't news. 'Can I pet the dog?'

"Of course you can. He's a nice dog. Go ahead."

Sonya wished she could see this dog the boy referred to, but all she saw around them was the dusty backyard. She watched Evan pacing close to Kellan's back like a bodyguard, and then it dawned on her. That "big white dog" the boy saw was Evan's gray wolf, standing sentinel over the vessel.

"Were you going to meet your grandpa, Jeffrey?" Kellan asked.

'Yes, but I thought I knew where I was going, and then …'

"You *did* know, you just got off track a bit."

'It's cold,' he said in a trembling little voice.

"Come inside where it's warm and have the hot cocoa," Kellan said softly. "We'll help get you to your grandpa."

Sonya watched in utter amazement as the tiny, filmy spirit took Kellan's offered hand and then slipped right into his body, easy as pie. Once they knew Jeffrey was inside, the three of them came quickly into the house. Evan shut the back door and threw the deadbolt.

Stopping in front of Sonya, Kellan took her hands and gave her a smile. "You okay? I know how freaky it is to witness this the first time."

She stared at his face a moment, then swept her eyes over his entire body. "That little boy's spirit is really *inside* you right now?"

Kellan only nodded, his long-fingered hands chilly in hers from being outside.

"I thought you would look different somehow," she said.

Kath put her hands on her brother's shoulders and smiled at Sonya. "Come on, Kell—sit in front of the fire where it's warm."

Evan came around behind him and slipped his coat off, hanging it on the wall hook. Kellan sat down on the kitchen floor.

"Is your kit in here?" Evan asked Kath, who nodded to him.

Sonya heard him rummaging in the bathroom and then he returned with a lovely wooden inlaid box about the size of a briefcase. He set the box on the floor where the Brochs now sat. Henry's large hand on her back gently urged Sonya to sit down at the island with Jewel, while he leaned in the doorway.

"It's all right if we're in here?"

Kath nodded to her. "Of course. He's just a little boy." She slid the box toward her and opened the lid. There was a half shelf inside with a shallow depression that held several small bundles of tied sage, and a pink cigarette lighter. Kath took one of the bundles and lit it, blowing on the end until the embers glowed.

Evan leaned on the kitchen counter behind Kathryn, at the ready should she need him.

Kath blew the sage smoke up over her brother's head and then moved the smoldering bundle in an arch over his whole body three times. "This vessel is a child of the light. He is protected by the light and cannot be harmed while he gives sanctuary to this lost soul. We ask the light to help us guide this boy, Jeffrey, to his family." She took a small shiny blue glass dish out of the box and set it on the floor, resting the burning sage bundle in it.

From the box, she took an object about the size of a brick that was wrapped in a white silk cloth. Kath removed the cloth to reveal a thick stack of cards with an intricate swirling blue design on their backs. Sonya had seen Tarot cards before, but none of this size. She watched Kath spread the cards out on the floor facing upward in a fan underneath the smoking sage. She put her hands on her brother's shoulders.

"Jeffrey, can you come talk me?"

Kellan sat up straight, looking in his sister's eyes, but his gaze had become slightly cloudy. And then the little boy's face seemed to overlay Kellan's, rising forward and out about an inch. Sonya could actually make out his profile. He was a tiny, frail child, about nine years old, with large eyes and a smooth, hairless head. He saw Kath and smiled at her.

"There you are," she said. "You okay in there?"

'Yes. It's warm and the cocoa is really good.'

Kath laughed. "You're safe in there for as long as you need to stay, Jeffrey. Can you tell me what happened to you?"

The boy proceeded to explain that he'd been sick for a long time and that he knew he was going to die, so he'd been talking to his Grandpa Joe who was 'already across'. His grandpa told him where to meet him when he passed on and that he'd be waiting. He gave Jeffrey specific directions of things to look for—landmarks and such—so it would be easy to find each other. Jeffrey told Kath he was supposed to look for a yellow road like in the Wizard of Oz. He was supposed to walk on that road and go toward where the sun was shining at the end of it.

"And your Grandpa Joe is there, right?" Kath said. "Where the sun is really bright on the yellow road?"

Jeffrey said that's what he'd been told. The problem was, when he actually crossed over and died, he couldn't find that road anywhere. Grandpa Joe said it was going to be *right there*, but it wasn't. He searched for hours and hours, and he hadn't seen anyone at all. It was getting dark and cold, and he was getting scared. Jeffrey started calling for help. That was when he saw Kellan's light.

Kath nodded emphatically. "I've seen this road. I know exactly where it is."

'You do?' Jeffrey's filmy eyes got big and excited.

"I *do*. You were very close to it; you just took a wrong turn somewhere and couldn't see it. I'm going to show you where it is right now." She smiled again and then reached down to the fanned cards; she selected one and held it up for him to see. On the face was the image of a woman in a flowing white robe holding up a massive star. "See?" Kath said. "The road is right there, around the corner, behind those trees."

Sonya watched as the little boy squinted into the face of the card, and then he suddenly brightened. 'I see it! I see the road!'

Kath smiled, her pretty eyes gleaming with moisture. "See how close you were? You can go right to it and call for your Grandpa Joe. We'll stay with you until you find him." She held the card up at the spirit's eye level and waited.

Sonya held her breath, watching in awe as the tiny spirit tugged itself forward and out of Kellan's body. Kellan lifted along with the spirit until it slipped free, as though they were connected by an invisible umbilical cord. Once the boy was out and floating again between him and Kath, Kellan relaxed.

Kath held up the card, still smiling at the small spirit. "Do you see your grandpa yet? That's him right there, isn't it?"

The little spirit raised his hands and waved them in the air. 'Grandpa! Grandpa Joe! I'm here! I see you!' And then he drifted right into the face of the card. He called out faintly once more before he disappeared. 'Bye! Thank you for the cocoa!'

"You're welcome," Kath said softly. "Be happy, little one." A tear tracked down her face, but she was smiling as she reached into the fan of Tarot again. She took out the card of the High Priestess and covered the Star with it. Kath held both cards between her hands and took a deep breath. "We send this spirit into the light of his loved ones. Look after him on his journey. We give thanks to the light for assisting us in our task. Blessed be."

Softly, Kellan said, "Blessed be."

They leaned toward each other and touched foreheads for a few moments. Kellan put a kiss on his sister's cheek.

"Good job, sissy."

"That's what it's all about." Kath was still smiling as she packed up her kit.

Kellan took what was left of the sage bundle and dropped it into the firebox of the stove. The sweet scent of it mingled with the pine smoke. They both stood and stretched, then hugged each other tight. He took the box from her and put it away.

Kath turned to Sonya. "I'm glad you got to see a happy one for your first."

Sonya had tears standing in her eyes. She recalled the first morning she'd sat in that kitchen with them as they explained what they were and how they helped the lost spirits. Kath had been almost dismissive about her own role in their task. "Some janitor, lady." Sonya breathed a little laugh. "That was incredible."

"She's a badass," Kellan said as he came back to the kitchen. He put his arm around Sonya's shoulders. "You're getting a *really* big dose of us in a very short amount of time. Are you sure you're all right?"

She gave him a hug, lingering with her face against his very warm neck. She could swear she caught a slight whiff of marshmallow on his skin. "Was there really cocoa?"

"There was to him," Kellan said. "When he got close enough, I could see things about him that would help make him feel safe. He loved hot cocoa and popcorn, and his favorite stuffed animal was a giraffe named Ike. If I'd needed to, I could have added those elements—but the cocoa seemed to be enough."

"How do you see those things, though?"

Kellan shrugged. "It's just there. In a similar way, Kathryn can see the cards she'll need to extract each spirit—the combination is always different."

"That's wonderful," Sonya said, again turning to her friend who was curled into Evan's side near the counter. "Amazing."

Kath smiled wearily. "It's all part of the package. We each have our given tools to make the transition as easy as possible for the lost ones."

"Does it hurt when they come and go?" she asked Kellan.

"Good ones don't bother me at all," he said. "I feel sort of full in a way, but it doesn't hurt. It's just—" he shook his head. "I've never been able to explain it in a way that anyone could understand. I know they're in there, but they don't crowd me. The benevolent ones feel warm."

"And the bad ones?"

"The bad ones feel cold; and most definitely crowd me. They burn my energy unless Kath binds them from doing so. If she ties them up, they can't pull on me."

"I see." Heart racing from amazement and adrenaline, she turned to Evan still leaning on the counter with his strong arm around his girl. "The white dog the boy saw was your wolf, right?"

"That's right," he said.

Jewel gave Evan's shoulder a squeeze from where she sat at the island. "Our Gray Wolf can sense the intention of an incoming spirit. If there's any hint of malice toward the vessel, out come the big teeth."

"I wasn't too worried about the little boy," he said. "But Kathryn and I are on watch for our unwanted guest. All spirits are stronger in the dark—especially the dark in Mount Iolite."

Sonya turned as Kellan stretched a bit beside her. He rubbed his lower back with his hands, flinching at a tender spot.

"What's wrong?" she said.

Evan stepped around behind him, placing his hands in the same spots. "Residue?"

"Mmm." He smiled at Sonya. "The spirits leave some junk behind sometimes—like a snail trail."

She frowned at that description. "Is that painful?"

"Not exactly, I just know there's something in there that doesn't belong. Henry's Aunt Tilly showed Ev and Kath how to get it out when we were kids. It's pretty easy."

Kathryn smiled as she passed behind her brother and Evan on the way to the living room. "Kellan prefers to have Ev do it, though; he gives a better massage."

Evan grinned, stepping into the bathroom to grab a bottle of lotion. "Come on, Peach. Stretch out on the floor in there."

Sonya caught Henry's little smile in her direction, noting that Evan had just used his special nickname for Kellan in Sonya's presence. During Kathryn's vision quest ceremony, he'd told Sonya that if that were to occur, it meant that Evan, the alpha leader of their tribe, had accepted her into the fold.

As Jewel followed her and Henry into the living room, she spoke quietly in Sonya's ear. "Look at you, in like Flynn."

Cheeks ablaze and heart still pounding from the events she'd witnessed, Sonya couldn't stop her smile. She kissed Jewel's cheek.

CHAPTER EIGHT

IN THE LIVING room again, Sonya sat on the small sofa with Jewel, next to where Kellan had stretched out on the floor. Evan straddled his hips and pushed Kellan's t-shirt up near his shoulders.

From the big brown chair, Henry said, "My godson Leonard has an excellent design for a blocking mark, Kellan. It would fit best right there on your back. He's been working on it for a few months and it will *only* keep out succubae."

Kathryn smirked. "You and I can hold him down while Leonard inks him."

With a little chuckle, Kellan said, "I'm not gonna argue. As long as it's only blocking that one entity."

"As promised," Henry said. "You'll like the design, too—it's pretty rock star, if I do say so myself."

Kath smiled in approval of Henry's selling point.

Evan squeezed some lotion into his hand and Sonya recognized the scent right away as the one Kellan preferred. The light fragrance reminded her of lemon trees in the sunshine and was a beautiful complement to Kellan's natural scent. Evan warmed the lotion between his palms. Sonya watched as he firmly smoothed it over Kellan's lower back, his long, strong fingers gently kneading. She felt the recent memory of that lovely skin under her own hands as she watched.

The potbelly stove had a good roaring fire, but the cozy living room was too warm for Sonya's taste. She shimmied out of her cardigan. Evan must have thought so as well; he paused to remove his t-shirt before continuing his massage.

Evan's extensive tattoo work decorated his carved, muscular torso. So did his battle scars. The pinkish-brown web reached over the ribs of his left side from hip to shoulder. Sonya only knew that he'd been stabbed and shot in an ambush of some sort, but she had no further details. Not wanting to be rude by staring at the scars, she admired his artwork instead.

She'd seen the mark of the USMC before—the eagle with the orb and anchor, and the waving *semper fidelis* banner. Evan's tattoo took up the entire spread of his wide shoulders and went halfway down his back. From where she sat, she couldn't quite see all of the wolf's head beneath it, but its long snout pointed down into the V of Evan's waist. Its relentless ice blue eyes glared.

In contrast to that ferocious image was the fat bloom of a beautiful, deep red rose curling over his chest on the right. Its crimson petals were drawn with such delicate accuracy they appeared velvety and lush. Sonya could almost smell its floral perfume.

When Evan reached forward to rub Kellan's shoulders, a dark vine emerged from the bloom, reaching down over the edge of his under arm. The spiked thorns were huge and sharp. Beneath the vine, high up on the flat of Evan's right bicep was the pinkish sphere Sonya hadn't quite been able to see the first day she met Evan at the Rhino; a succulent golden peach.

Kath leaned forward from where she sat on the larger sofa, tapping her finger to the peach with a grin. "Kell's head fits right there—always did; like that spot was made for him. It's 'the nook'."

"I love the nook," Kellan murmured. His eyes were closed in relaxation, but he was smiling.

Sonya had been wondering just how their cuddling activity worked and had imagined several scenarios since Kellan had told her about it the night before. With this new information, it was easy to picture them stretched out together; Evan on his back and Kellan tucked against his right side, head resting in the crook of Evan's strong arm. The image was at once soothingly sweet and hauntingly erotic; she liked thinking of it. Kellan's warm fingers wrapping around her ankle startled her out of her reverie.

He grinned at her, his eyelids heavy from Evan's ministrations. "I see your naughty wheels turning, little lady."

Blushing, Sonya laughed. "The grist for that mill is abundant at the moment."

Evan took hold of Kellan's lean hips and pushed his thumbs into the flesh on either side of his tailbone. His brow had a tiny knit of concentration. "Is it here?"

Kellan wriggled. "Bit lower. It feels like a tiny stone."

He shifted and pressed his thumbs again, making Kellan jump a little. Evan circled either side of the bone, then up over top of it. He used enough pressure to make pink indents in Kellan's skin as he drew his fingers down in a long, slow line to the tailbone. He repeated this several times, every time adding a bit more pressure, and stopping just above the cleft of Kellan's cute denim-covered butt. Kellan wiggled playfully with every stroke.

Sonya had seen a similar technique during her studies in Reiki. "You're drawing the energy down through his spine, but where are you sending it?"

"I'm gathering it first," Evan said. "And then I'll pull it up and out." He demonstrated by turning his palms upward. "Sometimes you can even see it moving around the room."

"Wow. And where does it go then?"

"Usually out a window," Kath said. "When I remember to leave one open." She stood up and went to the window over the pot belly stove that faced Jewel's house. She undid the latch and opened the wood frame a few inches. Cold refreshing night air blew into the over-warm room.

"Is that too cold for you, Kell?"

"No," he said in a buffed voice. "Feels nice."

Kath returned to the sofa, yawning as she sat down. "God, it's not even nine o'clock and I am toast. It's been a *very* busy day."

"Indeed," Sonya said with a little smile to her friend. "I'm pretty exhausted, too." She felt Kellan's fingers curl around her ankle again and when she looked down, his grin was triumphant.

She watched Evan work, noting how well he knew Kellan's tolerance for pressure, and just where to touch him to make him sigh. He'd stopped wiggling and was breathing deep and even, his lips slightly parted. Sonya loved the way his thick auburn lashes rested on his smooth, pink cheeks and thought of how she'd left him sleeping on their sofa earlier that morning. She longed to stroke his beautiful face with her fingertips, pet his eyebrows and tickle his whiskers until he fell asleep.

She was still sensitive from having him inside her, but all day as they'd worked on the thatching project, she'd smiled to herself whenever she became aware of the tenderness. It reminded her of their intimacy and his attentive focus. He'd been learning her with every kiss, every caress. Sonya had never known the sort of love they'd made; it was at once effervescing with erotic passion while still infused with such deep affection, it nearly made her weep. After seeing him and his sister with that little boy's spirit only moments before, she felt even more privileged to have Kellan's interest. But at the same time, she deeply feared that this extraordinary creature had already run off with her heart, whether he'd intended to or not.

Evan rubbed Kellan's shoulders underneath his t-shirt. Their breath was in sync, Evan's slate-blue eyes keen on his task. They were all quiet as he curled his fingers into loose fists as though he were scooping handfuls of sand, then opened his palms toward the ceiling. Sonya's hair was moved by a breeze that came from the opposite direction of the open window. She turned just in time to see a translucent flash of Virginia Broch.

Standing at the foot of the stairs, her arms folded over her narrow waist, flowered apron neatly tied, Ginny appeared to be supervising what Evan was doing. She faded a second later, but Sonya knew she was still there. As Kellan had said, she was always there.

The wood frame of the window creaked, drawing her eye back to it. A light, glittery mist lifted from the tips of Evan's fingers toward the open window. It moved quickly, slipping out into the night through the screen. He released a long breath and rubbed his hands together with a little smile of accomplishment. Kellan stretched contentedly beneath him.

"Better?" Evan shifted so Kellan could sit up.

"Yes. Thank you, brother." They sat on the floor facing each other, amber and blue eyes transmitting in silent communication. Sonya wished she knew what they were saying.

Jewel asked Kellan if he wanted her to give him a quick once-over.

"I think I'm fine, thank you," he said. "I do need to see a man about a mule, though." He got up slowly with Evan's assistance, then he stretched again. Kellan excused himself and went into the bathroom.

To Kathryn, Sonya said, "I just saw your grandmother over there by the stairs. She was watching Evan work. It was only for a second, but she was definitely there."

Evan leaned back against the chair, grinning up at Henry. "She was making sure I wasn't damaging her precious grandson."

"God knows," Henry chuckled. "You might've accidentally pulled out his spleen."

They all laughed, but Sonya was increasingly curious about Evan's interaction with Ginny. How often did he see her? Henry mentioned that she spoke outright to him, as she did with Jewel, but when and where did that occur? Would he be willing to discuss such a thing with her at this early juncture?

Their weary party dispersed for the evening a short while later and Kathryn offered to run Sonya home. They all felt uneasy about the unprotected road between them. Kellan, looking sleepy and spent, kissed Sonya in the doorway and asked if he could see her the next day. She whispered that she'd like that very much.

Wrapped up in coats and hats against the advancing fall chill, Kathryn drove her up Parker Drive and onto the compound. Thatching bundles had been left at the directional corners of her property and Sonya glanced at the one beside her driveway as they pulled up to the house.

"I really appreciate you guys doing that for me. It was such a fascinating process."

"Well, you're tribe now," Kath said, shifting her 4Runner into park to keep the heat running. "We have to protect each other. I mean, if you want to be tribe. Obviously, we all welcome you, but it's ultimately your choice."

This news made Sonya's heart pound for multiple reasons. "I'm honored, Kathryn. I just wish I knew that feeling was shared by your grandmother. She brought me into this, after all. I only know that she thought I'd be a good fit to you guys, but I don't know her verdict. It's obviously important."

For a moment, Kathryn had no reply. Her big dark eyes scanned the compound through the vehicle's windows, Evan's navy knit hat stitched with the Mammoth Lakes minaret logo tugged over her ears. "I can't imagine a single objection she might have, but what's more important is that *Kell and I* choose you. And now you've seen what we're really about. It's not all scary monsters."

In the low light from the dashboard, Sonya took in the details of the young woman behind the wheel. Kathryn Broch: rock star, witch, love of Evan MacTavish's life—one of them, at least. But above all of that, she was at the center of a small miracle. Maybe not so small to the disoriented souls she and Kellan helped redirect, but it was clear Kathryn regarded it as the task she'd been assigned; the simple fulfillment of a destiny. It didn't seem to overpower her life, it was just another component of it. Sonya found that simple fact astonishing.

Kathryn's full lips tilted in a smirk that was adorably similar to her brother's. "Are you trying to read my mind, yogini? It's a cross between a graveyard and a junkyard in there."

Sonya laughed. "I'm sorry, I didn't mean to be staring. I was just thinking how dumbfounded I am by you. How you balance all these elements of your incredible life and make everything appear effortless. I mean, you saved that little boy's soul tonight!"

"No, we didn't do *that*—his soul was already attended to by the light. He just lost his way in the crossing and we put him back on the right road. My brother and I are shepherds, not saviors."

Sonya reached across and took Kathryn's hand. Both their fingers were cold, but they squeezed tight.

"Nonetheless, you're amazing to me and it's a privilege to be your friend."

Kathryn pulled her into a long hug. Against Sonya's ear, she said, "I'm sorry you've been drawn into this situation with the hag. It stresses me out what might happen to you—and it would all be my fault."

"How on earth so?"

When Kath spoke again, her voice was tight with emotion. "I could have asked Grandma not to involve you—to keep you safe and out of all this—but I wanted you. I was being selfish and you might get hurt because of it."

"Kathryn," Sonya took her friend's face in her hands. "The decision to become your friend was entirely my own. I wanted you, too. I don't feel in any way influenced toward that."

"But you were." Kath swallowed, her long fingers curling around Sonya's wrists. "You were directed toward both my brother and me, and now ..." she breathed an unhappy laugh, "you're trapped in our creepy haunted snow globe right along with us."

Kathryn's vulnerability hurt Sonya's heart. She didn't know what else to do but keep hugging her to reassure her that all was well, that she wanted to be there for both of them, and to help if she could. This was Sonya's own choice, not merely the creative manipulation of a dead woman.

When they finally parted, Kath reminded her to keep her selenite stone with her at all times. Sonya was safe on her property and on any of theirs, but she needed to protect herself out in the world. Reaching into the pocket of her jeans, Sonya took out the gleaming white stone and showed her friend that she had it. She promised to never leave home without it.

CHAPTER NINE

REHEARSALS FOR THEIR upcoming Halloween show took most of the Brochs' time the following week. Sonya and Kellan had loose plans to get together but hadn't been able to connect, so she busied herself working around the compound. An errand to the hardware store in Mammoth reminded her of how this all began on the fateful day Henry Hunter had added a KKB flyer to the store's bulletin board just in time for Sonya to see it.

The same young man was behind the register when she rolled her cart up. She'd collected charming new porch lights for the guest cottages, some curtain rods for the kitchenettes, welcome mats and an assortment of planters.

"I remember you," he said with a smile. "You've got the yoga studio in M.T.I., right?"

"Good memory. I'm getting close to opening first week in November."

He nodded to the planters in her cart. "You were looking for a landscaper before. Did you decide to take it on yourself?"

"The big stuff is handled, but I wanted to try container gardening for some flowers. The deer ate all the last ones I planted, so I'm trying some different varieties."

From behind her near the wall of plumbing supplies, a familiar voice replied. "Sounds like they give their cute new bistro on the hill five stars." Evan grinned as he came to give her a hug and kiss on the cheek.

"Well, hello there," she said, delighted. It had only been two days, but she'd really missed seeing all of them. "What brings you to these parts?"

Bundled in a fleece-lined green plaid flannel jacket, work boots and khakis, Evan held up a new shower head in a plastic package. "Every winter something freezes way down in the mechanism of the one I've got and I end up having to take the whole damn thing apart. A plumber friend told me this model doesn't have that issue, so I'm going to change it out before the first snow."

"That's sounds complicated."

"Easier than fixing the old one every year. What're you up to?"

Sonya told Evan what she'd been doing at the compound. "Jewel suggested I try Russian Sage and Snapdragons because the deer don't eat those."

"Spider Flowers and Angelonias, too," he said. "Both colorful, but not to the deer's liking. That's what they have in the flower boxes around town in M.T.I."

The cashier was bagging the smaller items while Evan helped to arrange everything back in Sonya's cart.

"You need some help with all this? I'm off this afternoon and KKB are rehearsing. Happy to be of assistance."

Sonya loved that idea. "Thank you, Evan. I'd truly appreciate some help. But you have to let me buy you lunch in return."

"Deal. I just need to grab one more thing." He went off toward the back of the store while Sonya finished checking out.

She'd been hoping for a chance to get Evan's take on things, but hadn't figured out a way to approach him that wasn't awkward. This situation felt fortuitous.

Back out in the parking lot, he helped her load everything into the Rover. The wind had been picking up in the late afternoon, but was still quiet at mid-day. Bright sun flamed in the cloudless, cobalt sky, and yellow and orange leaves littered the ground.

Sonya sighed, taking it all in. "The Sierras have made October my new favorite color."

He grinned. "It never gets old—the fall colors and the first snow of the year."

"Looking forward to seeing that, too." She checked the time on her phone. "It's 12:20. Do you want to grab lunch here or head back to Mount Iolite?"

Evan's black aviators shielded his eyes, but she could still see his appealing little crow's feet when he smiled. "I've got a craving. Have you been to Corsero's Deli yet?"

Sonya brightened. "I've been driving by that little place for seven months and have never gone in. Am I missing out on something wonderful?"

"You are, and we have to remedy that," he said. "I'll follow you out."

As they drove back toward I-395, Sonya smiled at the red Jeep in her rearview. She was hopeful that Evan would speak freely with her alone. She had so many questions.

Running into him at that particular location in Mammoth gave her a moment's pause, though. Could Virginia Broch have a tether between their cabin and that hardware store? It seemed she was able to work quite a bit of connecting magic there, but it was miles from Mount Iolite. Perhaps the store sat on sacred land or atop an underground aquifer—some easy means for spiritual energy to traverse. Sonya had no idea. But it looked like Ginny's hand was working in her life again, and this time along the lines of Sonya's own wishes.

❧

Corsero's Deli sat on Mount Iolite's main drag wedged between a tiny local art gallery and the general store's hulking ice machine. The interior was no more than 15x20 and crammed tight with gleaming deli cases filled with all manner of meats, cheeses and tempting accompaniments. Over thirty curated sandwiches were available, and customers could also 'build their own.' House-made pizzas and calzones rounded out the menu with cookies and ice cream bars for dessert. A colorful selection of beer and wine was offered to complete the perfect picnic.

On the wall by the register was a small frame containing the first dollar the business ever made, and a worn wooden sign reading: 'Established in 1962; Never closed a day since.' Sonya wondered if that was really true.

A smiling, olive-skinned man in his early seventies came to the counter wearing a butcher's apron. He extended his hand in greeting to Evan and Sonya as they approached.

"Mr. MacTavish the younger, welcome. Good to see you. How're your folks?" His voice was so gravelly it almost broke when he spoke, and contained a hint of a Brooklyn accent.

Evan shook his hand warmly. "They're both great, thanks. I'll tell them you asked. How you doin', Glenn?"

"I can't complain because my wife always beats me to it." He rocked backwards with a chesty laugh.

"Please give Nina my best. I'm bringing you a new recruit today," Evan said. "This is Sonya Pritchard. She bought the Parker Compound earlier this year."

"Oh, of course." Glenn Corsero had dark brown eyes that seemed to sparkle from within. He held both of Sonya's hands in his and told her how pleased he was to meet her. He'd been unable to attend the town meeting held for her, but he was aware that she'd purchased the compound for a yoga retreat. They chatted about how things were going and how she was enjoying living in Mount Iolite.

With a firm pat on Evan's broad shoulder, Glenn said, "I've known this young man since before he was born. His pretty little momma used to come in here when she was pregnant with him because she *had* to have my wife's pickled sweet peppers. She told me the cravings kept her up nights."

Sonya laughed. "I'll have to try some of those."

"I'll set you guys up good. You must know Jackson Broch's kids," Glenn said to her. "The musicians, Kathryn and Kellan. Their cabin's right by you and they're definitely in town."

"They most certainly are." She could hardly contain her smile. "We've become very good friends."

Glenn was nodding. "Good people, the Brochs. My wife was friendly with their grandmother, Virginia, before she passed." His thick, silvery eyebrows drew down slightly. "Strange lady, if you ask me. She was always so dressed up with her fancy shoes and jewelry— here, in the freakin' woods." He chortled. "And she always wore black." He leaned in and lowered his voice so the customers enjoying sandwiches at the picnic tables outside wouldn't hear. "People 'round here said she was a witch."

Evan was grinning but had yet to comment. Glenn nudged his arm playfully.

"This boy knows the truth and he never says boo about it. Stuck like glue to the Broch kids since they were all pintsized." Glenn waggled his brow to Sonya. "Mark my words; he's gonna marry that pretty Kathryn. And soon! I see some towhead babies runnin' around in the next couple years!"

"I don't doubt that one bit." She gave Evan a wink.

Dismissing all this with a grin, Evan turned his attention to the menu board above the counter. "I want Sonya to try all your best stuff, Glenn. Let's get a large Italian with the works, a Club with extra bacon, and some sides of your beans, slaw and potato salad— plus as many of Mrs. C's pickles as you can fit in a bag."

Evan added a beer and a glass of wine and Glenn happily rang up the order.

With a wink to Sonya, the proprietor said, "I can't wait to see which one of my wife's pickles Kathryn craves when she's expecting. Her little friend, Gigi, was all over the spicy banana peppers. My wife said her baby probably came out pooping fire!"

This struck Sonya as strange since Kathryn hadn't mentioned that her dear friend Gigi had given birth to her twins yet. She made a note to ask Kath later, then smiled and shook Glenn's hand again. "It was lovely to meet you. I can't wait to try these sandwiches."

"You make yourselves comfortable out there under a heater and I'll have everything brought out for you."

Evan thanked him and held the door for Sonya to step out onto the patio in front of the store. A table was open near the art gallery side and they settled in close to the heater.

"You're ok sitting out here?" Evan said. "We can get everything to go and head back to the compound if you want."

"No, this is nice. I love the crisp air."

"Me, too." He tapped a quick message on his phone, then tucked it in his pocket with his sunglasses. "I'm telling KKB that I'm baptizing you at the altar of Corsero's."

"You might get a sainthood."

"I might."

"Glenn's a very sweet man."

"Yeah, I can't imagine M.T.I. without them. Glenn and Nina moved here from New York in the late '50s. All their kids were born and raised here. That man has seen it *all*."

"I love that he knew Ginny."

"Well, he knew *of* Ginny. His wife was much younger than Ginny and wouldn't have run in the same circles, even in a tiny town like this. Ginny kept to herself most of the time. Her eccentric dressiness and hermit tendencies helped perpetuate the witch rumors."

"Which were all true, of course."

"Absolutely."

A young lady in a red checked apron came out with their drinks. Evan told Sonya she was Glenn's granddaughter, Tamara.

"Glenn's whole family works at the deli in one way or another. His oldest son is the accountant, his youngest handles the food orders and works the counter. I went to school with both of them. And Nina makes all the sides and pickles herself. She's an *artist*. This is the first place Kath and Kell come when they arrive every year."

Sonya scanned their current location wistfully. From where they sat, the peak of Mount Iolite could just be seen over top of the village buildings. Tall pines, oaks and aspens lined the main street and crowded up the hillside from the village, branches rustling with birds and squirrels. Kids on bicycles and skateboards tooled along the sidewalks, dodging folks ambling through the quaint town in its autumn coat of gold.

"This must've been a magical place to grow up," she said. "Was it for you?"

Evan raised his beer to her. "For part of the year, it was excellent. For the rest of it, Henry, Gigi and Ginny made it bearable. Cheers."

"Cheers. Ginny? I thought she died when you and Kellen were eight." Sonya sipped her wine—a lesser brand with a bit too much oak on the finish, but certainly good enough for a picnic.

"She did. But I didn't meet her until after that."

Sonya was encouraged by his openness. "Jewel said I should hear everyone's stories of their first encounter with Ginny directly. Will you share yours?"

"Sure." But his smirk suggested he might not tell her the truth.

"Only if you want to," she said. "I've been warned that you can be a little cagey."

His eyes twinkled with amusement. "Did Kell tell you that or big sis?"

"Both."

Evan chuckled. "They have different methods for managing it—none of which gets them what they want, though."

"I don't know," Sonya teased. "My observation is they get *exactly* what they want from you. They love that you're challenging; keeps them on their toes."

"Kellan and I struggle less because we communicate easier. Kath is always making things black or white. I don't think like that, so we wrestle."

Taking a chance, Sonya leaned in and lowered her voice. "Is that why you haven't asked her to marry you yet?"

His brows lifted and he grinned. "Jewel told you about that, eh? That's actually not the reason, though." He dug into the coin pocket of his khakis, taking out a small glinting object. "Hold out your hand."

Sonya did, and Evan placed the most stunning engagement ring she'd ever seen into it. Jewel told her Ginny left her ring to Kathryn when she died; was this the same one? Kathryn had never mentioned that Evan had it. How could she not know?

"Oh my god!" Holding the gleaming platinum band up to the light, she admired the beautiful emerald-cut stones. A massive diamond —easily two carats—held court in the center, hugged by two slightly smaller sapphires, then two even smaller aquamarines.

The diamond had a faint purplish glow that she assumed reflected the flanking sapphires, but Evan told her to look beneath the raised setting.

"There's an iolite chip under the diamond," he said. "From a promise ring I tried to give Kath when she was eighteen. She wouldn't accept it because she was going overseas to school. She didn't want to hold me back in case I found someone else."

Sonya was a bit breathless looking at the ring. "This is gorgeous. And it's so perfect for her. I can just see it on her delicate hand."

"Me, too. But I'm hanging onto it for now. I need something from her before I put my knee in the dirt."

"Which is?" Sonya handed the ring back reluctantly and he tucked it away safe in his pocket. His grin told her he had no intention of answering her question.

"All right," she said. "Does Kathryn know what it is you need?"

"Sure. And she'll give it to me—eventually. In the meantime," he patted his pocket, "the ice stays on ice."

"You carry it all the time?"

"Every year while they're here. You never know when the moment will come."

Sonya squinted. "Wait, how long have you *had* that ring?"

"Since I was twenty-two," he said, sipping deep from his beer. "When I inherited it in trust from Ginny."

Her jaw dropped open and she wasn't able to close it right away. She took a steadying gulp of wine. "Ginny left that ring to *you*, not Kathryn?"

Evan shook his head. "No, she left it to Kath, but she intended it to pass through me. I memorized the passage from her will the day Big Jackson brought the ring to my parents' place. I'd only been back from Afghanistan a few months and was still recovering. My folks took great care of me."

In a soft voice, she said, "I noticed your scars the other night when you were working on Kellan's back. Kath told me you'd been both shot and stabbed, is that right?"

"Right." His internal wall dropping down was nearly audible. Evan's shoulders tightened. "I don't elaborate on those details, I'm sorry."

Sonya squeezed her fingers together on the table. "Evan, I didn't mean—"

He reached over and gently covered her hands with his. "Nothing to worry about. I just want to make sure any further questions are put away. It's not that I don't trust you, it's just … I don't like talking about it."

"Of course not. I won't mention it again."

He gave her a small smile, patted her hands, then settled back with his beer. He took a breath that seemed to clear the air in his head. "Kath isn't aware that Ginny gave the ring to me first. She thinks it's waiting for her in a vault somewhere under lock and key."

"Well, it is in a way."

"True," he smiled. "I'm pretty sure this proposal thing will go down any day now, so just keep all this under your hat for the time being."

"Of course. I'd never want to ruin a surprise like that for a friend. Best of luck with the big moment." A little rush went through her that Evan had confided something so huge. It was a good sign that he may trust her enough to open up a bit more.

Tamara came out again with a plastic tray overflowing with their food order. Glenn sent them another round of drinks on the house and they started unwrapping the goodies. Evan guided her through the various dishes, making sure Sonya tasted everything. The sandwiches and pickles were divine, but her favorite thing was the fresh, salty potato salad made with red onions, house-cured Kalamatas and a bit of boiled egg.

While they ate, she asked him about the passage of Ginny's will that accompanied the ring. "You said you memorized it."

He washed down a huge bite of the Italian with a swig of beer. "It said: *My engagement ring, the diamond and platinum band together, I bequeath in trust to Evan Michael MacTavish of Mount Iolite, California. My son, Jackson, Jr., will keep this item until such time as Evan MacTavish reaches the age of twenty-one (21). It is understood that the ring is to be given by Evan MacTavish to my granddaughter, Kathryn Victoria Broch, at the time of their betrothal. Should such betrothal not take place, the ring will be returned to my granddaughter.*"

Sonya swallowed a bite of coleslaw in a hard gulp. "You were eight years old."

He shrugged with a smirk. "Behold the Broch Witch's version of an arranged marriage, but we're taking our time getting around to it."

"Well, *you* are," she teased.

His eyes lit with a secretive little smile. "There are extenuating circumstances."

Sonya had no doubt. "Ginny was very specific about the components of the ring but didn't mention the other stones."

"Her ring was just the diamond and band. A jeweler down in Reno designed this setting for me based on Kath's photograph. I used my savings to buy the other stones because I wanted it to be spectacular."

"Aww," Sonya grinned. "Listen to you. Your girl told me there was a mushy romantic under this tough, mountain-man exterior."

This made him laugh. "She claims to hate it, but that's shit. Kellan, on the other hand, loves all my mush."

Sonya knew to tread carefully on this ground. What he'd said sounded like an invitation to proceed, but she didn't know him well enough to be sure. Evan hadn't become angry when she almost crossed the line before—he'd simply refused to let her. She determined that was manageable and forged ahead.

"Seeing as Kellan and I have become so close; may I ask about your relationship with him? I won't be offended if the answer is no. I understand it's very personal."

His nod was slow and speculative as he worked on a pile of baked beans, but the door was open.

She tried to keep her voice steady. "Mostly, I've wanted to ask if *my* relationship with Kellan bothers you in any way."

His dark blond eyebrows crinkled. "Why would it bother me? I'm happy you two are getting along so well."

The remark struck her funny and she breathed a nervous laugh. "Is that what we're doing— 'getting along well'?"

Evan grinned. "From what I understand, *very* well."

Blushing full out, Sonya groaned. "You know everything we've done, don't you?"

"No, Kell's not that guy. Never was, even when we were kids. I'd have to drag details out of him, unless something happened that he didn't understand. Then we'd have a long, revealing discussion while he sorted through it." He raised a brow. "Often too revealing, if you get my meaning."

"He is blabby for a man," Sonya said. "But I love that. Time just flies when I'm talking with him."

"I give him shit about chattering so much, but his thought process fascinates me. It breaks everything down to love, pleasure and happiness. Kellan can't understand how anyone would do anything that would bring about a different result."

"And yet, bar fights."

He laughed. "Testosterone is a harsh task master. He loves the rush of fighting."

Sonya smiled at that then circled back on her question. "You're sure, then? I'm not trespassing in any way?"

Those steely eyes fixed her but still glittered with a smile. "You may have misinterpreted what you've been told. Kellan's not my boyfriend or anything. We don't identify that way—never have."

"But you *are* lovers. That's how it seems based on what little he's told me."

Evan took a bite of the Club sandwich and chewed slowly, giving her statement a thorough mulling over. "That word doesn't quite fit. It's close, but only to a point."

"Yes, I understand you two don't go *there*."

He chuckled. "No, we don't. But the rest of it is the behavior of lovers, so I see how you arrived at that word. It's just not quite accurate."

"Is there another word that would be?"

He scratched at his blond whiskers then laughed. "None that I know of. This is a one-off situation that was sparked by Ginny when we were pups."

Sonya poked at her coleslaw with her plastic fork. "Jewel mentioned that she used a touch of magic to bond you boys. But she said, and I quote, 'Ginny may have put a little too much English on that eight ball'."

Evan's shoulders shook with his laughter. "Well, the lady had a mission. She needed the vessel and me to be completely bonded. That was going to happen with me and Kathryn anyway, but little boys are fickle with each other. Ginny had to make sure this would stick."

"Because she'd chosen you as their protector?"

When he looked at her then, his eyes were more gray than blue. "The way Ginny tells it, all vessel and outcaster pairs have a designated third—a guardian in the flesh in addition to their spiritual guardians. Ginny says I was chosen by the light for this duty. She was just acting as its agent."

"I see. And her action included the 'whammy' she put on you boys when you met?"

He nodded. "She's asked me many times if I want her to dial it back now that we're permanently bonded, but I don't."

"No? Wouldn't it be less complicated to not have that going on?"

A gigantic RV with a fishing boat in tow thundered past them on the main street. He waited for the noise to settle, then gave Sonya an impish grin. "The complication has never been a factor. It feels so damn good and makes Kellan so happy, I have never batted an eye about that. It's just *us*; the way he and I connect. We were affectionate from the jump before we were old enough for sexual feelings of any kind. But once all those hormones got boiling," he shook his head, "it was a freakin' freight train. He and I might even have wandered into these waters without Ginny's push."

"Really?"

"Really. But we'll never know." He held her gaze a moment, blue eyes intent and gleaming. "Was Kell the first man you've been with since your husband?"

Sonya's throat tightened slightly and she swallowed. "Yes."

"I hope he was worth it."

"He was."

Evan smiled and sipped his beer. "Now I'll ask you the same question, Sonya: does *my* relationship with Kellan bother you?"

Squaring her shoulders, she gave him a brave smile. "Ready to be astonished?"

"Hit me."

"Not only does it not bother me, but I find it intriguingly sexy."

His blond eyebrows went up. "Is that so?"

"Yes. That is so. So *there*." She laughed and took another bite of the crispy, vinegary slaw.

Evan shook his head. "You girls are funny. Kath thinks it's hot, too."

"Well, it's not any different from straight men enjoying watching two beautiful women together."

He considered this, also tucking into a bite of coleslaw. "I guess that's true. Hadn't thought of it that way. Would you like us to set up a viewing for you?"

Sonya's eyes went round and she gaped at him in cold shock—until she realized he was joking. She socked his arm. "Sure. I'll bring popcorn."

Laughing, he polished off his beer, then regarded her seriously again. "Just so we're clear: Kellan is my best friend with an added component, but I have no claim on him that could be trespassed upon. He's a free agent. And I'm happy you two are clicking. It seems to be good for you both."

Greatly relieved, Sonya took a sip of wine. The woody finish was growing on her. "Thank you for that clarity. I have no idea where it might go with us, or if it's going anywhere. But I'm very mindful of your deep existing relationship with him. Respecting that, and you, is important to me, Evan."

"I appreciate that. I just want Kellan to be happy and, so far, so good. But should you injure him in any way, *then* we'll have words, little lady."

Sonya shook her head. "I can't imagine how I might injure him. It's my heart that's on the line here."

"How so? Kell's a dyed-in-the wool sweetheart."

She hedged, not sure if it was safe to reveal her feelings. Would he tell Kellan what she said? What would be the harm if he did? "I know he is, but it seems this is just an expression of affection for him. He's physically attracted to me and enjoys my company, so he wanted to sleep with me. But I don't think he sees this the same way I do."

"And how do you see it?" Evan's intent gaze suggested he was reading her regardless of what words she chose. His protectiveness crackled in the air.

Sonya ventured to speak plainly. "I see it as a love affair. I mean, I've been courted, wooed and conquered. I'm giddy from his attention. That's a romance in my mind, but I doubt Kellan's impression is the same."

Evan's handsome face bloomed in a deep smile. She saw the little boy from those old photographs there, as well as the interesting, edgy man he'd grown into. Beyond his heart-stopping good looks, Evan was loving and complicated, and more than a little dangerous. She could easily see why Kathryn and Kellan each adored him so.

"Don't be so quick to doubt. That's all I'll say." Evan winked, then gestured to the remains of their lunch. "Should we take the rest of this with us and go hang some porch lights?"

Her heart raced with excitement from his remark, but it would do no good to appeal to him for more information. That much she'd learned. All in all, she felt their first private conversation had gone swimmingly. Sonya smiled at his suggestion and said, "Sounds good."

CHAPTER TEN

TAKING A BREAK from rehearsal, Kellan started for the door of their rented studio space on the outskirts of Mammoth. "I'm going out for a smoke."

Kathryn hooked the neck of his sweatshirt. "Show me your talisman."

He rolled his eyes and pulled out the black leather cord around his neck, waving the black onyx and red jasper stones dangling from it. Satisfied, big sis released him.

Before she'd even let him out of the car that day, Kath had done a quick sageing on the studio. She marked the outside corners of the building, including its two patios, with selenite, black onyx and rosemary that would serve as a temporary, but spiritually impenetrable fence while they were in residence.

They'd been using this studio since they were kids and first playing with other musicians in the Sierra's restaurants and lounges. Most of the local players lived in Bridgeport, Mammoth or Bishop, but they all congregated in this location to network and be among their own kind. The international 'rock star' Brochs were local royalty there.

Their favorite guest guitarist, Brady King, was working with them that day, along with the Skagg Brothers, Mark on bass and Matt on drums. The Halloween show was the biggest of the year for

KKB and had a special set list tailored to the holiday. They'd spent most of the day rearranging the iconic *Monster Mash* into a hard rock song, and the hard-rocking Hell's Bells into an eerie ballad during which Kath theatrically sawed the strings of her cello. Everything was sounding great.

Kathryn wandered out to the reception area where there were comfortable sofas and a fridge stocked with soft drinks. The owner, Kurt Monroe, sat in his office just off the lobby talking on the phone. She waved to him as she got herself a cold Diet Pepsi.

Kurt smiled awkwardly, and a blush crept up his thick neck. He was somewhere in his forties with a rounded middle and a nest of wild, tightly curly red hair. Horn-rimmed glasses sat on his large nose, but he still had an ever-present squint as though his prescription needed adjusting. He was soft-spoken and painfully shy and had always had an obvious crush on Kathryn. He flushed from his neck to his forehead every time she was near him.

In jeans and Kellan's oversized blue cable-knit sweater, she put her feet up on the Ikea coffee table and settled on the sofa to go through her emails. The text from Evan about taking Sonya to Corsero's made her smile. She was glad they were becoming friends; Evan could use a fresh perspective. Even though she believed such a thing would never cross Evan's mind, she couldn't resist teasing him just a bit.

Keep your hands off that pretty lady, son. My brother bites.

Immediately, Evan replied: *I taught him how, remember? How's the Halloween set going?*

Good. We're about halfway through.

See you for dinner?

She grinned. *Can I eat it off your naked belly?*

Impractical. I was thinking of chili. Evan sent a wink.

Killjoy. We should be back in M.T.I. by 7. Tacos at ours?

Can you make tacos with chili?

We'll find out. She sent him an emoji with a lecherous leer.

See you then. Now back to my full-scale invasion of the hot yoga teacher.

Kath sent an eye roll, a shit emoji and a kiss, and then a new text message came in. She switched over, but the sender's number was marked as 'unknown'. It appeared to be a video. She had good virus protection on her device and was bored enough to see what it was; probably just some stupid ad. She pressed play.

The grainy image skipped and jumped like the connection wasn't strong enough to play it, but Kurt's studio had excellent Wi-Fi. All her signals and battery power were at capacity. Still, the video crackled in and out, the images frayed and shadowy. She could make out a room with no windows, just a metal folding chair. The concrete floor gleamed with spilled, colorless liquid. Kath thought the video might be in black and white, but then she saw the bright, lush red of a rose tattoo she would know anywhere.

The camera moved seamlessly as though it were on a track. It panned slowly from Evan's naked right shoulder to his face—his 22-year-old face as it looked when he'd come back from the war. He panted, running with sweat, eyes wide with terrified shock. In the image, Evan was shaking his head repeatedly and muttering. And then he became agitated.

"He was just like Peach," he stammered, insistent. "So much like Peach!" His left hand came into frame, scraping over his mouth and whiskers and covering half his young face in glistening, sticky, bright red blood. Staring right into the camera, he began to lick those fingers clean.

The screen went black in her hand. Kath fumbled to turn it back on, but the faint light in the corner told her to connect to a power source. The battery that had been at 96% only seconds before was now flatlined. She dropped the phone in her lap and just sat there, trying to steady her hammering heart. But once the fear subsided, Kathryn got angry.

"God dammit, Evan! I *told* you this would happen."

She marched back to the studio to fish her charger out of her bag and then plugged the phone into the wall jack by the piano. The guys were either outside with Kellan or relaxing somewhere else in the studio, so she was alone. She sat on the floor and powered up the phone.

The video was gone. Nothing in the text folder, nothing in the archive, nothing in the cache. Vanished like it was never there. But it had been there and Kathryn had seen it.

The hydraulic hiss of the studio door made her jump. Her brother came in and spotted her sitting on the floor; he knelt beside her, concerned.

"What's with that face?" he said. "You look like you just got bitch-slapped by the devil."

"I think I did," she croaked, shaking her head at her phone. With a bitter laugh, she said, "apparently, the spirits have YouTube now, and I have a free subscription to the Hag Channel."

He frowned and reached for her phone, but Kath shook her head.

"The video's gone. I checked already."

"What was it?"

Kath hesitated, remembering a long-ago conversation with Henry over what Evan had told him about the war. It hadn't been much but what little detail had been revealed, Evan did not want shared with the Brochs—least of all with Kellan.

Kellan squeezed her shoulder. "Kathryn, was it some kind of omen or warning?"

"No, not even." She made a lame attempt to smile. "It was just saber rattling, a bunch o' bullshit meant to freak me out. Which it did, so score one for the succubus." She took a deep breath then gave him a real smile. "Never mind. I'm going to ignore it and move on."

His amber eyes were dark with suspicion. "Why are you hiding this from me?"

She met his gaze evenly. "Because, monsters. They're assholes. And we have more important things to focus on."

"Kathryn."

Voices out in the hall preceded Brady, Mark and Matt returning. The guys filed in and returned to their instruments. Still sitting on the floor by the piano, Kathryn reached over and cupped Kellan's face.

"Let this one slide, little bro. It was meant for me and it's no big deal. We've got music to make."

Kellan took her hand and kissed it, but he was still frowning. They got up and went back to work.

∾

She couldn't get that horrid video out of her mind. They rolled back into Mount Iolite just after 6:30 with their guitars tucked into the cargo hold of Kellan's Tahoe. A silver locket containing protective onyx and cat's eye stones dangled from a chain around his rearview mirror, swaying as they took the turns on Sylvan Road. All their cars had one of these talismans inside it somewhere. It was the cement of a blessing ritual that made a vehicle as safe as a church.

Kathryn saw the lights on in Jewel's place and her brother tooted the horn as they passed, tucking into their driveway next door. She and Kellan got out into the clear, chilly evening. Trooping up the front stairs with their instruments, his text notification chimed.

"Ev's still up top. Sonya's inviting us to do tacos up there."

"Sounds good to me—no mess to clean up." Kathryn glanced over to Jewel's warmly lit cabin and saw two other ladies sitting at her dining room table with her. She recognized Holly Naims from the vacation rental office in town, but the other woman had her back to the window. She had long gray hair that could use a good combing. Kath couldn't help picturing the hag sitting there, unbeknownst to Jewel, mocking Kathryn with her wily dexterity. She tried to put that out of her mind. The last thing she needed was to be jumping at shadows.

At the compound, they admired the new porch lights and cute curtains in the guest cottages and feasted on tacos made from Evan's famous chicken fajitas. Sonya barely ate a thing as she was still stuffed to the gills from Corsero's, but she seemed in very good spirits. Kath was happy to see her brother holding Sonya's hand and sitting with his arm over her shoulders while they chatted after dinner. She didn't think he realized it yet, but he was falling hard for the pretty yoga teacher. The whole situation felt good to his sister.

They left Kellan with Sonya and drove back down to the cabin after midnight. Kath had mentioned during dinner that she'd had another encounter with the hag, but hadn't gone into specifics. Since she'd minimized it for Kellan, she did the same with Sonya, but once she and Evan were alone in bed, she broached the subject again.

"I want to tell you about the hag's drive-by today."

Evan frowned in the tawny glow from the nightlight plugged in beside her bed. "I could tell you were holding back up there. I thought we were telling Sonya the truth about stuff."

"We are, but we're not telling my brother about this—at *your* request."

"I'm sure you'll explain that. Did you get another visit from that Tucker wench?"

"No. This time, the hag used my hot squeeze."

He groaned, rubbing his forehead. "Do I want to know?"

"Probably not, because it means I was right about that bitch telling me your war secret in her own nasty monster way." She recounted what she'd been shown in as much detail as she could recall. Evan listened with his brow anxiously knit but when she'd finished, he appeared relieved.

"That's just a load o' spooky horse shit, babe. Nothing you described has anything to do with my experience. This is good news, actually. It means she can't really read our minds—at least not thoroughly."

Kath squinted at him. "Nothing about it was accurate at all?"

"Not a thing. There were no windowless rooms with metal folding chairs near where my unit was stationed. Just tents, vehicles and foxholes."

She wasn't quite convinced. "What about before or after you got to your post?"

Evan sighed, clearly wishing she'd let this go. "Before, I was in basic at Pendleton and I shipped out immediately. After I was wounded, I went directly to the VA hospital in downtown LA. There were no windowless rooms like you described anywhere before, during, or after my deployment, Kathryn." He snorted mirthlessly. "And I've *never* liked the taste of blood—my own or anyone else's." He reached for her hand and squeezed it gently on top of the blankets. "This is just a smokescreen. The hag's got nothin'."

Kathryn studied his face in the low light as he spoke. He didn't flinch and his gaze never averted as people often did when they weren't telling the truth. But Evan was an expert at evasion. Not lying, exactly, just stepping deftly around facts he'd rather keep close to his vest. According to his mother, he'd been doing this since he learned to talk. This skill wasn't acquired; it was factory issue.

"All right," she said. "But it was still damned disturbing and too close to the bone. Even if she can't read our minds entirely, she can read enough to do serious damage."

Evan scooted close to her under the covers. "She can't read *anything* while we're in here, babe. Let's shelve it for now and get some sleep. I'm beat." He looped his arm around her and closed his eyes, effectively shutting down the conversation.

As much as she didn't want to let the subject go just yet, Kath was tired enough to go along. However, she was superstitious about good night kisses because one never knew when it might be the last. Evan knew this about her. Petting the soft whiskers under his plump bottom lip, she purred, "Where's my kiss, soldier? You know this drill."

He grinned, kissing the tip of her finger, then leaned in to kiss her lips. "Sorry. I don't know what I was thinking. Good night, babe."

"Good night." She smiled.

Moments later he snored beside her, but Kath lay awake for hours just watching him sleep. She couldn't stop seeing those disturbing images playing on her phone. Was Evan lying about them not being in any way accurate? Kathryn's outcaster gut niggled her, telling her to not only see what was presented, but to closely examine the negative space around it. Something significant was there in the absence.

On the edge of dawn, she finally fell asleep, but her mind continued moving the pieces of this puzzle to make them all fit. She dreamt first of the day's events, then some silliness about a toaster that popped out warm bedroom slippers, and then she was down in the hollow, dark tunnel of her subconscious. She had the sense of hyper awareness that humans only experience in a deep alpha state—

more awake than when truly awake. This was where she'd first gone to find the crow; this was where it always waited for her.

Darkness was all around, gravel crunched under her shoes and leaves rustled, then the long, soft sigh of the high wind moved through the starlit tips of the pines. She was in the middle of the backyard looking up at the cabin where all the lights were in dim nighttime mode—just a muted amber glow behind the curtains. It was never completely dark anywhere in Grandma Ginny's cabin. Nightlights glowed in every room. The darkness was not allowed to encroach on the fortress where her grandchildren slept.

Kathryn could see Sylvan Road between the cabin and the shed, and beyond it, the gleaming obsidian of nighttime Bonny Lake. The crow, the size of a mythical dragon, paced along the shoreline waiting for her to call to it. Its black eyes reflected the moon glinting on the lake water. A sound compelled her when she looked at her guide—not really a word, but an utterance in fricative consonants: *ttsschk—ttsschk*. Kathryn didn't know if that was the crow's name because names seemed nonsensical to it, but she murmured this sound whenever she saw it and the crow murmured it back to her. *Ttsschk—ttsschk*. This was their greeting.

The sweep of heavy fabric on the wooden boards of the porch made her turn in her dream. There was Grandma, at the picnic table, dressed in the full length black wool coat she wore for years before she died. It was highly tailored and nipped at the waist, its long bottom flaring in a pleated bell to the ground. Kath used to call it her 'Mary Poppins Coat'. Her neat black curls caught the moonlight as she was busy with something on the table. Kathryn moved toward her.

Even in the gloom, Ginny's manicured nails gleamed pink as she shifted bits of forest debris around on the green plastic surface of the table. Three pinecones identical in size made a perfect row off to the right, then a single aspen twig was laid by itself beside them. Ginny gave her granddaughter a secretive smile, her beautiful green eyes sparkling like emeralds. Kathryn's heart sang at the sight of her and she tried to tell Ginny how much she loved and missed her, but she had no words at her disposal. She gathered that she couldn't speak in this dream, only watch and understand.

Ginny pressed her right index finger to her rose-painted lips and kissed it, then brought it close to Kathryn's lips without making contact. In her spirit form, Ginny had to choose between the ability to touch and manipulate objects, and being seen in full visual manifestation. These two actions vibrated on separate frequencies and could not occur simultaneously. Even in a dream, she reflected these rules. She turned her attention back to her work.

Seven single pine needles were arranged in a soft sloping line beside the one aspen twig. Ginny made sure they were orderly. When she turned to Kathryn again, she held something in her elegant hands—a single fresh stem of white jasmine. Glancing back at the display on the table, Kath understood that it and the flower being presented noted a location in Ginny's collection of grimoires: Jasmine 3/17. She heard her grandmother's voice inside her head.

"This succubus is older than these mountains and knows beastly tricks. It attacked me once before you and Kellan were born, but I am not an outcaster. I hadn't the strength to send it on; I managed only to anger it. This is the reason it came at my family again when Kellan was a boy. It's learned so much from consuming human energy that it understands the dark pleasure of vengeance. It considers itself duly vexed by us both, my dear. Now it's got score-settling on its mind."

Still holding the sprig of jasmine in her hands, Ginny lowered her eyes. *"I'm sorry this has come to you at all, Kathryn. It's not fair to you."*

Kathryn shook her head. Without words, she tried to tell her grandmother that this was both their fight, not just Ginny's alone. And Kathryn had the outcaster advantage. She would set it right.

Still solemn, Ginny nodded that she understood. *"I'll be with you every step. There are nine parts to the magic you will need"*—she glanced at the display she'd arranged on the table—*"you'll find five in there. Know that you will each lose a piece of yourselves in this fight. It's inevitable. But what you lose will be balanced by greater gain."* Ginny smiled. *"Once you assemble all the parts, you must wait for the full moon. There is no choice in this, Kathryn. Do not be impatient. You'll need the power of that light to dispatch this spirit completely."*

Ginny held out the sprig of jasmine and Kathryn took it, holding it in both hands.

"I love you, my strong, black-winged angel. You make me very proud." And then Ginny was gone.

Kathryn's eyes opened to the gray dawn light in her grandmother's bedroom, the strong perfume of jasmine still floating around her. She was trembling with adrenalin, but not afraid. Evan's warmth and soft snores beside her comforted her instantly, but she knew she had to work fast while her memories were fresh.

She reached for her notebook on the night table and jotted down every detail she could recall from Ginny's critical communication.

CHAPTER ELEVEN

EVAN WAS ALREADY up and moving around down in the kitchen when she woke again a few hours later. She heard her brother's voice down there, too. It was just after 10:00.

Kath got up quietly, wrapped up in her robe and crept to the chest of drawers opposite her bed. Underneath, a large leather suitcase was tucked that contained all of Grandma Ginny's grimoires, as well as all of Kathryn's own. She kept any spells she wrote when she wasn't in Mount Iolite neatly organized on her laptop, and then transferred them in handwriting to these beautiful books when she arrived at the cabin. These volumes were sacred and precious and had to be kept inside Ginny's fortress.

The books were arranged with their spines facing up so their identifying botanicals were easy to see. In the light coming through the rose-patterned curtains, Kath found the spine adorned with a sprig of jasmine. This one was old—from Grandma's thirties. Very carefully, Kathryn opened the delicate vellum pages and turned to the entry marked March 17. Ginny's elegant, formal cursive tracked over it in neat lines.

When it first appeared hovering over me, the succubus told me it craves the feast of a witch, even a weakling like me. I warded off that attack with my selenite talisman and the luck of the coming dawn. The daylight syphons its strength immediately, but it can still manifest. The second time it attacked, I surrounded myself with an inferno of sage smoke, which irritated the creature enough to push it back, but only temporarily. When it came again last night, I added two pinches of ash of myrrh and four drops of betony oil to dried oak and birch leaves, three each. Burning them together in a clay pot was a most effective deterrent. It cursed about 'that disgusting stench'—called it 'witch's stink', and wouldn't come near it. That gave me enough of a barrier to lay down a ring of black salt—much to my husband's dismay. He didn't see the creature when it came. He still thinks all of this is so much malarkey and I'm just making a mess in the house.

Unfortunately, every incantation I tried only drew its foul mockery. It appears I can bar it from entering our property, but I can't send it on. I just don't possess the tools. There are tribes with holy men nearby who would know what I need, but I have no in-road to them. They would have no reason to share their magic with a white woman unless I'd been vetted by one of their own. I can only hope that this spirit will tire of only being able to watch me.

Kath made note of the selenite talisman and the ingredients for the smoke barrier. At the time she wrote this, Ginny was still thirty years from making the acquaintance of Shaman Fred Hunter and his wife, Tilly. She was on her own against this monster trying to drain her rich life force. Jackson, Jr. was only a toddler, not strong enough to catch the eye of this spirit.

Grandma explained to them that the life force of humans burns brightest when we're first born, then dims through early childhood when the energy is needed to grow our bodies. It flares again at puberty when it gains strength from the powerful urge to procreate, and then settles to the brightness it will have throughout that individual's life. At the moment of crossing, the energy becomes blinding as it draws itself into the collective light and moves to the next part of the journey. But the light of spiritual practitioners has a different make-up; the fuel for its fire a different source.

Energy feeders covet these delicacies and pursue them relentlessly once they've been discovered. From what Kathryn and Kellan had learned, the hunt wasn't based on the winning of a prize as might be a human's motivation—just on the consumption of the light. What they didn't know was what happened to these entities afterward. It's easy to assume they would grow stronger, but they'd never seen one after it fed. They always disappeared.

The stairs creaked, and she leaned into the bedroom doorway to see Kellan coming up, yawning and scratching his messy hair. He smiled at her.

"Hey, sissy."

"Hey. Is there anything left of Sonya?"

He grinned and sat on the floor inside her doorway. "Nothin' but bones and a big grin. She had a video conference with some folks at her bank this morning, so I lit out." He yawned again. "I'm nappy, though."

She poked him in the thigh with her pen. "No rest for the randy."

Evan started up the stairs with three mugs of coffee nestled between his fingers—one black, one white and one stupidly sweet. Kath took hers gratefully and sipped it. In his flannel pajama pants and a gray t-shirt, Evan sat next to Kellan on the floor of the hallway between their bedrooms.

"Ginny stopped by this morning," he told Kathryn. "She gave me all the stats from your dream visit in case you missed anything, but"—Evan nodded to the case of grimoires—"looks like you're on top of it. That's Jasmine 3/17 you've got there?"

Kath held up the book to show him the spine. "It's mostly just a recipe for smoke, though—well, smoke the hag freakin' hates, so that's something. Did you share all those stats with Kell?"

Her brother nodded as he sipped his coffee. Kath almost asked if Evan told Kellan about her vision on her phone, but she knew better. He'd never share such a horrific image with his Peach because he wouldn't want the guilt of having put it there. She didn't particularly want that guilt, either. There was no reason Kellan needed to know unless the images had a grain of truth to them. Kath would have to wait and see.

Picking up on her thoughts, Kellan said, "Any more love from our hag after the video you two mother hens won't tell me about?"

"Nothing on my end," she said.

Evan shook his head. "She hasn't tried anything on you, right, Kell? Other than appearing to you out on Swamp Rock a few weeks ago?"

"Not that I know of, at least. I haven't had any dreams or seen any ghosts from childhood."

Kath didn't think the hag would use the same tactic on the vessel; she was too clever. "I wouldn't look for her to repeat those. She'll try something else, if she comes at you at all. She is saving you for an entrée; can't have you all banged up."

Kellan yawned again. "Damn. I'm gonna grab a catnap. Wake me if anything interesting happens, 'kay?" He got up and shuffled into his bedroom, setting his coffee on the night table near the door. Kath saw him give Evan a little grin. "Nook?"

Evan winked then leaned across to give Kathryn a kiss. "You need me?"

"Nope," she smiled. "You boys enjoy."

Following Kellan into his bedroom, Evan closed the door halfway, but didn't shut it. It wasn't as though Kathryn would be offended. She could just see them crawling into Kellan's unmade bed, fluffing pillows and settling. As she went back to her notes, she remembered all the times she'd found them adorably curled up and snoozing in a tangle of limbs. To this day, neither of them ever slept sounder than with each other.

When she'd carefully tucked the grimoires back under the chest, Kath went downstairs to shower and get dressed. She thought about what Grandma Ginny had said in the dream: how they would lose part of themselves during this fight, but what they lost would be balanced by greater gain. Had she meant that in a big picture way, or a personal one? Kath was always left wondering after her dream visits with Ginny, but she knew that was as it should be. This outcaster was at her best when deciphering a mystery. It activated all her skills and made her see into the corners of things. That was why Grandma had been giving her puzzles since she was a child.

Kath wanted to talk to Sonya. Even without being told all the details of what they were up against, she wasn't missing much. In fact, her slight distance from the situation gave her a clearer perspective in some ways. Kath sent a text. It was a gorgeous day; would Sonya be interested in a picnic lunch out on their dock? Right away, her friend called her.

"Hey there, lady," Kath said with a smile.

"Well, good morning!" Sonya's voice was lilting and happy. "Aren't you up early for a Broch?"

"I had kind of a weird night—slept in fits and starts. There's a lot going on and I'd like to talk to you about it. Do you have lunch plans?"

"Is this about that video the spirit sent you yesterday?" Sonya said. "The one you wouldn't elaborate on because you're trying not to freak me out?"

Kath sighed. "Not just you, my brother, too. I'm sorry to be so secretive; I promise I'll explain things."

"There's actually something I want to ask you about, also. Jewel and I were just about to head up to the Rhino for lunch. Can I persuade you to come along for some day drinking and greasy fries?"

"Twist my arm," Kath laughed. "But we should drive, remember, just for now."

"Understood. I'll scoop you both up shortly."

⮌

Pool balls clacked as the ladies entered the Rhino. A group of young men Kath didn't recognize were making boisterous bets on the outcome of the game. It was just after noon and the place was packed; the only available table was beside the short end of the bar near the pinball machines.

They all greeted Max behind the counter as they settled in. He leaned between two gruff, weathered regulars nursing bottles of Bud, and called to the ladies. "Ketel and tonic, Dewar's rocks, Jack and Diet?"

Jewel gave him thumbs up and a grin. "And keep 'em coming."

"You got it. Sandie's on her own today so please be patient."

"We're not in a hurry," Sonya assured him.

Kath spotted some familiar faces in the bustling restaurant and figured she'd do a lap a little later. Part of keeping their small-town celebrity status was pressing the flesh with the locals. It helped fill the venues when they played.

Sandie charged through the kitchen's batwing doors at the back with five plates balanced on her thick arms, weaving around the pool players to get to a table in the center. She spotted the ladies in the corner as she served the food, sending them a smile. When Max set their drinks on the edge of the bar, Kath went up to collect them.

Wiry and quick with skin tanned to the point of freckled leather, Max hadn't changed much since the Brochs and their friends first started hanging out there as kids. With his well-worn, dirty green Rhino Bar cap turned around backwards, he told Kath he was really looking forward to the Halloween show. "My wife's been working on her costume for two weeks."

"Awesome! Can't wait to see everyone all dressed up. We've got some fun surprises in store this year; should be great."

"As long as Kellan sings 'Werewolves of London,' I'll be happy. I love that little dance he does on the piano bench." Max's quick impression looked less like Kellan's popular oily-hipped dance and more like a person in the last seconds of slipping on a banana peel.

Kathryn cracked up. "Spot on, my man!"

The barkeep took a little bow. "Where's he been, by the way? Haven't seen him in here for a few days."

Glancing over her shoulder at Sonya, Kath smiled to herself. "He's been busy socializing. I'm sure you'll get sick of seeing him in here before we leave. He swears you make the best Long Island Ice Tea on the planet."

"He's drunk enough of 'em to know." Max chuckled as he went down the bar to another customer.

Kath carefully corralled the three glasses between her fingers and started back to the table. A woman wearing heavy, sickly-sweet perfume brushed hard against her on the right, so close that the drinks sloshed a bit before Kath could set them down. Annoyed, she turned to unload some snark—but no one was there. Their table was off by itself in the corner and the nearest bodies were a group of big, burly men, none of whom were even looking in her direction. She touched Jewel's shoulder.

"Did you see a woman bump into me just now?"

Her graying eyebrows knit and then her ever-present smirk took over. "Spoilin' for a bar brawl, young lady? Get a drink in you first—helps you take the punches."

Kath snorted, but she kept searching the crowded room. She hadn't seen the woman, just smelled her nasty perfume; she could be any one of the many female patrons there. Something about that sickening fragrance was familiar, though. Kath couldn't quite place it.

"Kathryn?" Sonya's delicate hand alighted on her arm. "Are you okay?"

"You didn't see anyone, either, right?"

Sonya shook her head. "It's just us in this corner. Come on, sit down."

"Yeah," Jewel grinned. "If some bitch starts shit with you, we've got your back." She raised her glass and waited for them to toast with her.

Kath sat beside Sonya, still suspiciously scanning the room. They touched their glasses together and drank and then Sonya spoke softly.

"Was that the hag again trying to scare you?"

"She doesn't scare me; she pisses me off. If she were trying to scare me, she'd—" Kath suddenly remembered where she'd smelled that horrible perfume. It was the night Evan brought Kellan home passed out drunk and carrying a different succubus—one so strong, it nearly killed them both before Kath sent it on. The hag had not been near them that night—Kath was sure of it. Making her smell that perfume was just another example of this entity's ability to see inside their minds. "Damn it." She rubbed her forehead and took a big sip of her strong drink. "She's saber-rattling again. Reminding me what she's capable of."

"Reading your thoughts?" Jewel said.

"It would be unwise to think she couldn't read all our thoughts." Kath looked from one to the other of her friends. "Anyone close to me and Kell is fair game."

"How does one put a fence around one's brain?" Jewel said, leaning in.

"You got me. If you figure it out, pass it on. Right now, I'm pretty sure we're all open books—and this monster is a fan of horror stories." Kath sat back in her chair and steadied herself before telling them exactly what the hag had shown her in the video on her phone. She left no detail out. She wasn't worried about how Jewel would take it, but when Kath looked right into Sonya's pretty green eyes, she was surprised to find them only slightly wide.

She swallowed a gulp of her vodka tonic. "And Evan denied that was an actual event?"

"He said there was no truth to it whatsoever."

Jewel snorted. "You'd need a wheelbarrow for the grain of salt you should take *that* with."

"I know." Kath drained her drink then turned to the bar to get Max's attention. He pointed to the fresh round already sitting there waiting. "I love this man." Kath got up to collect their drinks as Sandie finally made her way toward them with a stack of menus. She stopped to give Kath a hug at the bar.

"Always happy to see you, girl." Sandie threw a nod toward the loud group near the pool table. "Gotta herd of douchebros running me ragged back there. You ladies lunching, or nibbling and drinking?" She helped carry the drinks back to the table.

"All of the above."

"Best kind o' day."

Kath sat down and then felt her phone vibrate in her pocket. Evan sent her a photo of Kellan passed out asleep with his cheek resting right on Evan's peach tattoo. The fingers of Evan's right hand were softly entwined in Kellan's chestnut hair. His message read: *A niblet for the hot yoga teacher.*

She chuckled, sent him a heart and a kiss, then leaned over to show Sonya the image. Jewel and Sandie were engaged in a merry chat and not currently paying attention to them. Kath watched her friend's eyes soften and get a bit misty as she looked at the photo. A quick flash of unease crossed her face but didn't linger. Finally, Sonya smiled.

"Adorable doesn't cover it; sexy doesn't even touch it."

Kath grinned. "Ev said you two had a great talk yesterday."

"Yes. He was far more open than I thought he'd be since we don't know each other all that well."

They paused to order nibbles and another round and then Sandie returned to the demanding group in back. Jewel leaned in to see the photo on Kath's phone.

"Aww. Kellan's in his happy place. I saw Evan go up to the compound with you yesterday, Sonya. What were you kids up to?"

She swirled the ice in her glass with an impish grin. "Cougars have to keep their claws sharp, don't they?"

They laughed and Jewel raised a toast to that notion.

"Evan was just helping me with some odds and ends in the guest cottages," Sonya said. "But I got the chance to learn a lot more about him. At least, I *think* I did—it's hard to tell when he's pulling my leg."

"I'm sure Kathryn can tell the difference," Jewel said.

"I wish," Kath muttered. "What did he share?"

Her pretty green eyes twinkled with her smile. "I finally got the story of how he met Ginny—at least, I think I did. You tell me if I got the truth."

Kath put that pushy unseen perfume wearer on the back burner for the moment and stretched her legs out under their table. She and

Kellan had heard Evan tell this story at least a thousand times and knew every incredible detail of it. She was curious to see how much he actually told Sonya and what he might have chosen to omit.

"That story, I know. I'll fill in the blanks if there are any," she said.

Sonya settled back in her seat. "He was such a huge help to me. I couldn't thank him enough. I just sort of stood there handing him tools and listening to him talk."

Kath grinned. "He was a little tipsy when Kell and I got there for dinner. Good call to lube him up with alcohol. He gets chatty and noisy when he's drunk."

"Most people do, but I assure you it wasn't intentional. At lunch, we talked about his and Kellan's relationship and we cleared the air about me crossing any lines. That was a huge relief since Henry warned me that trespassers were eaten on sight."

Sandie brought them a plate of nachos and checked on their drinks. They all dug in to the steaming chips.

"I'm glad you guys talked about that," Kath said. "Ev hadn't said anything to me about it so I wasn't sure if he had an issue. Good that it's out of the way."

"Definitely," Sonya said. "Not that I'm assuming anything with respect to Kellan." She paused to sip her drink. "Anyway, when we'd started on the curtain rods, I asked him about his first encounter with Ginny."

Kathryn shook her head. "He tells it like a movie—every scene, every line. Cracks us up."

"That's exactly how he did it." Sonya munched another chip before she repeated Evan's story as he'd told it to her, word for word.

CHAPTER TWELVE

EVAN MACTAVISH AND Henry Hunter had only been friends for a few months.

As the only two children being collected by the school bus from Mount Iolite Junction, they had lots of time to get to know each other. Henry was finishing seventh grade and Evan's acumen had got him bumped up a year into third grade. Their age difference made them an unlikely pair, but they'd bonded right away.

It was early summer and the days before the end of the school year were long. Henry would pick Evan up after school and they'd ride their bikes down to the park at Robbin Lake. There were always lots of kids there as the park flanked several of Mount Iolite's resort hotels. It was safe and well-supervised by employees from the resorts. Each evening, the park staff lit a bonfire in the large stone pit near the shore and the kids—locals and resort guests alike—would roast marshmallows.

Evan had just turned eight. He and Henry rolled into the park around 6:30 that afternoon and got into a game of kickball with some other kids. While Evan was running after the ball near the trees that edged the shoreline, he saw a woman sitting on some rocks down near the water. She had a fishing pole and a tackle box, and he could see the sun dancing on the rippling waves right through her.

Evan had kicked the ball back into the game and stopped there on the shore, staring at this bewildering image. The woman had her back to him and appeared to be dressed in a fishing hat and a light black windbreaker. He'd blinked and stared, trying desperately to make sense of the fact that she was transparent. What was going on here? For a second, he thought he might be looking at some sort of sheer poster advertising the mid-summer trout fishing contest, but then the woman turned and looked right at him.

She smiled. Evan held his breath. He could feel her gaze, almost like she was searching around *inside* him, but she was barely visible in the late daylight.

Evan swallowed and cleared his throat. He called out a hello.

The woman only smiled, but it was a kind smile. Evan liked it. She made him feel safe somehow. She nodded toward the ground near Evan's feet and he reluctantly looked away from her to follow the direction of her gaze.

Lying in the scrubby grass was an ordinary house key. It was all by itself, not on a key fob or tied to a string like Evan sometimes saw other kids wearing around their necks. It was just lying there. He figured it must belong to the woman on the rocks and that she wanted him to bring it to her. He grabbed the key quickly and looked up to where she'd been sitting.

The woman was gone.

Confused, Evan searched the whole shoreline for her, but she'd vanished. He frowned at the key in his hand, wondering what he should do with it. It had no markings on it or any indication of what it might open. He thought about just leaving it where he'd found it in case the lady came back to look for it. In fact, he'd almost done just that. But before he could place the key on the ground, Henry had called him back into the kickball game.

Evan tucked that key into the pocket of his shorts and forgot all about it until his mother found it on laundry day.

❧

"So far, so good," Kathryn said as she piled a chip piled high with olives and salsa. "But we're not at the creepy part yet. He tends to embellish there because he's secretly a drama queen."

Jewel laughed heartily. "I remember when Ginny told me her side of this story. She said she'd been impressed by his bravery, considering he was only eight. Any other kid would have run screaming to his mommy if he saw a ghost."

"Not our Evvy-Ev. He *loves* seeing ghosts." Kath winked at her. "Onward to the day

Evan found the lock for that mysterious key."

Sonya grinned and carried on.

❧

Evan was lying on the couch in the living room reading a comic while he waited for Henry to come by that Saturday afternoon. His father, Pete, was in the big chair next to him, the newspaper opened over his lap. The TV was on but neither of them was really watching it. Cindy came in from the laundry room and knelt beside her son.

"This was in your pocket, honey." The key glinted in her palm. "Do you know what it goes to?"

He'd forgotten about that key entirely until he saw it again, then the whole experience of how he found it came rushing back. He replied simply: "It belongs to a ghost lady I saw at the park."

Pete MacTavish folded down the corner of his newspaper. "What was that, buddy?"

"A ghost lady." Evan sat up to take the key from Cindy. "I thought it belonged to her, but she went away before I could ask her, so I put it in my pocket." He'd smiled at his mother like the whole thing had been well explained and then put that key in the pocket of the jeans he was wearing.

"I see." Cindy and her husband shared a wary glance.

Pete said, "Where did you see this lady, Ev?"

"At the park on Robbin Lake the other day—Tuesday. She was sitting on some rocks fishing, but I could see through her, so … she was a ghost, right?" He'd frowned at his father, not sure why this was so difficult to understand.

Cindy cleared her throat. "I suppose she *could've* been a ghost. Or maybe you had the sun in your eyes and didn't quite see her right?"

Evan knew that wasn't what happened. The sun was on the other side of the mountain at that time of the day so it wasn't shining in his eyes. "I saw her," he insisted. "She was there. But I could see through her. And she made me see this key on the ground."

"Okay." Pete decided to go along with this story. "Any idea what it goes to?"

"No. But she wanted me to see it. She sort of pointed at it so I would look down at it. I thought she wanted me to get it for her, but then she was gone."

Pete folded the newspaper and set it on the coffee table, leaning forward in his chair. "Did anyone else see this ghost lady?"

Evan shrugged, not sure what that had to do with anything. "I dunno."

"You were with Henry that day, right?" Cindy said. "Did he see the lady?"

"Nope. He was playing kickball."

Evan's parents exchanged another uneasy glance, but then Cindy showed one of her forced 'mommy' smiles. That meant she had no idea what to do so she was stepping away to regroup.

"It's okay, honey. I'm sure the lady wasn't trying to scare you."

"I wasn't scared," he'd said, indignant that his mother would suggest such a thing. "I just want to know what that key goes to. Maybe the ghost lady needs it."

Cindy nodded with a patient smile. "Maybe. But let's not go around town trying to unlock everyone's doors, okay?" She gave him a kiss on his forehead and then started back toward the laundry room.

Evan hadn't thought of that option until his mother mentioned it. It really wasn't a bad idea. Of course, he'd have to be very careful and not get caught. Some people in town had big, mean dogs. Henry would help him. With a plan beginning to brew in his eight-year-old head, Evan picked up his comic book and stretched out on the couch again to wait for Henry.

Sonya paused for a few bites of the salad she'd ordered for lunch. "He seems very close to his mom and dad. It's sweet the way he talks about them."

"Pete and Cindy are great," Kath said. "Before Pete retired from being a ranger in Yosemite, he used to get us into the park free every summer. My dad *loved* hiking there. Cindy's a great cook, too."

"So they'll be good in-laws?" Jewel teased.

Taking a bite of her bacon cheeseburger, Kath gave her a wink. "For someone."

Sonya rolled her eyes and went on.

Evan and Henry rode their bikes into town later that day and got cold drinks at the general store. Sitting outside on the shady steps, Evan took the key out of the pocket of his jeans and showed it to his friend.

"A ghost lady gave me this." He explained the rest of the story about his encounter that day at the park.

"How come you didn't tell me then?" Henry said. "I was right there. Maybe I could've seen her, too."

Evan didn't really have an answer to that. "I don't know. I guess I didn't think about it. But I have to find out where it goes. The lady might need it."

Henry scrutinized the key in Evan's hand but didn't touch it. He tipped back his bottle of Snapple for a deep drink. "My uncle will know. Let's go ask him."

Excited, Evan pocketed the key again. He always found it fascinating to talk to Shaman Hunter and looked forward to his mystical insight on the key. It came from a ghost, after all. That made the key itself sort of mystical.

The boys rode down into the village where Fred and Tilly Hunter kept a small ranch style home on a double lot. The backyard contained two wide greenhouses where Tilly grew fruit and vegetables that she sold at the local farmer's markets. Also in those greenhouses were the shaman's store of healing herbs and plants. Fred liked to sit in a wicker chair out in the yard between the two greenhouses where he could hear the wind in the trees. The boys found him there that hot Saturday afternoon.

"Uncle," Henry had said as they approached. "Gray Wolf has a question for you."

Fred Hunter set down his glass of iced tea and turned to smile at the boys. He wore jeans and a white t-shirt. His thick, black, shoulder-length hair was run through with strands of silver and tied back from his weathered face with a strip of buckskin. The two feathers tattooed behind his right ear reached all the way down his tanned neck. He shook Evan's hand politely, as was his custom.

"Good to see you, Gray Wolf. You're growing tall."

Pleased by the compliment, Evan said, "Thank you, sir. Good to see you, too."

"How can I help you today?"

Digging the key out of his pocket, Evan held it out to the shaman. "A ghost lady gave me this a few days ago in the park at Robbin Lake."

Fred took the key with a meditative nod. He held it up and squinted, articulating the long, deep scar under his right eye. He'd told Evan once that the scar came from an eagle that tried to carry him off out of a high-country meadow when he was a boy. The key flashed in the sun light as the shaman turned it in his fingers. "A ghost lady, you say?"

"Yes, sir. She was on the shore sitting on some rocks. It looked like she was fishing. I could see *through* her, but I could still see her fine. She seemed nice."

Fred had smiled at this detail as he tucked the key into the palm of his hand. He squeezed it in his fingers like he was trying to wring water from it. "What is your question, Gray Wolf?"

"Henry said you would know where this key is supposed to go."

"Oh, yes," Fred said brightly. "It goes to the back door of a cabin down on Bonny Lake." He promptly gave the key back to Evan.

The boy blinked, confused. "It does?"

"Most certainly."

"Which cabin, sir?"

Fred took Evan's hand in both of his. They were rough-looking from working in his garden, but the skin had a soft, papery quality. "You will know it when you see it. The ghost lady will show herself in the window."

This was exhilarating news, if the tiniest bit frightening, but Evan made sure to show no fear. It was imperative to him to live up to the strong spirit name Shaman Hunter had given him, and a wolf was never afraid. "Who is she?"

"She is the gatherer," Fred said. "You are being collected by her." He patted Evan's smaller hand gently and smiled. "This is a good thing, Gray Wolf. She is a very fine lady. Don't be afraid."

"I'm not afraid, sir," he'd said, but in truth he was. Evan wasn't sure he liked the idea of being 'collected' by a ghost. Did that mean he would have to die?

As was always the case, Fred Hunter guessed his thoughts. "You will not die for a long time, Gray Wolf. Certainly not on this day. The ghost lady isn't really dead, either; she is just in a different form of life. Go see her. She's hoping you will visit."

Evan swallowed and looked up at Henry with big, round eyes. "Will you come with me?"

"Sure," Henry said. He looked to his uncle. "Is this cabin down on the waterfront or on the road above?"

"On the water," Fred said. "Sylvan Road. You will see it. But, Henry, *you* will not see the ghost lady because today she is there for Gray Wolf. She can only show herself to one person at a time. Go and help him find her."

"Yes, uncle." Henry grinned at Evan and playfully ruffled his spikey blond hair. "Let's go see your ghost."

Evan smiled but inside he was growing more anxious by the second. He thanked the shaman for his help and he and Henry got back on their bikes.

They rode through town to the left turn by the Rhino and coasted along the dusty road toward Bonny Lake. Sylvan Road cut to the right into dense aspens and pines, making the road shadowy and cool even at midafternoon. When they came to the first of the lake front properties they slowed and walked their bikes.

They passed several cabins, some with people staying in them and others closed up and waiting for their owners. As they approached the fork of Sylvan Road and Parker Drive, they saw a woman off to the left sweeping a long flight of stone stairs. When they got close enough, Evan thought he knew her, or had at least seen her somewhere recently. He couldn't quite remember, though.

The woman leaned on her broom and waved to them with a friendly smile. "Afternoon, boys."

They both said hi and smiled politely as they walked by, heading to the right of the fork to stay on the lake front. When they were out of earshot, Evan whispered to his friend.

"Do you know that lady?"

Henry smirked. "That's not a ghost, Ev."

"Duh, but do you know her?"

Glancing back, Henry shook his head. "I haven't seen her before."

Evan looked back, too, that feeling of having met her growing stronger. The woman started up the stone stairs where a big brown dog waited at the top, happily wagging its tail. Evan liked dogs.

The boys passed the next cabin, the one that sat right inside the fork of Sylvan and Parker, and saw that it was closed and shuttered; no one staying there. As they moved on to check out the next house, Henry suddenly stopped. He stared back at the cabin inside the fork with a strange frown.

"What?" Evan turned in the direction of Henry's gaze.

"I thought I saw the curtains move in the front window."

Evan stared at that window but saw nothing. The curtains were drawn and the house was quiet. "I don't see anything."

"Huh. Never mind." Henry started up the road again.

Hesitating another moment, Evan kept his eyes on those curtains. Fred had said the ghost lady would show herself in a window—was this her? While his focus was there, he saw something out of the corner of his eye, around the back of that cabin. When he shifted his attention, he took in a quick breath. His heart began to pound.

The ghost lady was there near the back of the house, but she wasn't see-through then. He could see her just like any other person—as clearly as the living woman sweeping the stairs next door. But he remembered her features from when he saw her at Robbin Lake Park and this was, without a shred of doubt, the same lady. She stood with her arms folded in front of her; she was looking right at Evan and smiling.

"Henry, look."

Having gone up the road a bit, Henry stopped and turned back. "Those curtains moved, didn't they? I *knew* I saw that."

Evan swallowed. "I see her. She's there behind that house."

Henry came back to his side, squinting at the cabin in the fork. "Okay, well … I can't see her, but my uncle said I wouldn't. You should go over there."

"Yeah." Evan's feet had grown roots where he stood. He was frozen, but not really in fear—just uncertainty. He was afraid the lady might vanish again if he got too close to her.

"Uncle Fred said not to be afraid," Henry reminded him. "She's just a lady. I don't think she'll try to kill you or anything."

"No, I know." Evan took a shaky deep breath. "Watch my bike?"

Henry took hold of the handle bars and gave his friend a reassuring smile. "Don't worry. I'm sure it's cool."

Evan nodded but he knew his eyes were round and anxious. He screwed up his courage and started walking toward the cabin in the fork. Behind him, he heard Henry moving their bikes out of the road to rest against a tree. Evan wondered if the woman next door could see them and if she thought they were up to mischief around this empty cabin. He hoped not. He didn't want his mission interrupted.

He walked up the side of the green painted cabin, under what was likely the kitchen window and up onto the slight rise of the wooden back porch. There was a shed to the right and a picnic table to the left behind the house, near the back door. The ghost lady stood in the back doorway, holding the screen door open.

"Hello, Evan," she said in a voice as clear as any he'd ever heard. He wasn't too sure what he thought a ghost would sound like, but he figured it would be different from a living person. This lady sounded just like anyone else.

"Um, hello?" He'd been annoyed that his voice came out shaky and small. He cleared his throat. "You know my name?"

The lady smiled sweetly. "I do. And my name is Virginia Broch. Now we know each other."

"Okay. It's nice to meet you, Mrs. Broch."

"And you, dear," she said. "Just to make sure: you know that I'm a ghost, right?"

Hoping it was the right response, Evan nodded. "Yes, ma'am."

"Right, but there's no reason to be afraid of me, like Fred Hunter told you. He and I are good friends and he knows me very well."

Evan smiled weakly. "He can vouch for you."

With a tinkling little laugh, she said, "That's right, he can. I'd like us to be friends, too, Evan—you and me."

"How come? I'm just a kid."

Virginia's smile had brightened. "Well, yes, but I believe you're quite a special kid and I'd like to be your friend. If it's okay with you, of course. Friends have to choose each other."

His curious eyes had been moving all over her, taking in her black pants and her flowered apron, her shiny black hair. She had what looked like a big diamond on her left ring finger. Her eyes glowed like green marbles. She was kind of beautiful. Evan had no idea why this ghost lady would want to be friends with a little boy, but he wasn't about to argue with her.

"Uh, sure," he stammered.

"Good!" She seemed very pleased by his decision. She leaned in the doorway, still holding the screen out of her way. "I like my friends to call me Ginny."

"Okay."

She'd watched him for a moment, seeming to take in all his details as he'd done with her. "You know you won't be a kid forever."

"I hope not," he said with a nervous laugh.

"No, you'll grow up very soon—sooner than your parents would like, I'm sure. And you'll be a tall, handsome man."

Evan liked this prediction. "Cool! As tall as my dad?"

"Oh, at least," Ginny said. "And you and I will see each other a lot, I think. You can come visit me anytime you like. The key I gave you opens this door right here." She pointed to the lock on the back door.

"Oh!" he said, digging in his pocket for the key in question. He held it in his hand, still trembling with adrenalin. "This is your house?"

"That's right, honey."

"Are there other ghosts here, too?"

Ginny seemed to consider this question carefully. "My husband stops by sometimes, but just to make sure everything's okay. He doesn't stay long. My family visits here often, though—and none of them are ghosts yet."

"They're alive—I mean, living people?"

"That's right. My son and his children like to come up here and go fishing. My grandkids are your age, actually. I'm sure you'd like them."

Evan smiled. "That's cool. There aren't a lot of kids up here."

"That's true. Do you like to fish?"

"I love it!"

"This is a beautiful spot for it," the ghost of Virginia Broch said. "We have a dock right out in front of our cabin. You and your friend, Henry, are welcome to go fishing there—even if my family isn't here. It's way out on the water and has a good fishing hole in front."

"Thank you, ma'am. You know my friend Henry, too?" This confused Evan.

"Yes. I met him in the general store a few months ago. That was actually *before* I died. Ask him. He'll remember."

"And how did you—" Evan stopped himself, thinking it might not be nice to ask a person such a question.

Ginny smiled. "I had a heart attack, dear. It was very sudden and there wasn't any pain; one moment I was alive, the next I wasn't."

"Wow." Evan's eyes were wide and fascinated. He remembered how he could see through her down on the shore of Robbin Lake and asked her why she was so solid now. Ginny explained that her strength came from their cabin and the land it sat on, and that the farther away she got from it, the harder it was for her to appear.

"That's why we'll always have to meet here to talk to each other," she said. "So you can see and hear me. I hope that's okay."

This concerned him. "Well, I probably can't come all this way alone. My parents only let me ride around town if I'm with Henry."

"Henry is always welcome, too," Ginny said.

"Okay, good."

Ginny glanced over her shoulder into the dark kitchen behind her, as though someone had called her name. "I'll need to go now, dear. But you keep that key safe, all right? And use it to come visit me any time you like. When you come, I'll be here and we can talk just like this."

"I'll keep the key safe, ma'am." Evan really wasn't sure what they would have to talk about, but he figured Ginny must have something in mind.

She was watching him closely and then she said, "Sometimes, I might call you to come see me if I have something I need to tell you."

"Like on the phone?"

"Well, not exactly," she said. "I'll find another way to let you know that I'd like you to stop by. We'll decide on that later, okay?"

Evan had nodded and then looked at the key in his hand again; he tucked it into his pocket. "Okay."

"Good boy. You enjoy the rest of your day, now. Take care of the people you love."

Evan smiled and nodded. "Yes, ma'am. Goodbye."

"Goodbye." Ginny shut the door.

For a moment, Evan just stood there on the back porch gaping at the door and wondering if he'd just dreamt all of that. There were scrubby trees between this cabin and the cabin next door with the stone stairs. He could see the woman through the brush up on her patio playing with her big dog. Once again, he tried to remember where he'd met her, but it just wasn't coming to him.

A little dazed, he'd walked back around the other side of the cabin to where Henry waited with their bikes. Bonny Lake rippled cobalt blue in the hot afternoon sun.

"Well?" Henry said. "You were gone a long time. Did you talk to her?"

"Yes." Evan sat on his bike and leaned forward over the handle bars. "She was nice. Her name is Virginia Broch. She said she'd met you before."

Henry's expression went slack. "Your ghost lady is *Virginia Broch*?"

Alarmed by this reaction, Evan just nodded.

Henry plopped onto the seat of his own bike. "I did meet her. She asked me to look after her grandkids, Kathryn and … the other name was kinda weird, I don't remember it. But she asked me if I would help her look after them. I thought they were in the store with her and she just wanted me to make sure they didn't break stuff or something, but they weren't there. I thought it was kinda batty that she asked me to look after kids that weren't even with her."

"That is kinda weird," Evan said. "She told me about her grandkids, too, but they aren't here right now." He could tell Henry was distressed by this memory, but he wasn't sure why. He waited for his friend to continue.

"She looked really healthy to me," Henry said. "I mean, not like she was sick or anything. It's weird that she just up and died."

"She said she had a heart attack," Evan told him. "It was really fast. I wanted to know how she died so she told me that."

"Oh." Henry blinked but his expression was still confused. "So where *are* these kids?"

Evan shrugged. "They don't live here. She said they'd be coming up soon to go fishing."

Henry nodded slowly, obviously thinking hard about something he didn't share at the moment. Instead, he turned his bike out toward the road. "Will you tell me what you and Virginia talked about?"

"Sure, but it wasn't really all that interesting," Evan said and then he chuckled. "I *was* talking to a ghost, though. That's pretty dang cool."

Henry laughed. "Wanna head over to the park and see if they have the fire pit going yet?"

"Sure." Evan turned his bike and followed Henry at a slow cruise back up the slope of Sylvan Road. He glanced at Virginia Broch's cabin as they passed, but it was closed up and quiet. He figured she was resting after using so much energy talking to him for such a long time. Evan didn't know why he thought that, but he did.

They rounded the bend in front of those long stone stairs and that big brown dog trotted down to greet them. It seemed friendly with a happily wagging tail; it ran a little ways alongside them. The woman was standing halfway down the stairs, smiling as she watched her dog chasing their bikes.

In a cheerful voice, she called out, "Rosie, leave those boys alone. Get on back here."

Evan looked over his shoulder to watch Rosie turn tail and lope back to her owner. She was a good dog, he could tell. When she returned to the woman on the stairs, the woman was laughing as she reached down to pet Rosie's ears. The expression finally tripped the memory trigger in Evan's mind. He remembered where he'd seen her.

"That woman took my picture at the fireman's barbeque," he told Henry as they rode over the rise that emptied Sylvan Road into town.

"The lady with the dog?"

"Yeah. I saw her taking my picture and I gave her a dirty look."

"How do you know she was taking *your* picture? The whole town was there; maybe she was just taking pictures of everyone."

Evan frowned. "'Cuz she was. I know she was."

Henry chuckled at him. "You're paranoid."

"Whatever." Evan rode ahead a little bit, annoyed that his friend didn't believe him.

He remembered the moment so clearly because he'd *felt* someone looking at him. When he'd searched around Evan saw that woman pointing a camera at him and he got mad because he didn't want some stranger taking his picture. He gave her a dirty look hoping that would make her stop, but instead she just took another picture. He remembered the woman thought his dirty look was funny. She'd laughed and then stuck her tongue out at him.

Evan *really* hadn't liked that, so he turned his back and ignored her. If she took any more pictures of him, he didn't know because he stopped paying attention to her. She was just some wacky old lady, right? Only a wacky old lady would be taking pictures of some kid she didn't know at the town barbeque.

But that wacky old lady lived next door to his new and interesting ghost lady friend. Evan couldn't help wondering if she'd ever seen Ginny. Maybe he'd ask if he ever saw her outside with her dog again.

CHAPTER THIRTEEN

TO KATHRYN'S SURPRISE, the story was entirely intact. At least as much of it as she'd ever heard.

Jewel chuckled deeply. "I love it. After all these years, that little snot is still pissed at me for taking his picture when he was eight."

Sonya nibbled the last of the fries on Kathryn's plate. "He really didn't leave anything out?"

"Nope," Kath said. "He must have been in a rare forthcoming mood."

"I was a very attentive audience," she laughed softly. "Evan and your brother have the gift of gab in common—excellent storytellers. The more my eyes widened, the more theatrical he became. Honestly, though, if I'd experienced that as an eight-year-old child, I'd have been traumatized. Evan just took it in his stride."

"He still has that key," Kath said.

"He showed it to me," Sonya brightened. "He said you guys have changed the front door lock a few times, but never the back and that's the key he uses to get in when you're not here. When Ginny sends up his smoke signal from the potbelly chimney."

"That the old lady next door tells him about," Jewel said, raising her glass.

"Exactly. It's wonderful to finally have all these pieces fitting."

"We're just getting started," Kath said with a small, wary smile.

The restaurant was packed and noisy for lunch service; patrons were even waiting outside for tables to open. Sandie came to collect their plates and deliver a fresh round of drinks, then Jewel leaned in. Her expression went serious.

"Sonya, honey, did you tell Kathryn about the wind? I think it's important."

"Wait, *what* wind?" Kath frowned, her belly tightening. "Is this what you wanted to talk to me about?"

"Yes." Sonya poked at the lime wedge in her fresh drink. "It was late last night, about 2:00am, when I came down to use the bathroom. Kellan was asleep upstairs, so he didn't experience any of this. I hadn't heard any wind all night and then all at once leaves were whirling around, branches and pine needles flying against the windows—it was so loud! But when I looked outside, the trees around my property were stock still. The wind appeared to be isolated to my courtyard, like my own personal tornado. We don't have tornados in this area, though—I Googled it."

Kath didn't like this one little bit. "Was our thatch moved?"

"That's the disturbing part," Sonya said. "I opened the front door to see if there'd been any damage and found the thatch bundle you guys left near my driveway sitting right in the center of the porch. Only that one, though. I took a walk around with a flashlight and the other three were undisturbed."

"Did you put it back in the driveway?" Kath said.

"Yes, right away—and I said the incantation again, too." Sonya took a breath. "But if it was moved to begin with, was the barrier broken?"

Kath shook her head, even though she was troubled. "Most likely not. The purpose of the thatching is to set the magic like an invisible fence from the sky to the ground along your property line. We left those four corner bundles as extra precaution, but if the ritual was successful you wouldn't actually *need* them. The wall is a done deal."

"And it was only for a moment," Jewel pointed out. "She put it back right away."

"Yes." As much as she was trying to, Kathryn knew she didn't look or sound convincing. "What bothers me most is that the hag waited until you came downstairs to make sure you saw the wind display in the courtyard. Your bedroom is on the other side of the house; you wouldn't have seen the tornado effect from there, even if the noise woke you." She took a thoughtful sip of her Jack and Diet. "No, that old bitch wanted you to know two things: one, that she was watching you, and two, that she's not afraid of our magic."

"Maybe not affected by it, either?" Sonya hazarded.

Kath said that would be highly unusual. "But anything is possible. That much, I've learned."

"So, what does all that mean? Am I being targeted?"

Kath squeezed Sonya's hand. "Like I said, it's unwise to think the hag can't see inside all our heads. She can easily observe that you and Kellan have become lovers and that you and I are close friends. But we don't know how much she can see of what's on the inside—yet. Right now, based on what she's shown us, my gut tells me she's only getting bits and bobs. Sort of like channel bashing on a television where you only view snips of the shows as you go by. It's enough to see what's on, but you don't know the story." She took a deep breath to steady herself. "At least that's what I hope is happening. Of course, it's also possible that she knows everything and is just doling it out in fragments to throw us off."

"Great," Jewel muttered.

"She hasn't done anything to you, has she?" Kath asked.

"Not that I'm aware of. But if I was this monster and wanted to cause drama for the outcaster bitch that locked me in a tree, I'd concentrate on her brother, her squeeze and her best buddy. The old lady next door would make me no never mind—and no monster would be dumb enough to trifle with a shaman."

Kath smirked darkly. "I love how you've learned to think like a monster after all these years."

"Comes in handy on occasion."

Recalling the women she'd seen in Jewel's cabin the night before, Kath said, "Just to make sure—I did see *two* ladies at your place last night, right? Holly Naims and another woman?"

"Affirmative," Jewel said. "That was Holly's aunt who's visiting from Colorado. Nice lady, even if she didn't like my stew."

"Okay, that was irking me." Kath picked at the edge of her cocktail napkin.

Frowning, Sonya said, "You were thinking the hag could just pop into Jewel's house after you just reinforced the thatch?"

"She's a monster, hon. We're really only able to guess at what they can do. Magic is 1% mystical and 99% intentional. Our intention is to block her, but we don't know how truly effective that is. I wanted to make sure there were two ladies with Jewel because being a pop-up imposter seems to be this hag's jam—at least for me and Ev."

In a soft voice, Sonya asked if Kathryn had learned anything more about Evan and Lisa Tucker when they were young.

Kath laughed sheepishly. "I haven't learned anything more because I'm too much of a wuss to ask. Besides, it'll piss him off regardless of the answer. My man does *not* like to be questioned."

"Nonetheless," Sonya said. "It would be good information to have."

"Wait," Jewel said. "Are we talking about those two little bleach blonde sluts from Irvine? The ones who chased your brother and Ev around like rabid dogs for four summers?"

Kath nodded, but her teeth connected in her mouth. "Do you remember seeing the older one—Lisa—around with Evan when we weren't here?"

Jewel snorted. "*Hell* no. It looked to me like the only thing that little skank liked about chasing Evan was making *you* watch her do it. Where would the fun be without her target audience? Besides, she was disgusting. I don't care how horny Evan was back in those days—he wouldn't have screwed *that* sleaze with another guy's dick."

That was some relief, at least. Kathryn knew Jewel Early never missed anything gossip-worthy that occurred in Mount Iolite— especially if it had to do with the Brochs. At Ginny's request, she was ever watchful on their behalf.

Sonya said, "I'd still ask. If the hag is using this as a tactic to drive you two apart, then you should discuss it and take it off the table."

"I've tried that logic with him already," Kath said, "with zero joy."

"Boy, he's a stubborn one."

"You have no idea."

"Right, then," Sonya said. "Any words of advice now that the hag has *me* in her crosshairs?"

"Yeah," Jewel said dryly. "Think clean, happy thoughts."

Kath smiled, patting Sonya's knee. "Keep your eyes open; watch your six; and carry that selenite stone all the time."

"And keep an eye on Kellan when he's alone with you," Jewel said. "Remember, this old bitch is hungry for a vessel snack. That's her objective. Getting revenge on his meddling outcaster is just icing."

"Kellan is vulnerable, but mostly because he's careless," Kath said. "We all need to watch out for him a little more than usual. But don't let that interfere with the lovey-dovey." She put her arm around Sonya's shoulders and pressed a kiss to her temple. "Keep right on enjoying each other. It's working nicely for you both."

"I think I can handle that," Sonya said, her cheeks flushing pink.

Kath tried to make light of the situation even though her warrior senses were shifting to high alert. The concentrated wind storm showed the hag was indeed targeting Sonya, even if it was just with scare tactics. Kath knew her friend would be careful, but careful was probably not enough.

She needed to talk to Henry.

After making sure Sonya and Jewel got home safely, Kath spent a few hours with the guys back at the cabin. All was well and quiet for the moment. When the sun went down, she'd texted Henry and asked for his counsel. He invited her to come over for some spiked tea.

"The thatch must not be working if the hag could create that spectacle for Sonya." Out in the enclosed porch of Henry's house in the village, Kath stretched her legs close to the small wood burner in the corner. The early evening was frigid, but clear and fresh. Stars gleamed like diamonds in the waning moonlight.

Puffing on a pipe his uncle made for his birthday, Henry stared out toward the silver-black glitter of Robbin Lake. "I don't think the thatch failed, it's just not juiced up enough. The hag is stronger than we first realized. The virtual fence is slowing it down some, but its current volume can't keep the entity from interfering with the environment inside the compound. That's good information for us. It's fascinating, too, from a scientific point of view."

Kath snorted. "The only point of view I want is watching that thing's ass blowing through a portal. And if it can mess with the environment inside the compound, what's to stop it from doing the same at our places?"

Henry shook his head slowly, exhaling a soft cloud of sweet smoke into the cold air. "Ginny's magic is on your cabin and Jewel's, too. Ev and I stoked up our own houses pretty good, but maybe we ask Virginia to protect the compound?"

Kath frowned, irritable. "We should be able to protect the compound, Henry—just us, all by ourselves."

"I'm glad to hear you talk like that," he said with a small smile. "Your grandmother will be, too. You know she wants you to rely on your own skills more when you're here in M.T.I."

Curling her gloved fingers around the mug of tea in her hands, Kath sighed. "Do *you* think that's what we should do? Ask Grandma to help?"

"No. I think we should do it ourselves." He gave her a sidelong grin in the low light coming from the living room lamps. "Where's the Golden right now?"

"With Ev back at ours; safe and sound. But I'm sure he'll be spending lots of time at the compound now that he and Sonya are dancing."

Henry grinned. "A good thing all around. Okay, let's think about this from the beginning. In your dream, Ginny told you there were nine parts to the magic we'd need to get rid of the hag. You said she gave you five."

"Correct. The selenite talisman, the smoke repellent recipe and the clay pot she burned it in. The full moon is four. She said we'd have to wait for it to do the ritual." Kath breathed a bitter laugh. "She was forceful about my not being impatient; she knows I want to do this as soon as possible, full moon notwithstanding."

"But you'll be a good little soldier," he teased. "The full moon light is the most potent. If Virginia says we need it, we do."

"Agreed. The ring of black salt is the fifth element in the grimoire. But we still need to find the other four."

"Well," Henry puffed on his pipe. "The full moon is in six days—two days *after* Samhain and your gig. We've got a little time."

"Yeah, but we don't know what horrid shenanigans it might get up to in the meantime. Part of me wants to just let it get hitched to Kell and then flip it immediately."

Henry shook his head hard. "No—that's too dangerous. We don't know how quickly it can drain the vessel. My guess is far too quick. Gray Wolf will never allow that, anyway."

Under her breath, Kath muttered, "*I'm* Kellan's outcaster."

"And *we* are your tribe." Henry leaned forward in his rocking chair. "I won't let you put Kellan in danger any more than Evan will. You're a badass, Kathryn, but I'm taller. Don't make me punch you."

She laughed at the mere idea of standing up to the mountain of Henry Hunter physically. "It's not in my DNA to put my brother in harm's way—have no fear. I'm just saying. It would be so much easier if I could do what know *how* to do already, instead of having to concoct an untested plan."

"We have time, as long as we keep everyone safe. We're getting a good idea of this thing's strength based on its behavior. We know it can appear in daylight, although not for long; it can read our thoughts and manipulate electronics quite proficiently. It can produce full, detailed manifestations of people we know."

"Know and *hate*," Kath muttered.

"Mmm, yes." Henry was quiet for a while, squinting out at the lake. The little fire glowed through the stove's window, sending shadows flitting around the porch. "I'm sure that's significant. Succubae are drawn to weaknesses in their chosen victims, cracks in the armor. You have two cracks in yours. We need to anticipate what this monster might do to exploit those." He blew a perfectly formed smoke ring into the air. "What would you do if you were the hag?"

Only one thing came to her mind immediately and Kath hated it. "I'd turn those two weak points against each other and make the outcaster choose."

Henry shook his head, frowning. "Good guess, but I don't think that's chemically possible. Gray Wolf and the Golden would never turn on each other."

"Not of their own will," she said. "But we don't know if this thing has the power to influence behavior, or worse, to possess a human."

Henry shivered in his rocking chair. "Yuck. But now that you mention it, I'm sure Evan told you that we were called in this summer to assist Darien's group on a possession case down in Bishop."

"He did." The details Evan had shared about the case fascinated Kathryn at the time, but thinking of having to employ those methods on someone she cared for gave her a cold chill. It reminded her too much of that bitter old man who wouldn't let go of Kellan last fall—the one she had to pull out like a low-level demon. That meant forcing a human soul into eternal darkness, rather than on to its destined path. As a disruption of the natural order, it was brutally difficult.

"That possession was crazy," Henry said. "Freakiest thing I'd seen in a long time—until your vision quest."

Kath brightened. "You're saying my crow out-weirded a demon possession? Damn!"

"Yep," he laughed. "Seriously, Darien was amazing through it all. She was able to see the entity's thoughts enough to anticipate its next move. If she could do that with a demon, she might have some insight on our hag." He raised an eyebrow to her. "I can almost guarantee she'll want to read you, though—since the succubus is focused on you. Would you be willing? I know she freaks you out."

Kath sipped her tea with a wry grin. "I'm always afraid she'll see my sexual fantasies or something."

"She does, but she chooses to be discreet. At least that's what she told me."

"Fabulous. It's a good idea, though, if she has time for us."

"I'll call her in the morning." He paused to pack his pipe again. "What have you used on the other succubae you've encountered recently? You said there had been a few."

Kathryn thought back to the three she had to extract from Kellan earlier in the year. "I always used the Magician card because it works best on rapists—it's been very effective with these entities."

"Is that your pull card or your seal?"

"Pull. The seal changed every time, but I remember them: Hierophant, Temperance, and The Tower. The third invader did something weird—it kept showing itself to Kellan in the image of Evan, trying to make him allow it to feed."

Henry frowned. "So, it read his thoughts?"

"Yes, but that's happened before when spirits are hitched, or are close enough to make the connection. It's like a light comes on inside him and illuminates the things he likes."

"Kell needs to bust out that lightbulb," he smirked.

"Right? I can use the Magician for the pull, but I won't know the seal until I'm there with her. I see it in their eyes but not until the exchange has already begun."

Henry gnawed the end of his pipe. "I wonder if Darien could see it in advance."

Kathryn had never tried to find the extraction cards prior to doing a ritual, but a highly tuned clairvoyant might have no trouble with that at all. Darien Taite held a PhD in Parapsychology and had even been studied herself for her incredible psychic abilities. "I like it. I'm happy to drive down to Bishop to see her."

"I'm thinking we're going to need the full magical arsenal set up and ready to go before we even bring the hag into the environment. Working quickly will be essential."

A light went off in Kath's head. "The environment itself is probably another of the nine elements."

Henry touched his finger to his nose. "Yes. I'm concerned about the salt ring, though—now that we know this entity can create powerful winds. We'll need a way to keep the salt in place."

"Such as? It has to be in contact with the ground."

He added another log to the little fire then tapped his pipe bowl over an ashtray. "Let me think on it. Would you consider the Tarot cards one or two elements?"

"One," Kath said.

"All right, then we still need two more."

Kath made a list on the note pad on her phone, then read over it again. "Samhain is between now and then. What can we only get on that day?"

"Ash from your ritual fire."

"That's good." She added it to the list with a star beside it, noting it as a solid but unconfirmed possibility. After that, though, Kathryn's mind went blank. She let her head fall back against the rocking chair and looked out at the stars, chewing her bottom lip in thought.

"We've got a bit of time," Henry said. "Ginny might share something with one of us between now and then. And hopefully Darien can be of help."

"Yep." Kath slipped her phone back into her pocket as Henry refilled his pipe from a small wooden box on the porch railing. "What's in that stuff, anyway?"

His dark eyes twinkled. "It's Uncle Fred's special mix. Try some?"

"Will it turn me into a shaman?"

Lighting the bowl for her, Henry grinned as he passed her the pipe. "No, but expect to see pink elephants wearing kimonos in your dreams."

Kath chuckled as she brought the pipe to her lips. She'd take that over horrible images of a crazed, blood-covered Evan any day.

CHAPTER FOURTEEN

RUMBLING DOWN SUNLIT 395-South, Kathryn watched the sloping valley through the Jeep's passenger window. Between the rolling expanses of deep green popped stands of aspen blazing gold, and clusters of oak flaming red. Yellow desert flowers edged the highway and hawks floated against the azure autumn sky.

Henry and Kellan were analyzing the latest season of *Game of Thrones* in the back seat while Evan drove them the 45 miles to Bishop. Kath yawned to clear the pressure in her ears as they descended the fierce Sherwin Grade, taking them roughly three thousand feet down to the high desert floor of Mojave in less than ten minutes.

Evan's strong hand touched her thigh, slowly stroking toward her knee. He gave her a sexy wink. "Nervous to see the scary mind reader?"

Kath smirked. "Darien does give me the wig, but we need her right now. I'm glad she could see us so quickly."

"Interesting she wanted us all to come," he said.

"I'm sure she has her reasons."

In town, the vast fairgrounds rolled by on the right with horses and riders doing paces in the large corrals. The four-lane road through the town center was always congested with a mix of locals, truck drivers and tourists making their way through the largest small town in the Eastern Sierras. As the last stop before heading up into the mountain range, Bishop was a bustling hub of restaurants, markets, sporting goods retailers and tattoo parlors. While there were a few national chains represented, most of the businesses were small and owned by area locals.

Evan turned down a side street near the auto parts store and guided the Jeep along a roughly paved road toward a row of houses. Off the main drag of the interstate, it was so quiet Kathryn could hear the wind moving through the aspens that dotted the sidewalks. The sweet smell of sage baking in the desert sun reminded her of childhood days fishing on the lakeshores with her dad.

"This is it, right?" Evan peered over top of his aviators at the address painted high on the side of a small white house. The neat yard was shaded by an old oak and a low red picket fence encased the lush grass and flower bushes.

Kath recalled Darien's mention of that identifying feature. "That's definitely it. She told us to park in the driveway."

Evan rolled the Jeep in, stopping behind the closed garage door. A four-foot sneering stone gargoyle posted at the entrance to the garden path wore a wooden sign around its thick neck that read: I Eat Curmudgeons.

"That's excellent," Kellan chuckled as they made their way up to the front door. He gave a friendly pat to the head of the snarling statue of reference. "He doesn't look so mean. We get him laid, he'll be our buddy."

Kath shook her head as she tapped the door knocker. They heard rustling inside, then light footsteps on a wood floor. Darien Taite, diminutive and frail with age, came to the door with a radiant smile. Her long gray hair lay in a dense rope braid over her right shoulder. The roundness of her pale hazel eyes was amplified by her thick spectacles, making her storied inner vision seem even more palpable.

At just under five feet tall, she was nearly swallowed by her hooded, flannel house coat that flowed down to her well-worn brown Ugg boots.

"Kathryn Broch, come here, you lovely little witch." She opened her arms and Kath bent down to embrace her. "It's wonderful to see you again."

"Thank you, Darien. It's great to see you, too. We really appreciate you fitting us in today."

"My pleasure. I was intrigued when Henry told me about your situation." Darien lifted on her toes to try to get her arms around Henry's huge shoulders, but even fully bent over he couldn't get down low enough. They laughed at this and he kissed her delicate hands.

"You look beautiful, Darien," he said.

"Now, now"—the older woman wagged a finger—"nobody bullshits a psychic—not even a shaman." Darien turned to Evan who had removed his sunglasses in the shade of the porch. She extended her hand, waiting for him to close the distance, all the while scanning him from tip to toe with a speculative frown. "Mr. MacTavish, we need to talk first. Come in and find a seat."

"Yes, ma'am." Evan smiled sweetly, but Kathryn could tell that unnerved him. It unnerved her, too.

Darien stood aside while Henry and Evan went into the house, then she opened her arms to Kellan. "Come down here, beautiful, glowing thing. Give me a kiss on the cheek."

Kellan went to one knee, eye to eye, and pressed a soft kiss to Darien's cheek before drawing her into a warm embrace. She gave him a good squeeze and held his face in both her hands. From where she still stood in the doorway, Kath could see those hazel eyes diving deep into the amber of Kellan's, swimming in the ocean of information there. Darien smiled.

"Always in so much love, Kellan Broch—every time I see you. You're in love with the entire world."

He laughed softly, letting her continue investigating.

"You've made a place for someone special, though; a beautiful, green-eyed lady. I see her light all around you, encasing you." Darien lowered her chin. "You are nearly her every thought at the moment. Did you know that?"

"No," he said, but his eyes sparkled. "I'd think she'd be getting sick of me by now."

Darien laughed. "That won't happen for a very long time, if ever. Come in, dear. Let's all sit in the living room. I have tea for us."

The small house had many windows, but most were covered in dark blue silk drapes. The living room, adorned with fresh cut roses from her garden, was the center of the floorplan. Velvet-covered sofas were comfortably arranged before the large hearth, bright with a roaring fire. Framed photographs of Darien's family and many friends jostled for space on its polished wood mantle. A silver tea set gleamed on the Queen Anne coffee table. They all waited for their hostess to choose her seat, then got comfortable around her.

Evan sat across from her as she began pouring the tea into charming blue china cups. She handed him his cup first.

"Sugar and milk are just there, if you like."

"I take it straight up, thanks."

"Of course." Darien smiled at him then handed Kathryn a steaming cup and saucer. "Men have simple needs, dear. Don't overcomplicate this one just because he's secretive." She gave Kathryn a wink.

Kath felt her cheeks heat up and hoped it was dim enough in the room to hide her uncharacteristic blush.

After giving Kellan and Henry their cups, Darien reached across the table toward Evan. "Give me your hands, handsome devil."

He set his cup down and gently cradled Darien's small hands in his. For a time, she just stared into his slate blue eyes while the fire snapped on the hearth, but then she promptly let go of him. "We should speak privately, dear," she said with a quick smile.

Evan glanced at Kathryn. "I have nothing to hide from present company."

Her eyebrows shot up. "Excuse me?"

Darien patted her knee. "Don't fret, dear. Even if he told you, the story wouldn't be quite right. He doesn't remember it clearly for several reasons." She nodded to Kellan. "And you shouldn't hear it at all, regardless of your bravado. It will haunt you in a way that does more harm than good. Understand?"

"Yes, ma'am," Kellan said, but Kath could see he wasn't convinced.

Pausing to stir some honey into her tea, Darien gave Henry a smile. "Tell me more about the intruder in your midst."

"As I mentioned, we have a very old, clever succubus. We've been told we need certain magical elements for a banishing ritual, but we don't know them all." He nodded to Kathryn. "Her grandmother gave us five parts, we've been able to gather two, possibly three more, and were hoping you might have some insight on what remains."

"Fill me in from the top." Darien sat back on the sofa while Henry and Kathryn shared the backstory and the details of the hag's interference so far. Kath described the dream conversation she'd had with Ginny. Darien listened carefully to everything, then looked across to Henry. "You're hoping I might be able to tune into this being, like I did with the demon this summer?"

"That or anything else that might be helpful," Kath said. "My grandmother likes to give me puzzles to work through because it gets my brain going, but I'm frustrated that she didn't just *tell* me everything I need here."

Darien shook her head crisply. "Virginia isn't playing with you, dear. She didn't tell you the other parts because she doesn't know them."

Kathryn blinked. That had simply never occurred to her. "Oh."

Setting her half-empty cup on the tea tray, Darien took Kathryn's hands. Another moment of quiet concentration, and then she let go. "Yes. That's it. Virginia doesn't know. The way she sees it is like a game of mahjong—simples and honors. She sees open places for tiles, but has none to put there. It seems that your grandmother witch is being blocked by this succubus. It's managing somehow to obscure Ginny's focus. It has a sore spot for her since she outsmarted it when it first attacked. And then you, the upstart little granddaughter witch, locked it up in a tree for two decades." Darien chortled. "This hag is not happy with you Broch women."

"Then it's definitely about revenge and not just about consuming Kellan's life force?" Evan asked.

"That's where you're misinterpreting its desire. Kellan's life force is just the gravy, not the meat. The hag needs to put these foul witches in their place." Darien shook her head, absently tugging her long gray braid. "The trouble it's having is that you're not just a witch, are you, Kathryn? You're an outcaster—a naturally occurring slayer of evil things."

Kellan smirked at his sister. "We need to get you a hard rockin' theme song."

Darien just smiled. "You are something this succubus hasn't encountered and isn't sure how to destroy. And make no mistake; destroying you *is* its key motivation. It already knows the best way to distress you is to torment the ones you love. It's taking all these side roads to learn your response to the different affronts. It's figuring out what *really* gets under your skin before it makes its big move. Don't give it any help."

"I'm not sure how to avoid that," Kath said. "I mean, it's reading our minds."

"Yes," Darien said. "And obviously, your vessel and your handsome beau are at the forefront of your mind at all times. I see them there now." Her thin lips turned in a playful smile. "I see what you're thinking of doing to this lovely young man later, too. Tsk tsk."

Evan laughed. "As long as it doesn't involve chains or handcuffs, I'm good."

Darien winked at him. "Don't lie, Evan. You'd let her restrain you and enjoy it."

Kellan burst out laughing, almost spilling his tea, while his sister blushed like a school girl. Tying Evan up and having her way with him was a relatively recent desire, but had definitely taken up fantasy space during private time.

Looking across at Henry, Kath muttered, "I thought you said she was discreet."

Darien laughed as she stood up from the sofa. "I'm just tuning into you, dear. I won't share anything else of that nature; I promise. I don't even have the vocabulary for what's going on in that corner of your brother's mind."

Kellan batted his lashes, unabashed, and Darien shook her head.

"I know this originated with Kathryn and her grandmother, but it's all of your problem now. I asked you all to come because I think a group reading is the best idea. You see, our thoughts function on different levels—the deeply personal or secret level, the general interaction level, and then on the group level. This is our collective consciousness at work."

"Amazing," Kellan said. "And that explains a lot."

"Indeed. Your tribe is very connected. I simply need to find the frequency you share so I can tune in and meet you there. Just like our more private thoughts, there are often blind spots and gaps we create without knowing. You've been working on this problem for some time now and may be missing things that are right in front of you. Sit back and enjoy your tea; give me just a moment to find your radio station."

Darien folded her hands in front of her and began pacing around her living room, widdershins. Kathryn tried to relax and calm her thoughts so she didn't cause any unnecessary psychic noise. Glancing at the others, they seemed to be doing the same. Evan caught her eye and grinned; Kath blew him a kiss.

Stopping at the window, the slight old woman stared out at the oak in her front yard. "The wolves and the owl are showing me where to stand so I can hear you all. It'll just be another moment." Darien lowered her chin briefly, took a deep breath, then turned to them with a smile. "You don't see it, but there are dark wings as wide as an airplane around all of you. They emanate from Kathryn, but they also watch over her." She raised a gray eyebrow to Kath. "That is the biggest damned crow I've ever seen, young lady."

"It's a beast."

"You haven't known it long so you're not familiar with all its capabilities yet. It's not just a spirit animal, it's a spirit *guide*. The crow has watched you your whole life, waiting for you to connect to it, and it's stepped in when it was essentially needed. You may not have been aware of it during those times—or you may have blocked it out because it frightened you."

"That happened when I was a kid and this succubus first attacked Kellan," Kath said. "The crow came in to help me, but I'd never seen it and was terrified of it. I blocked out the entire interaction for over twenty years."

"I see," Darien said. "But it waited for you until you were ready. I have an image of Henry at your side when you made that connection."

He looked up at their host. "I guided Kathryn on a vision quest a few weeks ago. It was truly amazing. After she made the connection to the crow, she levitated. High. I almost had a heart attack."

Darien laughed softly. "The guide was showing its charge what it can do for her. It certainly didn't mean to frighten either of you. You've been practicing with it, Kathryn?"

"Yes."

Nodding as she paced the living room again, Darien moved behind Kath on the sofa.

"It exhausts you, I know. But it has a lot to tell you. Take your vitamins and stay with it." She winked, then began pacing again, that time toward Kellan. "Golden one, you have little to do with all these protectors hovering around you."

"That is so," he said with a rueful grin. "My mother calls them my enablers."

"She's not far off," Darien said. "You need to watch your own backside more often, especially now that you have someone so drawn to you. She's your responsibility also. I see her face, but her name … it's a song?"

"Almost. Sonya," Kellan said.

"Ah, Sonya, yes. Her light is around all of you, but mostly the Brochs. She's close to you, too, Kathryn?"

"She's become a great friend."

"She admires you all very much. Her energy is part of your collective now. Your healer is coming through, also."

"That's Jewel," Evan said.

"Right, the nurse." Darien returned to her seat and poured herself some fresh tea. "I have your frequency now. There are others that vibrate here—some that are far away. Across oceans."

Kath nodded. "We have some very close friends who help us in Scotland; Mae, Lily and Brodie."

"Mmm—a cook, a dressmaker, and a photographer."

As always, Kath was amazed at Darien's accuracy. "Yes."

"And the one who left you recently to have a child—two children, twins. They aren't born yet, but they'll come before Christmas. What's her name?"

"Gigi," Kath and Kellan said together.

"Yes, Gigi. She was tribe for a very long time and has a deep connection to you Brochs—a *blood* connection." Her hazel eyes honed in on Kellan. "These twins are not her first born."

Kellan just shook his head, his expression suggesting he'd rather Darien not elaborate.

She raised her hand for his patience. "It's inevitable that that bird will return, young man. You left the trail of breadcrumbs with that intention."

Kellan nodded only once, his expression and its request unchanged.

"All right," Darien acquiesced. "That's everyone on this station, I believe. Let's see what I can see." The clairvoyant closed her eyes.

The fire snapped cheerfully and the oak tree shimmied in a breeze out in the front yard. Somewhere in the house a noisy clock ticked.

"I see a window blowing inward; glass and wood flying, children screaming."

Kath met her brother's eyes, but said nothing. She hated that memory.

"It was vengeance then, for Virginia getting away from it." Darien's eyes were still closed and she shivered slightly. "It was so angry at you for binding it, Kathryn. That bitterness seethed and festered for twenty-three years. It was plotting all that time. Listening to you when you'd come to the mountains; learning about your experiences. It bided time." Her hazel eyes suddenly fixed Kathryn in earnest. "Its plan is formed, but I can't see a clear image of it. There's violent wind and rushing water, but not at the same time."

Frowning hard, Kath said, "Sonya had an experience with a terrific wind two nights ago at her home. My brother was there with her, but he didn't see it."

Darien's focus glazed as she concentrated. "I'm seeing it now, through Sonya's green eyes. Yes. That was a clear message." She reached for Kathryn's hand and held it tight. "Your friend needs to be very careful who she talks to and where she goes. Her home is safe and yours, as well, but she shouldn't go far. Your thatching is effective, have no fear of that, but this creature is able to reach through it and manipulate the interior environment."

"She can breach it?" Henry said, concerned.

"No," Darien stated, then squinted, as though she were trying to hear a faint noise coming from far away. "It can *move the air* inside the barrier, but it can't change the temperature. In other words, it can move things but not set them on fire. Understand? Its capabilities are most definitely hampered by your magic. But from what I can see, it cannot cross the thatch itself in any physical form. You still have that advantage."

Evan leaned in. "Would it help to strengthen the thatch?"

"Not worth spending the energy. It's already as strong as it can get on your collective power. This old thing is simply stronger than what you've got. What you need to focus on is where this entity is weak. It knows *your* weaknesses too well—all of yours."

"How do we learn that?" Kath said. "It's not like she'll sit down with us for drinks."

Nodding slowly, Darien sipped her tea. "I see her in the guise of that girl from your past—the ill-groomed blonde one."

"Lisa Tucker," Kath said with a slight grimace. The name actually tasted bad in her mouth.

Darien's hazel eyes drifted to her. "The answer to your question about her is no, dear girl. Don't let it trouble you further."

Kath let out an audible sigh.

"What question?" Evan said.

"Never mind." She and Darien grinned at each other.

"Now, as far as what you need for your ritual, I see the things already collected. From Virginia: a stone talisman, a mixture of smokes—Henry, don't you and Evan use something like this on an old one in Mount Iolite?"

"Yes, my uncle gave us a very effective smoke mixture for a local entity we call Old Red Eyes. That mix makes its victims invisible to it, so it gets bored and moves on. Virginia's recipe has some similar ingredients, but its purpose is to repel, not conceal. I believe we want the succubus to be able to see us, right?"

"Oh, yes—Kathryn needs to have eye contact with it," Darien said. "All right, the other things Virginia gave you are a terracotta pot to burn this mixture in, a ring of black salt, the power of the full moon, the location itself—which should be the same place where you did your vision quest. That's a place of great power from the earth."

Kath nodded. "It was Sonya's property."

Darien's brows drew together in concern. "Your friend wants to do whatever she can to help you, but she doesn't know the danger she's in."

Kellan flopped back in his chair. "This is because of me."

"It's because of your family blood, dear. Nothing you could do about that even if you wanted to." Darien turned to Kath again. "I can't see both cards, but I see the best Tarot for you to use as a seal."

"That's the information I need," she said. "I've used The Magician to pull all the other succubae that have attacked Kellan this year, so I was planning to use it again."

Darien frowned at this news. "There have been *others* like this one?"

"Not as strong, but strong enough in different ways. There's been sort of a wave lately. Four altogether before this old business returned."

"Huh." Darien stroked her braid, staring at a spot on the coffee table. "I can't see why that is just yet, but I'll ruminate on it. But if you're confident with The Magician as your pull card, use it. I see the Three of Swords as your seal."

Kath didn't understand. "I never use suit cards for extractions—only major Arcana."

"This time, you'll play a different song. The suit card will work; you'll see when you're in the moment." She gave Kath's knee a maternal squeeze. "You made a note of something when you and Henry last discussed this—an item you weren't sure was right."

Henry leaned in. "Ash from your Samhain ritual fire."

"Yes," Darien said. "That's a keeper." She took a slow, deep breath, her frown increasing. "The last item will make most of you uncomfortable. I know you don't employ the black aspects of magic."

Kath shook her head. "Black magic repeats threefold on the caster; those are shit odds I'd rather not play."

"Understood." Again, Darien leaned toward Evan and reached for his hand. "You'll be in charge of this last element, handsome devil. As the alpha, your stomach is stronger and it won't be as difficult for you to carry out."

"Yes, ma'am. What do we need?"

Those magnified hazel eyes touched on Kellan, Kathryn, then back to Evan. "The blood of the three. You'll need a good amount of it and it has to be equally let. Have your nurse help you to get that right. Before the full moon, you'll be told how to use all these things—maybe by Virginia, maybe another; I'm not sure. But you have four days left before the moon. You'll know by then." She sat back with a sigh, as though she'd just set down a heavy burden. "That's all I have to tell you at this time, my friends."

Kathryn knew her eyes had gone round, and they stayed that way for nearly the entire drive back to Mount Iolite. They'd thanked Darien for all her help and piled back into the Jeep, but everyone was silent and lost in thought. As they passed the turn off to Mammoth Lakes, she let out a long, frustrated groan.

"White light practitioners don't let blood. It's against our credo. Maybe Darien's wrong."

From the backseat, Henry cleared his throat. "I wouldn't put too many eggs in that basket, Blackwing. Darien's vision is chillingly acute. I've never once known her to be wrong."

Kath turned in her seat to see Kellan staring out the window, his amber eyes cloudy with unease.

"I don't love it, either," he said to her. "We've never let ritual blood. What if something goes wrong?"

Evan caught his eye in the rearview mirror. "For instance?"

"I don't know, I just don't like it. It's smacks of hoodoo and gives me the freakin' creeps."

"I'm with ya," Kath said. "But it's not like we're murdering a goat or anything. It's just our own blood."

"A 'good amount' of it," Evan reminded her. "Equally let."

"Yeah." She tried to smile at her brother. "I'll read up on it; try to limit novice mistakes, at least. I'll make it as okay as possible, baby bro." She rested a hand on Evan's arm as he drove. "You good with being the head vampire?"

He grinned crookedly. "They always have the best wardrobe."

Kath laughed, turning back to her brother. "Don't worry, Kell. It's all gonna be okay." She lifted her gaze to Henry. "Right, shaman?"

Henry's smile was sure and true, and it made Kathryn believe him when he said, "Right, outcaster."

She turned back toward the road, watching the horizon.

CHAPTER FIFTEEN

"IS IT SNOWING there yet, Aunt Sonya?" Isla, her eldest niece, was obsessed with the snowfall she'd never seen down south in San Diego. Sonya and her older sister, Shannon, had been planning their visit to Mount Iolite for Isla's upcoming tenth birthday, but much of its success was predicated on whether there would be snow.

Standing at the sink overlooking the courtyard, she leaned forward to see the slope of the hillside behind the compound. That morning's forecast warned of the first big storm of the season and a leaden belly of cloud had been rolling in all day, gathering ominously over Bonny Lake. "Not yet, pumpkin, but it's going to start any minute. You should see these clouds!"

Excited, Isla said, "Send me pictures! I can't wait to get there. How long is it now?"

"It's coming up quick." Sonya peered at the calendar on her phone. "The day after Thanksgiving is only three weeks and two days away."

After another round of girlish squealing, Isla returned. "How come you're not coming down for Thanksgiving? We could all drive back up together."

"I know, but I've already accepted an invitation from my friend, Jewel. I'm helping her cook for her huge family, so she needs me. She'll be feeding twenty-one people and three dogs!"

"Wow!" Isla gasped. "That's an army!"

"I know! But I'll see you and your mom the very next day. And then it'll be your birthday!"

The little girl giggled as she clapped her hands. "Two digits, *finally*! I thought it would never happen."

"Don't rush it, my love. Life goes fast enough as it is. Meanwhile, Halloween is this weekend. What did you decide to be—the princess or the wizard?"

Her niece had changed her plan altogether and would now be going as a ninja. "The costume is *way* cooler; I even have a sword."

"I love it—girl power!"

"Totally!"

Sonya smiled. "I have to dress up this year, too, actually."

"Grown-ups go trick or treating up there?!"

"No, I wish! My new friends here are musicians and they have a performance on Halloween night where the whole audience comes in costume."

"How fun! What're you gonna be?"

"I'm not sure yet." She wandered into the guest bedroom to her main closet and rolled the door open. "I was thinking maybe an angel. Remember the dress I wore for baby Christopher's baptism?"

"Oh, yeah—when Aunt Selena made you his godmother. That's a beautiful dress!"

"It is." Sonya reached to the back of the rack for a clear plastic garment bag and laid it out on the guest bed to unzip. The dress was a simple, off-white crepe shift with bell sleeves made of intricate lace inlaid with pearl beads. The hem had a layer of floaty chiffon cut in a lettuce-edge that gave the dress liquid motion. "I could make wings out of paper and hanger wire and paint them with glitter. That might look neat. I'll send you a picture so you can tell me if it works."

"Cool!" On Isla's end, Sonya heard her older sister's voice saying it was her turn to talk to auntie. "Mommy's here for you. I'll talk to you later, okay?"

"Okay, sweet girl. Have fun trick or treating. I love you."

"Love you, too, Aunt Sonya! Bye!"

A moment later Shannon was on, still talking to her daughter about helping with dinner. "Don't go too far away, young lady. Hi."

"Hi." Sonya put the dress back in the closet for later. "We were discussing Halloween costumes."

"She told you about the ninja?" Sonya could hear the eye roll in Shannon's voice. "I see broken things all over my house from that plastic sword. Anyway, are you going stir crazy in the woods yet?"

"Not at all. I'm in heaven. I can't wait for you and Isla to see it." She started the kettle and leaned against the counter with her phone. "I have a little news; I'm seeing someone."

"Oh my god! Let a person sit down first!" Shannon crowed, then her tone softened. "I thought you didn't want to date again after Rob died."

"I thought so, too—and then this happened. His name is Kellan Broch."

"Sounds like a Viking. I'm sure he's *very* attractive."

"He's beautiful." Sonya's cheeks heated up at the thought of him. "And get this scandalous detail: he's younger than me—by a lot."

Shannon sounded mildly alarmed. "How old exactly?"

"Thirty-four."

Lowering her voice so her curious daughter wouldn't hear, Shannon said, "it's coming clear to me now, little sis; you moved up to the hinterlands to cougar on hot young mountain men."

"My secret is out," Sonya laughed. "They're thick on the ground in these parts. Can't walk two inches without tripping over one."

"Uh huh. What does this toddler look like?"

"Hang on, I'll send you a picture." Sonya pulled up her phone's gallery and selected one of her favorite images of Kellan from the KKB website: lounging in front of a roaring fire in a cuddly white sweater, his long fingers curled around a mug of something with whipped cream on it. The firelight ignited the gold in his amber eyes and made the strands of auburn in his tousled hair glow. He'd told her that Evan took that photo last year, but she wouldn't be elaborating on that situation for her sister. "Okay, sent."

While Shannon paused to look at the photo, Sonya spooned her favorite rose hips tea into a pot. There was a grin in her sister's voice when she returned.

"Holy crap, *he's gorgeous*! Did you take that of him?"

Sonya explained about the Brochs' musical career and where the photo had come from. She and Shannon were close, but for the moment she only wanted to share the safer details about her new friends; their exciting rock star lives in Europe, their lovely cabin with the rich family history, their wonderful, welcoming friends and how close she was also becoming to Kellan's sister, Kathryn.

"All kidding aside, I'm grateful for them," she said. "Jewel has been a godsend, but I'd been a little blue lately nonetheless. The Brochs and their friends are brightening everything up."

"And then some," Shannon teased. "No, really, I'm thrilled to hear you're having fun. I've been worried about you up there all alone."

"I know you have." Sonya looked out the window as the kettle started to hiss. From her vantage point, she could see the edge of the thatch bundle near her driveway, still safely in place after the wild, supernatural wind the other night. She'd most certainly leave those details out for Shannon as she hoped it would all be cleared up by the time her sister and niece arrived. "This is still the right thing for me, though. I'm very happy here, even before the Brochs. I can't wait to show you around so you can see everything I've done in person."

"From the photos you've sent, it's been quite a transformation—the property and you. I'm so happy to hear it, Sonya."

The kettle boiled and she poured the water into the pot. The fragrant steam carried a hint of sweet lemon, reminding her of the scent of Kellan's skin lotion. She smiled thinking of how his lovely skin felt against her own. She couldn't wait to see him later that night.

"So, is this serious or just for fun?" her sister said.

Stirring the tea leaves, Sonya sighed. "I went into it thinking it was just a fling, but things are going so well that I'm not sure now. They're only here for three months in the fall, so it's hard to imagine it becoming too permanent."

"You love to travel—go visit him in Scotland!"

She'd been thinking a lot about that, but hadn't wanted to bring it up for fear Kellan would think she was being clingy. "I have two months with him before they go home. We'll see how it goes."

A door closed on Shannon's end; Sonya guessed she'd gone into the downstairs bathroom for some privacy. Isla was a precocious nine-year-old and seemed to always overhear things her mother didn't yet want to explain.

"Listen, don't let fear get in the way if you're thinking this might be something great. If it's widow guilt, don't even go there; Rob wants you to be happy."

"I know that." Sonya fought back inevitable tears as she brought her tea to the sofa in front of the fire. "I think he'd like Kellan, actually. They have some similar traits."

"I can only imagine any guy that looks that good is at least decent in bed," Shannon said. "Or he'd better be."

Sonya chuckled. "He's delicious all around. Kind, charming, great sense of humor, terrific kisser. And he treats me like a goddess."

Her sister laughed, delighted. "This is *wonderful*, honey. Will we get to meet him when we're there?"

"Absolutely. All of them, I hope. Oh, before I forget—I was filling out some insurance paperwork earlier and I listed you and my neighbor, Jewel, as my emergency contacts. Hope that's okay."

"Of course it is. You're spending Thanksgiving with her, right?"

"Right."

Shannon laughed a little. "Selena and I have been trying to distract Mom from dumping a guilt trip on you."

"She knew I'd planned to stay here for Thanksgiving, anyway—even before Jewel invited me. It's right in between my first two bookings and I didn't want to stress myself out by leaving town."

Shannon said they all understood. After everything Sonya had been through, her family just wanted her to be happy. "We'll miss you bunches, though, no guilt intended."

"You'll be here the very next day."

"I know. Isla's beside herself." Shannon laughed. "You'd better talk to the mountain gods and get some snow going or this kid's gonna be a pain in the ass all weekend."

As if on cue, a low rumble of thunder vibrated the windows of her house. "Well, things are looking good on that front. I should send you a photo of the sky right now."

"I'd rather see another picture of your sexy little Viking."

Laughing at herself, Sonya said she had more than she cared to admit. "There is one other I'd love for you to see. Let me find it." She faced the screen and tapped the gallery app, but it didn't open right away. When she tapped again, the whole screen grayed out for a second before it cleared, and then her camera opened on its own.

"Hang on," she said into the speaker. "I think the storm's making my phone act crazy. Gimme a sec."

Sonya pressed the button to close the camera, but it didn't respond. She'd turned the lens inward earlier to get a snapshot of herself standing next to the giant wood-carved bear on the Robbin Lake boat docks, thinking it would be a fun Christmas gift for her parents. When she shifted the phone to access the controls on the side, her face flashed on the screen. But there was something strange about her eyes.

Her hair was loose that day and slipped forward as she peered down at the lens. Her eyes were still green, but their shape was off— too round, and edged in deep shadow as though she were far older than she was. Thinking the angle might be distorting her image, Sonya held the camera up and looked at it straight on. It was her face for sure, but it appeared ages older, like she'd jumped ahead in time forty years.

Heart pounding, she couldn't look away as the skin of her cheeks began to sag into hanging wrinkles; her green eyes went dull and sunken, and her lustrous strawberry blonde hair shriveled to tangled wires of gray. Sonya gasped and when her mouth opened, all her teeth were rotted and chipped.

"Sonya?" Shannon's voice startled her terribly and she dropped the phone on the sofa. "Sonya, did I lose you? Hello?"

The phone lay on the cushion beside her, but the camera had shut itself off, displaying the normal app screen. Sonya's heart thundered in her ears.

"Hello?" Shannon insisted.

"I'm here," she croaked. "Just a sec." Sonya was terrified to touch that thing again, but she grabbed the phone and pressed the button for the gallery. As though there'd never been a mishap, the photos came right up. Her fingers trembled violently, but she selected the one she was after and sent it to her sister. "Sorry, took me a minute to find it."

"You sound out of breath. Did you just do a lap around your courtyard or something? Oh my god, *look* at this freakin' guy! Could he be any hotter?"

Shannon's exclamations made her laugh involuntarily, which was a good thing. It calmed her racing heart. "He is crazy cute."

The image her sister was looking at Sonya had taken herself. She'd been sitting with Kellan out on her front porch while he had a cigarette, just as the sun was going down behind Mount Iolite. A warm pink glow surrounded him as he'd turned toward her camera. Bundled in a flannel and brown scarf, his small smile was intimate and sultry like his thoughts should carry a parental guidance warning. She loved it.

"God," her sister sighed wistfully. "It's been about a million years since a man looked at me like that—and none of them were ever this sexy. Good goin', sis."

"Thanks." Sonya made sure her smile could be heard in her voice, but she'd walked into the bathroom to look in the mirror. She was relieved to find her reflection the same as it had been that morning: rested, smooth-skinned, pink-cheeked from the brisk autumn cold; hair still strawberry blonde and soft, teeth still straight and white. That was definitely her in the mirror, but who had that been in the camera?

After solidifying their plans for Shannon's visit, they ended the conversation saying they'd speak again before Thanksgiving. Sonya sat on the sofa and held the phone in her hand for a moment. The good blaze crackling in her fireplace warmed the whole room as heavy clouds crept into the tree line outside. Bonny Lake reflected a portentous gloom. Sonya stared at the phone until she worked up the courage to open the camera again. The lens was still pointed inward and she held her breath as she angled it toward her face.

There was nothing unusual about the image that time, beyond her current expression of dread. She let out a shaky breath and turned off the camera. She knew she hadn't imagined that. It was the middle of the day, she was sober as a judge and had a great night's sleep. There was no reason for her to be seeing things. Sonya concluded there was only one possible explanation for what she'd witnessed. She texted Kathryn.

Remember that target we thought might be on my back? It was just confirmed.

The quick reply asked if she was all right and Sonya assured her she was. Kathryn then wrote: *pack an overnight bag and drive down here soon as you can. Please stay with us tonight.*

Hating being afraid in her own home, Sonya cast a bitter glance around the room. "Leave me alone, you bitch," she muttered into the quiet. Then she told Kath she'd be down shortly.

The rain started as she gathered her things, pelting the windows from every direction. The forecast had called for high winds and rain at first, then a potential for snow overnight. She'd been looking forward to the first snow of the year. Sonya and Rob had first driven through the Sierras during the summer, and she'd only seen a few holdout dirty patches of last winter's snow when she first toured the compound with Annie Schon. She hated being distracted from that by this monster.

It was just after dark when Sonya drove down to the Brochs' place with her overnight bag and a bundle of nerves. Kathryn took her out of the blowing rain on the front porch and into the living room. She hung up Sonya's coat then sat her on some throw pillows in front of the potbelly.

"Tonight, we drink bourbon." Kath slipped a tumbler of ice and amber liquid into Sonya's hand then sat with her on the pillows. The little fire snapped, soft Celtic music flowed from the stereo and candles flickered on the coffee table. In Virginia Broch's cabin, all appeared quiet and well. Sonya tried to tune into that.

Kellan and Evan had been out in the shed restocking the firewood and they thudded back inside through the kitchen. The sound made Sonya jump even though she knew it was them. Her nerves were a mess. She took a big sip of the sharp alcohol as Kath squeezed her hand.

"It's all right, just give yourself a minute. Drink that up and then tell us what happened."

The guys joined them after filling up the wood box and they all listened to every detail of Sonya's experience with pointed concern.

Evan had been inspecting her phone while she spoke. "Your battery wasn't dead after?"

Sonya frowned. "No."

"Weird. It must have drawn energy from some other source up there."

Kellan sat forward in his father's chair. "Darien said the compound was a place of great power from nature. There's probably pockets up there we don't know about—maybe even portals."

"Who's Darien?" Sonya said.

Kath told her about their visit to the clairvoyant in Bishop and what information they'd gathered about the upcoming ritual, among other things. "Darien isn't for the faint of heart," she grinned. "But she's dead accurate so we're following her instructions. It may help to know that we have everything we need for the ritual now, we just need to figure out how to apply all the elements. We've been working on it all day; I think we're really close."

"That does help," Sonya said with a weak smile, but the statement was true. If they had a solid plan, she believed they would win.

"The full moon is in three days," Kellan said, reaching for Sonya's hand. "We'll do everything we can to keep you safe until then. I promise." He brought her hand to his lips and kissed it. "Try not to worry, pretty lady."

Sonya cupped his jaw gently in her hand and smiled for him. Between his genuine sincerity and the warm buzz from the whisky, she was finally feeling better. Evan topped off their drinks before he and Kellan went into the kitchen to start dinner. Kath glanced after them then spoke softly to her friend.

"You really okay?"

"Getting there."

Kathryn's smile faded quickly. "I'm so sorry this is happening to you, sweetie. I feel horrible about it."

"It's not your fault. This is just … a byproduct of being close to you two. I've accepted that. I certainly don't blame you, Kathryn."

In the kitchen, the guys were at the counter rinsing green beans and slicing lemons. They stood close and spoke softly to each other, their expressions troubled and pensive. Sonya assumed they were discussing their supernatural problem, but she couldn't help noticing the press of their shoulders and the intimacy in the glances they exchanged. Kellan was obviously distraught over this happening to Sonya, as was his sister. She heard Evan assure him it was going to be all right. He pressed a lingering kiss to Kellan's forehead. She watched those beautiful amber eyes slide closed for the duration of the contact.

Kath had been watching her watching them. She offered a wan smile, but didn't say anything right away.

Sonya whispered to her. "In all the drama, I hadn't given a thought to the sleeping arrangements here. Kellan's been with me at the compound every night we've stayed together, other than the first night when we were here alone." She glanced again into the kitchen. "Should I expect him to be in with Evan tonight?"

Kathryn looked down with a little shake of her head. "I never know the answer to that myself when Ev's here. The situation is always fluid with them. But I went ahead and made the master up for you so you have your own space, just in case they do crash out together."

Relieved, Sonya smiled. "Thank you. I don't want to interfere with the flow. This is your sanctuary. I want you all to do what's natural, not fuss over me."

"Understood and appreciated," Kath said. "But what's most natural to my brother and me is to care for the people we love. Why don't you take your stuff upstairs and get settled in? Take a few deep breaths. You're safe here."

Sonya thought that was a grand idea. She collected her bag and started for the stairs.

Kath said, "There's a bathroom up there, too—make yourself at home. For the master, take a left at the landing and keep going until you see the lake. Come down whenever you're ready."

Sonya thanked her again and went up.

At the landing, she'd stopped and glanced at the four open doors. Having never been up there, she didn't think they'd mind if she took a quick peek into the rooms.

Kath's was the room directly in front of the stairs, lit by a small night light plugged into the outlet by the door. Heavy floral curtains covered the one large window; she felt a light, cold breeze and smelled the rain outside. Heat rose from the stoves downstairs and she figured Kath liked to keep her room cool for sleeping. A small dresser was littered with bits of jewelry and half full water glasses; an empty pink china tea cup sat beside a notebook on the only night table.

The queen bed was unmade and rumpled with pink sheets and a pile of quilts, four big pillows tossed around and a black sleep mask on the corner of the mattress to shield Kath's night owl eyes from the terrible dawn. Tucked in under one of the pillows, Sonya spied a small pink vibrator. She laughed softly because it would never occur to Kath to hide that toy away in case one of their many guests might see it; she truly could not have cared any less. Sonya envied both their comfort with sexual expression and hoped she was relaxing from their example.

Kellan's room was also lit by a night light. Sonya realized just then that every room in their cabin had this low, ambient light. She wondered if that was so they could always see where they were going, or if there was some deeper reason for not allowing full darkness anywhere inside.

She leaned on the doorway of Kellan's room and glanced to the window that faced her own property. It was covered by a heavy curtain, but not open to the night breeze. He must like to have his room a bit warmer than his sister did. Sonya looked around.

His scent was strong in there; a delicious combination of the sweetness he always had and the faint musk of his pleasure. She knew that scent well by now. His bed was also unmade but his sheets were light brown. A stack of quilts was pushed down near the footboard where he likely kicked them off while he slept. From the few times she'd lain beside him overnight, she knew he was a squirmy belly sleeper and that he got very warm. She'd felt his heat radiating even when he was a few feet away.

On the night table near the door was a cup of cold coffee, and a small leather journal with a braided string attached to close it; but it wasn't closed then. She bit her lip, considering how guilty she might feel if she took a quick peek. Then again, Sonya knew Kellan would understand her curiosity.

She sat on the bed and gently opened the journal without moving it on the table. She turned a few pages. In the light from the hallway, she could see that on some he'd written snips of what looked like lyrics or poems; on others he'd scrawled snatches of music. This wasn't a diary, but a catcher for those great ideas that always seem to come to artists in the dead of night. On the first page, there was an inscription in beautiful cursive handwriting: *For my son to capture the magic ~ Dad.* She smiled and let the journal fall gently closed.

Sitting on his bed, Kellan's warm, earthy scent was wonderfully strong. She leaned down and pressed her face into the scrunched pillows, breathing in. As had happened periodically since they'd become lovers, a tiny trickle of moisture seeped from inside her; spillover of his heavy, creamy ejaculate left behind. With Rob, she'd always hated the mess of oozing after sex, but with Kellan it seemed like a primal, claiming mark. He'd put his seed in her; she was *his.* Sonya swallowed, shivering with a combination of emotional panic and fresh lust. She stood up and brought her things into the short hallway, heading for the row of windows that faced Bonny Lake.

Kath had left a bedside lamp on for her in the master. The room was bathed in its warm yellow light. The king-size bed was neatly made with fresh linens and fluffy quilts. She set her bag on a chair just inside the door and went to see the view from the windows behind the bed.

The storm had been churning up white chop on Bonny Lake all day, but the faint moonlight coming through the cloud cover gave the water an eerie internal glow. The silhouettes of the trees seemed to hug close to the waterline for protection, but the storm buffeted them regardless.

Rain pattered on the front porch below the window and she looked down to see the rocking chairs creaking back and forth. Ghosts watching the rain fall on the lake or just the wind? She forced herself to smile at that idea. With a succubus hag closing in on her, ghosts were the least of her concerns at the moment.

She retrieved a cardigan from her bag by the door. Downstairs, she heard Kathryn laughing as Evan told her and Kellan about an awkward encounter with a former high school teacher outside a liquor store in Bridgeport. She glanced around the master bedroom once more before going down to join them, taking note of the clutter-free surfaces and the simple window blinds, obviously Jackson, Jr.'s preferred décor.

She tried to imagine the room when it belonged to Ginny. Would she have had flowered curtains like those in Kathryn's room? Little knickknacks of cute forest critters, fresh wildflowers in delicate vases mingling their perfume with the fragrant pine smoke from the stoves? How would this room have been softer when she lived here alone after her husband's passing?

Sonya realized she and Virginia Broch had some significant things in common; not only had they both experienced widowhood, but they both dearly loved her grandchildren. Momentarily overcome with bourbon-fueled emotion, Sonya let a few tears track down her face. They felt good; cleansing, even. She wiped her eyes then sighed into the quiet master bedroom.

"I'd love to know your thoughts, Mrs. Broch," she'd whispered. "Are you glad you brought me to them?" Sonya listened a moment, but there was no reply from the ghost. She smiled nonetheless. "Well, I'm glad you did, for what it's worth. Thank you."

Sonya went downstairs.

✦

After they'd polished off the bottle of Maker's Mark Evan had picked up for them in Bridgeport and watched the first Godfather movie in its entirety, Sonya had nearly forgotten about her frightening experience with her phone. She and Kath had been sharing the sofa and a bowl of kettle corn while the guys stretched out together on the floor in front of the pot belly. The bourbon had them all tipsy and Kellan fell asleep just after midnight with his head tucked into 'the nook'.

Evan tried to stay awake to keep chatting with the ladies, but he nodded off soon after. Kath put a quilt over them and stocked up the fires, then she and Sonya went upstairs. On the landing, Kath turned to her.

"The evening's events have given you your choice of beds—Kellan's or the master. Wherever you're comfortable."

Sonya gave her a hug, noting the soft fragrance of lavender in Kath's thick hair. "Thank you, sweetie. I'll tuck into the master. I'm practically asleep standing here."

Kath grinned. "I told you bourbon was the thing tonight. Get some sleep and let me know if you need anything." She went into her room, softly closing the door.

The master was warm from the evening's fires, but Sonya wondered if she'd need another blanket later when they'd gone out. Too tired to worry about it then, she crawled into the big bed and was asleep almost instantly.

CHAPTER SIXTEEN

SONYA WOKE FROM a long, uninterrupted sleep at 8:30, but didn't open her eyes just yet. A soft floral perfume wafted by her nose then disappeared. The only sound she heard in the Brochs' cabin were the purring snores coming from Kellan's room. Warm under a stack of quilts, she stretched and finally opened her eyes.

A new quilt had been added to the bed during the night. Kellan must have checked on her when he came upstairs. On the night table next to the lamp, was a small vase of blown glass filled with wildflowers. Fat raindrops glinted on their bright pedals. Sonya smiled as she sat up, imagining Kellan going out to collect them in the wee hours between cloudbursts. She couldn't hear the rain and figured it had stopped; she'd look out the windows after attending to more urgent matters. She got out of the snug bed, stepped into her slippers, and tiptoed to the bathroom.

As she quietly returned to the hall, she saw Kath's door was still closed. Far too early for a Broch to be moving around. Kellan's door was open just a crack. Sonya peeked inside.

Evan lay on his back with Kellan tucked in on his right, his head resting on Evan's bare chest. The 'nook' clearly had the same relaxing effect on them both; they were deeply asleep. Kellan was facing the door, his curvy lips parted and relaxed, silky pieces of chestnut hair tumbling over his brow. The covers were up to their waists but she could see he was still in the pajamas he'd put on after dinner. Part of her thought she'd find them naked, but then they'd all been exhausted last night. They appeared so content and peaceful; just looking at them soothed her. She crept down the stairs.

She'd expected to find the cabin chilly because the fires would have gone out, but a cheery little blaze snapped in the pot belly stove. She remembered Kathryn closing the vents on both stoves to contain sparks before they went up to bed, but now they were open to disperse the heat. In fact, the entire bottom floor was warm and cozy. Sonya knew the others were upstairs very much asleep and had been for some time by the look of them, so who was tending these fires?

As she approached the door to the kitchen, Sonya stopped cold. Her heart raced. The fully manifested figure of Virginia Broch opened the kitchen stove's narrow fire box and wriggled a fresh log inside.

She was solid as any real person; Sonya could even see the gentle folds of her cotton flowered apron tied over her trim black trousers and light black sweater. A delicate pair of black kitten heels peeked out from the hemline. The morning light creeping in around the drawn curtains caught the highlights in her shiny black curls. The only giveaway that this wasn't a real person was the fact that Ginny didn't use a pot holder to touch the molten handle of the firebox.

Once she'd stoked up the little blaze with an iron poker, Ginny replaced it on top of the stove and wiped her hands on her apron. She then turned to Sonya still frozen in shock in the doorway. Ginny smiled.

"Good morning, dear," she said in a strong, clear voice that had just the slightest rasp to it—very similar to the one in both Kathryn's and Kellan's voices. "I trust you slept well."

Sonya swallowed but her throat was bone dry. She realized she'd wrapped her arms around herself and had been squeezing in stunned anxiety. She'd been repeatedly assured there was nothing to be afraid of; Ginny was just a lady. A guardian, not a frightener. And this was *her* house. Sonya let her arms down.

"Good morning, Mrs. Broch. I slept very well, thank you."

"It gets cold in the wee hours, so I brought you another blanket," Ginny said.

"Oh, that was you. Thank you very much. I … slept like a stone."

"You needed it." Ginny glanced at the copper kettle sitting on the stove burner—an item that had not been there when they'd all cleaned up after dinner the night before. "I can make you a cup of tea, but I'm afraid I can't manipulate the coffee machine. Spirit energy is incompatible with electrical appliances."

Sonya found that fascinating. "Which is why electronics malfunction when spirits are near."

"That's correct," Ginny said. "Would you like tea?"

"Thank you, ma'am, but I think need coffee." Sonya laughed nervously as she took a step toward the counter.

"Of course." Ginny stood aside to let her get to the coffee maker by the stove.

Sonya's fingers trembled as she opened the container of ground coffee and fumbled with a fresh filter. She filled the pot with water at the sink then poured it into the machine's reservoir, all the while feeling Ginny watching her every move.

"Please don't be afraid, dear," the apparition said softly. "As my dear ones have told you, I mean absolutely no harm."

Sonya turned the coffee maker on and then leaned against the counter facing the vision of Ginny. "I know you don't, Mrs. Broch. I just need to get used to this unusual situation."

"I understand. Just keep taking deep breaths until you relax. And please, call me Ginny."

"Thank you." Sonya's fingers gripped the edge of the counter for support as she took in the being before her. While Ginny was solid, she had a slight shimmer all around her reminiscent of special effects used in older movies—before they made the space between an actor and the green screen seamless. It made her appear superimposed on the room rather than part of it. Sonya supposed that made sense as she wasn't *really* there.

"You have questions?" Ginny said, her emerald green eyes dancing with inner light.

"So many. I don't know where to start."

"Have a cup of coffee and sit down. Let yourself settle." Ginny nodded to the back door where the storm glass was covered by a thick shade. "We got the first snow of the season last night. Take a look. It's beautiful."

"It snowed?" Sonya turned around at the sink and lifted a corner of the kitchen window shade. She could see the Brochs' shed from there and its roof was crowned in gleaming white. The trees surrounding the property sparkled with fresh powder. "How lovely. My niece will be thrilled."

"She's coming soon, right?" Ginny said. "Day after Thanksgiving?"

Sonya blinked at the apparition. "That's right. How did you …?"

Without answering the question, the elegant ghost held the back door shade aside to look out. "I love the winter here. The forest goes so silent and still as it rests."

The coffee maker chuffed on the counter, sending fragrant steam into the air. Looking down at the fire burning in the stove, Sonya said, "Ginny, how are you able to light these fires?"

"Because I have a strong sense memory of doing so," she said. "Through that I can manifest the making of fires in these stoves in the same way I can manifest this image of my physical body." Ginny smiled. "They say that in heaven we revert to our most beautiful selves. This representation of me is a combination of how I looked in my thirties and how I looked before I died—which wasn't half bad for an old lady." She cocked her head playfully. "Does that make sense?"

"Yes," Sonya said. "It's amazing."

"Ah, yes. All of life is amazing; the front and back of it, the in and out of it, the many ways it can be experienced."

Hesitantly, Sonya said, "Did you really choose to go when you did so you could be of more help to your grandkids?"

"It had to be done." Ginny's expression clouded slightly as she turned to face Sonya again. "My son, Jackson, Jr., loves his children deeply, but he has so much fear about their spiritual lives. He doesn't understand how important their task is."

"Jewel explained some things to me," Sonya said. "That every sixth generation of your family line has a vessel and an outcaster born into it."

"That's correct."

"And your son knows this, doesn't he?"

"Of course. I wrote everything down along with a detailed family tree and gave it to him the day he married Michelle Gibson. I considered it a gift, but he was none too pleased to receive it. All of that material is here, in fact, upstairs in the loft. Jackson wouldn't keep it in his home, but he knew his children would want it one day. If you're interested, you should take a look. It's in a yellow hat box in the loft closet."

"I'm *very* interested, thank you," Sonya said. "Your family fascinates me beyond words."

Ginny waved her manicured hand in the air, the soft pink polish glinting in the kitchen light. "We're just people, like anyone else. We simply got a different assignment from the fates."

Sonya was listening, but her eyes kept moving over the visage of Ginny and marveling at the incredible detail.

With the quirk of an eyebrow, Ginny said, "Are you wondering if you're dreaming?"

"Actually, *no*," Sonya smiled brightly. "That hadn't occurred to me. I think I was even expecting you."

"I'm glad. Get your coffee and let's sit a moment. We don't have much time."

Sonya poured herself a cup of the fresh brew, pleased that her hands had finally stopped shaking. She joined Ginny at the island where they sat across from each other. Ginny folded her fingers together, but primly kept her elbows off the table. The massive diamond of her wedding ring glowed like a tiny star on her hand. Ginny saw that it caught Sonya's eye and she held her left hand out to better show it.

With a wry smile, she said, "My husband used to tell people he won this ring in a card game and that the wife came with it."

Sonya laughed and then instinctively reached to take Ginny's hand, but she stopped in mid-air. "I suppose I can't touch you, can I?"

"Probably not. You may feel a sensation like static electricity if you put your hand near mine, but not solid mass. You're welcome to try. Evan tries every time, even though the result is always the same." Ginny laughed softly. "His head is harder than Kellan's."

Very carefully, Sonya reached her hand toward Ginny's and tried to connect their fingers. Even though she could see Ginny's hand clearly, her own went right through it as though it were air. There was a brief sensation like someone squirted her with a spray bottle—just the faintest touch of sprinkles.

"Amazing," she said and then laughed at herself. "I keep saying that; I really need to brush up on my vocabulary."

Ginny smiled and left her hand flat on the table so Sonya could see her ring clearly. "Evan's made a beautiful ring for my Kathryn using this diamond and band. He said he showed it to you."

"He did. It's stunning and so perfect for her." Wondering when Evan had last spoken to Ginny, Sonya inspected the simple platinum band and the six-prong setting around the gleaming solitaire. The pristine minimalism of the ring in its original form seemed ideal for its graceful wearer. "Beautiful."

"Thank you. I always loved it." Ginny smiled as she turned her hand under the light to flash the diamond. "I hope that proposal happens soon. Evan's taking forever."

Sonya suddenly wondered if the others in the cabin could hear them. She was about to ask when Ginny leaned forward.

"They're all still asleep, but if they were awake they'd be able to hear you, but not me. Right now, in order for you to see me like this, I'm tuned in to your personal frequency. That means they cannot hear or see me at the same time because their frequencies are different."

"I see. Is that true for all ghosts?"

"I believe so," Ginny said thoughtfully. "I don't actually encounter many others, to be honest."

Sonya found that surprising. "No? What about your husband?"

"Oh, he's here. Sometimes. Mostly he just stops by the cabin to make sure it's all right—hasn't been broken into by a bear or flattened by another avalanche. We're not often here at the same time, though."

Taking a much-needed sip of her coffee, Sonya never took her eyes off her surreal companion. "People always assume we reconnect with our lost loved ones when we die."

Ginny's finely lined brow lifted. "Which is most assuredly true for others. Jackson, Sr. and I are still very connected and in love, but his idea of the perfect afterlife didn't include a constant tether to our living grandchildren. He can be found fishing at the high elevation lakes nearby. Gem and Agnew are his favorites. We see each other in a version of the evenings we shared here at the cabin when we used to read before the fire or try to best one another at Scrabble." She smiled. "I look forward to those times, but my experience of time is quite different from yours. I don't have a sense of day and night, only then and now."

Sonya was listening so intently she forgot to breathe. "I have no idea why, but that makes perfect sense to me."

Ginny's emerald eyes sparkled with a smile. "I knew it would, dear. That's why the light chose you. And please know that your husband is well and happy and he's waiting for you."

Sonya swallowed. "You've ... seen Rob?"

"We crossed each other recently when he saw me skulking around your perimeter." Ginny laughed lightly. "He thought I had shenanigans in mind, so I had to explain what I was doing to put him at ease. Once he understood, he was very supportive."

Unable to respond right away, Sonya struggled not to cry. Ginny saw this and her lovely eyes softened.

"Dear, I'm sorry to upset you. I know how you miss him, but please know he's just fine. And that he watches over you all the time. He's so happy you've fallen in love again."

The tears were there before she could stop them. Sonya covered her mouth but it took a few tiny sobs before she could pull herself back together. She reached for a napkin from the holder on the island and dabbed at her eyes.

Ginny watched her the whole time with an expression of remorseful concern. "Forgive me, Sonya. I'm a bit removed from the trappings of emotions now and I forget how intense and close to the surface they are."

She shook her head, blowing her nose delicately. "Not at all, it's fine. I haven't cried over Rob in a few months, so this was probably backlogged."

A creak overhead made Ginny look up. "That's Evan. He's not awake yet, just shifting. His arm is falling asleep under Kellan's head."

Sonya composed herself and drank some more coffee. She knew they didn't have much time and didn't want to waste her opportunity with Ginny. "You said the light chose me? You told Evan that, too."

"Because it's true. I saw the colors on Evan as a little boy, even before I died, and I knew he was the designated third. I'm very grateful to him, actually. He never flinched about his duty; just accepted it and did it as best he could. I genuinely trust him with their lives." Ginny leaned close again. "You can, too. Evan is very strong. After his misstep last year, he'll never abandon them again. He needed to go through that to know."

"To know what?"

"That he cannot live without them, nor they without him. The light connected them forever. He was struggling with that on several levels, which is why he panicked in that terrifying moment. But he's overcome it. His commitment is complete."

A log settled in the kitchen stove and Ginny stood up to add another. Sonya watched her there, picking up a new log from the wood pile, opening the fire box with no potholder, and shoving the log in to catch. She closed the fire box and wiped her hands on her apron, then rejoined Sonya at the island. Ginny smiled.

"Feeling better?"

"Yes, I'm fine. May I ask how you knew the light had chosen me? And what, exactly, it's chosen me to do?"

"I'm afraid I can only answer the first part," Ginny said. "I knew because you had the right colors; they represented what the children were missing in the tribe since Gigi left. You're a patient teacher with a genuine desire to heal. My grandchildren are often uncertain and insecure. They need to be reassured of their gifts and strengths. Gigi was good at that; they trusted her and believed in her. Still do, of course. But her time within their circle has ended and she's on to the next path of her life." Looking down at the ring on her finger, Ginny's eyes went misty. "I had thought she and Kellan would marry at one time, but I was just being foolish and old-fashioned. They were just children when they were in love. They were in no way prepared for what came to them."

Sonya blinked, confused. "What came to them? What do you mean?"

Ginny met her eyes directly. "I invite you to take a look at what's in the yellow hat box upstairs, dear. Many of your questions will be answered by those materials. You'll have a little time after I go this morning—before the children wake up. Enough time, I'd think. But I need to tell you a few other things right now."

Curling her fingers around her cup, Sonya braced herself. "About this succubus?"

Ginny appeared to sigh. "That horrible thing. I'm so sorry it's fixated on you. It's my fault because it saw me around you long before my grandchildren came up this fall. I'd been keeping an eye on you, making sure the local entities didn't bother you while you were getting settled. I knew that thing had broken the bonds

Kathryn put on it and was afoot again. Once you experience an energy like that, you never forget. I probably drew it to you unknowingly just by my proximity. But now that you're involved with the children directly, well … you have a good understanding of what that means."

"Unfortunately, yes. Is there anything I can do to make it go away? Or keep it away from all of us?"

"Not by yourself, dear." Ginny gave her a maternal smile. "This is a job for the tribe as a unit. It will be your first experience working with them. You'll learn a great deal." Her expression went grave and she glanced over her left shoulder toward the bathroom hall, as though someone might be there listening. "But be ever so careful, Sonya. This spirit is clever and wicked. It wants to harm me and my granddaughter and the best way to do that, is to harm Kellan." Those emerald eyes fixed her. "You have been added to those he cares most about. That puts you in the same danger as the others, but with less experience to defend yourself. Do *everything* they say without fail."

Sonya's entire body was tense. She breathed deeply, trying to relax, but to no avail. "Could this thing kill one of us? Is it that strong?"

Ginny only sighed.

"I see." Sonya frowned grimly into her coffee. "Not just danger, but mortal danger."

Smiling with reassurance, Ginny said, "You only have a few days before the full moon and then they'll dispatch this thing for good. After that, things should go back to normal—or, at least back to the way they were before. Nothing in Mount Iolite is ever 'normal,' per se."

Another creak overhead drew their attention, but then Sonya met the apparition's eyes again. "Do you know why I've been drawn to them, Ginny? In what way I'm meant to help?"

Glancing quickly into the bathroom hallway again, Ginny lowered her voice as though she were saying something she shouldn't. "You are here to love them, my dear. And to be loved *by* them. That entails many things, big and small. It's not just one task or one function. Much will be asked of you during your time with their tribe." She smiled gently. "But I have every faith in your strength, Sonya. You will learn and you will thrive."

Sonya also lowered her voice to a whisper, though she wasn't sure why. "Do you see the future?"

Smartly, Ginny shook her head. "I only see then and now, child; then and now. You'll find in the coming months that true soothsayers are few and far between. Humans are not meant to know their individual destiny. We are only meant to grow in the process of finding it."

She gave Sonya one more bright smile before she stood and headed for that darkened hallway that seemed to beckon her. "The yellow hat box, dear. You haven't much time. We'll meet again soon." She took a step into the hall, then glanced back over her shoulder. "By the way, the flowers were from me—the ones on the night table upstairs now, and those on your front porch the day before my grandchildren arrived. I wanted you to know you were welcome, Sonya. I, for one, am very happy you're finally here."

Fresh tears blurred her vision of Ginny disappearing into that darkness, but Sonya whispered 'thank you' into the then empty room nonetheless. Bewildered and exhilarated by what she'd experienced, she took a moment to compose herself and dry her eyes. Then she refreshed her coffee and went quietly upstairs to the Brochs' loft.

CHAPTER SEVENTEEN

THE YELLOW HAT box caught her eye immediately. It seemed to have a slight glow to it as she approached the shelves and cupboards in the loft space between the master and the other bedrooms. Sonya heard Kellan's now familiar snoring and Evan's alongside it. Kathryn's door was still closed. Reaching up between a wicker basket and a turquoise blue hat box, she slid the yellow one down and took it into the master with her. She closed the door quietly.

Sonya opened the blinds over the bed to let in the daylight, pausing to admire the crystalline blanket of fresh snow weighing down the branches of the old growth pine beside the cabin. Down on the front porch, the rocking chairs were sprinkled with a mix of snow, fallen aspen leaves and pine needles that had been tossed by the wind. Clouds still filled the sky over Bonny Lake, only letting the sunlight through as a shadowless, flat gray.

She sat on the bed and took a few sips of hot coffee before drawing the covers around her for warmth. Sonya carefully slid the lid off the yellow box. Inside were three envelopes: a simple 8x10 manila, a white letter size with the name 'Jackson' written across it in lilting cursive, and a heavy brown expandable envelope. That one was sealed by a string wound around a brass bracket pressed into the stiff paper.

Starting with the white one, Sonya eased a four-page handwritten letter out of it. She sat back in the pillows and held the pages up to the window light.

My Dear Son,

On this day of your marriage, my gift to you is the history of our family. I've told you pieces of these tales throughout your life, but never comprehensively. Today, I share the whole story with you in hopes it will inform your decisions about your future children.

Ginny described at length everything that was known about the Concanon bloodline and when the first vessel and outcaster pair was born into it in 1477. Every sixth generation saw a new pair. She told of the tasks they faced, their notable triumphs and failures, and of how each previous pair met their respective end. Most of the pairs perished together in the act of transitioning a non-human spirit. While a few pairs died at different times, none outlived their counterpart by more than a year throughout the five hundred and forty years of written accounts.

Sonya had been given this information by Jewel, Evan, and Kathryn herself, but something about seeing it written in Virginia's hand gave it fierce gravity. This was the truth. She drew her knees up toward her chest under the stack of handmade quilts and continued to read.

You, my dear Jackson, are the fifth generation of the current Concanon line. This means your children will contain the next vessel and outcaster pair. You've made an excellent choice in Michelle Gibson; she will make a strong partner for you and be a loving, devoted mother. Please share this information with her so that she may also be prepared. I will leave this to you, but if you have not told her by the time your children begin to show their colors, I will be forced to do so myself. The mother of a vessel and outcaster must be well-informed of their needs.

You have always been resistant to the presence of spirituality in my life, but you also know in your heart of hearts that the things I believe are real. We exist in tandem with many other dimensions and countless other beings that cross in and out of our lives constantly. Whether or not one chooses to believe these others exist does nothing to change the fact of their existence. There will come a time when you simply must accept this. For the sake of your children, who are unborn magical beings themselves, please find a way to be open.

I enclose a detailed Concanon family tree. Please keep this for my grandchildren as they will need this information.

My wish for you is for a joyful, blessed life with the beautiful bride you take today. You are my only child and most precious to me.

Your loving mother,
Virginia

Wiping tears off her cheeks, Sonya reached into the box for the manila envelope. The large stack of vellum pages inside contained a meticulously itemized, hand-drawn family tree tracing the Concanon lineage over eighteen generations. A small Roman numeral noted each generation making it easy to track the patterns of six.

At the bottom of the tree was the branch where Virginia Concanon married Jackson Broch in 1937. One branch from them lead to Jackson, Jr., and then to his marriage to Michelle Gibson. Below were two branch lines for their offspring, Kathryn Victoria in 1982 and Kellan Vincent in 1984, and below that was the last line of the tree. This had been written in a different hand and led directly from Kellan.

No marriage was indicated, but the name Gigi Elena Perez was enclosed in parentheses. Beneath was the name Melody and a date of birth of November 2, 2001. Beside that was the notation of the numeral I.

Sonya stared at the page as pieces fell together. When she'd first asked Kathryn if she and Kellan wanted children, she'd noticed a brief but undeniable stiffening in Kath's demeanor. As they were brand new to each other at the time, Sonya hadn't pressed for more information. Glenn Corsero's mention of Gigi craving his wife's hot peppers during her pregnancy made sense now. He wasn't referring to Gigi's current pregnancy, where she was carrying twins, but rather to her *former* pregnancy when she was a teenager. Gigi had her first child with Kellan.

"Right," Sonya said to herself, reaching for her nearly cold coffee. She drank it anyway, taking deep breaths to steady her heart. Kellan had a child somewhere—but where? Would he or Kathryn tell her if she asked? *Should* she ask? These questions tumbled in her mind as she put the family tree and the handwritten letter carefully back in their envelopes. She reached for the brown accordion envelope and unwound the string closure.

The thick folded document inside was Ginny's last will and testament. Sonya hesitated before removing it, not feeling right. She had already seen what she'd been invited to see in that hat box. Burning curiosity aside, this document was private and not hers to read. She put it back in its envelope and resealed the string, then tucked everything back into the box. For a moment, she just sat there looking at it.

A creak of floor boards and a light tap on the door preceded Kellan popping his bed-messy head in. Upon seeing him, every jumbled, anxious emotion that had been churning inside her was pushed aside in favor of a rush of passionate affection. Just out of bed and rumpled from a good long sleep was one of Sonya's favorite presentations of Kellan Broch. He gave her a sweet, sexy smile and came into the room, closing the door quietly behind him.

"Hi," she said as she held the covers back for him to climb under with her.

He snuggled close and gave her a soft kiss. "Hi." His skin smelled of sleep, warm buttered croissants, and Evan. Sonya was surprised she'd made note of Evan's scent, but she had. The clean, woodsy, dry-desert aroma lingered on both Brochs constantly.

Kellan's whiskers needed a trim but tickled deliciously against her neck as he put a kiss there. "Sorry I crashed out last night. Bourbon does that to me."

"Now I know it does that to me, too," she said. "I peeked in on you a while ago; you boys looked so peaceful."

He grinned, scrubbing his hand through his spiking hair. "We get *good* sleep together. Did you sleep okay? You look a little pale."

She breathed a laugh. "I've had quite a morning. I finally met your grandmother."

Amber eyes widening, Kellan lifted up on his elbow. "Really? How is she? Did you get to talk to her?"

"She's seems very well, I suppose. And yes, we had a wonderful, long talk. A very … informative talk." Sonya nodded to the yellow hat box on the bed. "She invited me to take a look at some of the things in there. I certainly wouldn't have gone poking around without permission."

His gaze lingered on the box a moment and then his brow knit very slightly. "The family tree and that letter Grammy wrote to Dad the day he married our mom?"

"Yes, and your grandmother's will, also—but she didn't say I could look at that, so I didn't. Just the other stuff. That was quite a letter to get on one's wedding day."

He smirked. "Right? 'Dear Son, your kids will be freaks who die young. Happy Wedding. Love Mom.'"

Sonya laughed but shook her head. "She really needed him to know. I understand why."

Kellan's attention remained on the box a moment longer, then he took a deep breath. "You saw the tree, then?"

"All eighteen generations of it. It's truly astonishing."

He met her eyes. "If you saw it, then you know there are actually nineteen."

She touched his chest gently through the soft cotton of the t-shirt he'd slept in. "Yes. I'm sorry if you didn't want me to know that, but it seemed your grandmother did."

"I don't mind you knowing. I would've told you eventually since we're getting so close. That's not the kind of secret lovers should have."

Sonya's heart raced, not knowing what he meant by that. "I suppose not."

"Does it bother you?" His dark eyes gleamed with concern.

"Sweetie, why would it? It was ages before I met you. And you were just a kid. How old were you guys exactly?"

"I was sixteen and Gigi seventeen." He glanced out the window over the headboard. "The little girl will be seventeen next month."

"Melody," Sonya whispered.

Kellan's small smile was melancholy. "Yeah. Even though we decided to give her up for adoption, Gigi insisted that she have a name. She didn't want us going through our whole lives referring to her as 'the baby'. We figured the people who chose her would change it, but she'll always be Melody to us."

Sonya felt his tension and sadness and drew him close. With his head on her chest, she caressed his hair, silky and fragrant from sleep. "I'm sorry you had to lose her."

"Me, too." His voice was quiet and tight with emotion. "But there was no way we could have raised her or even provided for her. We did the only thing we could to make sure she had a good life. We talk about her all the time, though; wonder what she's doing, where she lives. What kind of music she likes." When he looked at her, his amber eyes were wet. "That psychic we saw—Darien—she said it was inevitable that Melody would come back to us one day. She will, too; I made sure of it."

"How?"

"When those ancestry tests came out and people could buy them pretty cheap, I did a few of them so my DNA would be available on different databases. If Melody goes searching and does one of those tests, boom: she'll find Dad."

"That was smart."

"Well," he said. "We didn't want to let her go. We had no choice."

"I know." Sonya kissed his forehead gently. "That must be quite a bond between you and Gigi."

He smiled. "Not only tribe, but family."

"And Melody is the first generation of the new cycle."

"Yep," he said, and then with a sarcastic grin, "Only five more until the next lucky couple gets to enjoy these *amazing* cosmic benefits."

Sonya shook her head. "It is amazing. But I can only imagine how difficult it is to have that hovering over you all the time. Never knowing when the next lost spirit will call out and need you. Not to mention all the unsavory visitors. In her letter, Ginny said the vast majority of the previous pairs had died while transitioning a non-human spirit. That's terrifying."

Kellan didn't seem affected by this statement. It wasn't news, after all. He laid his head on the pillows beside her. "Did Grandma tell you anything about the succubus? Any advice?"

Frowning, she said, "Mostly she reiterated what you all have already told me: it's old and clever, it's smarter and stronger than the arsenal we currently have and I, especially, need to be extremely careful. But she seemed completely confident the spirit would be dispatched by the ritual. That was comforting, if in a dark way."

He nodded. "I'm very happy she said that. My outcaster doesn't like to use untested methods when my life is on the line, but she has no choice here. She'll think it to death but it's still gonna be a crap shoot."

"Are you afraid?" she said softly.

Kellan glanced at the closed bedroom door, then whispered to her. "Kath couldn't stand knowing that I was, so I'll never admit to it. She'd lose her shit and that's helpful to *no one*. But between us, pretty lady—I'm afraid. This one's a Big Bad."

Sonya cupped his handsome face in her hands. "I have absolute faith in your sister and your team. Your grandmother does, too. They *will* take care of it—and you."

He gave her a slow, soft smile then kissed the inside of her wrist. "I believe you."

She thought of all the things Ginny had shared with her; primarily the purpose Sonya was meant to serve. "Your grandmother told me the light chose me, like it did Evan; and that I was meant to love you two and be loved by you. But beyond that, she didn't give me much information about what I can do to help you both." She sighed. "I wish she had."

Kellan's smile appeared to light his eyes from the inside at first, and then Sonya realized that light was slowly radiating from everywhere around him. Muted, like candlelight at first, it grew in a shimmering field along the surface of his skin. It pulsated rhythmically, and she understood it was following his heartbeat. The light was part of him but encompassed him as well—an organic fire burning without heat. His eyes glowed gold and orange, then suddenly emerald green just like Virginia's—and just as the eyes of his spirit wolf had done when it visited Sonya in her studio.

She sat up in the bed, gaping in awe and gently traced his skin with her fingertips. The shimmering light reached about six inches from him and reacted to her touch, parting like vapor when her fingers moved through it. It had no heat of its own but seemed fueled by the thriving life of his strong, young body.

"I can see it shining in your eyes," he said. "Grandma's letting you see my light."

Sonya was speechless. All she could do was stare and run her fingers through the glistening, radiant glow. Of all the incredible things she'd witness during her brief association with the Brochs, this was by far the most astounding. Ginny was finally allowing her to see The Golden.

"It's … beautiful," she stammered. "I had no idea. My god, no wonder everything flocks to you."

"But you came without seeing it," he whispered. "You saw me."

Sonya supposed that was true. She *had* seen him in his photographs and on their music videos; she'd seen and been drawn in by Kellan Broch the man, not the mysterious spirit warrior. She felt the tears on her cheeks, but she was smiling so hard, it hurt a little. She reached for his hand and held it tight.

Holding her gaze with his sparkling, golden eyes, Kellan repeated the promise he'd made through his wolf that day in her studio. "No harm."

She touched her forehead to his and closed her eyes, weeping. She returned that promise and then sealed it with a kiss.

CHAPTER EIGHTEEN

ON THE MORNING of Samhain, Kathryn went to the wardrobe in her room for the burgundy velvet ceremonial robe Mae's wife, Lily, had made for her in Edinburgh. Lily worked as a costume designer for a local theater company and had altered many of Grandma Ginny's elegant opera dresses for Kath to wear on stage. She called them the "Gold Dust Woman Gowns."

Lily had made this garment as a birthday gift for Kath out of vintage fabric she'd found in Glastonbury. It had flowing long sleeves and a draping hood, and connected down the front with intricate, slightly tarnished silver buttons. Kath loved this robe. It hugged her body so perfectly, she felt she wasn't wearing clothing at all.

She tiptoed past Kellan's room to the loft where she took down a turquoise blue hat box that had belonged to Ginny. She glanced at the yellow one beside it and smiled thinking of Sonya's joy at finally seeing Kellan's light. Kath knew that meant she'd not only been accepted by Ginny, but that Sonya had also made the choice to come into their fold. It was a done deal; Sonya Pritchard had become their sixth.

She'd taken the news about Melody well. Kathryn was glad she finally knew about it; dancing around the subject had been exhausting. Sonya had been sympathetic and understanding and that put Kellan at ease. Kath had never seen her brother happier than he'd been since he and Sonya bonded. She never expected him to fall in love because he never stayed with a partner long enough. Kath thought it was fitting that he'd found love in their sacred place on the mountain. It felt right.

Inside the blue hat box were several velvet bags containing various ritual elements to be added to an altar for special ceremonies. Samhain was the highest holiday for witches; the day when the veil between the living world and the others was the thinnest, and communion with spirit was easiest. Kellan honored her traditions with deep respect and participated however she asked him to, but he was not a witch himself. The intentional practice of these ancient pagan rites belonged solely to Kathryn.

Carefully removing the amber colored velvet bag, she placed the box back on the shelf. Kathryn kept a small altar on the east-facing windowsill down in the cabin's living room. To an unknowing observer, the items there would appear to just be unusual knickknacks, but each represented something specific and powerful. Kathryn peeked in on her brother sleeping soundly in his bed before she crept down the stairs. She wouldn't need his help for her ritual that day.

The lighting of the stove fires on Samhain morning was ceremonial. She added drops of sage and rose oil to the paper she crumpled under the kindling and spoke soft prayers to the spirits of the mountains and the white light to infuse the fire with power. When the flames had caught and were growing, she scraped a bit of its ash into her hands and rubbed them together. She went to the altar.

A steady icy rain had fallen the last two days, washing away what was left of the first snow. Kathryn looked forward to its return. The snow reminded her of sitting in the kitchen with Grandma Ginny with a good fire going in the stove, watching the weather churn outside the window over the sink. During one of those cold days when the children couldn't play outside, Ginny had first taught Kathryn to read the Tarot.

She hadn't intended to teach her granddaughter to see fortunes, but to understand the meaning of each card and how they might aid in the transitioning of human souls. Each outcaster received a different tool of divination when they were very young, and most were given enough time in childhood to master the tool before being called to use their gifts. Kathryn had gravitated toward the Tarot since before she could walk, plucking them out of the spreads Ginny would do for friends and holding them up to her little face to see inside them. Ginny gave Kath her first deck when she was nine; a mere year before Ginny died. She'd used that deck and none other ever since.

That morning, she placed two cards on the altar to infuse them with the strength of her magic: The Magician and The Three of Swords. She added the items in the velvet bag: a pearl-handled athame she'd found in Prague, an obsidian arrowhead Kellan found in the nearby mountains, and a lead toy soldier Henry bought for her at an antique store in Bishop.

The shop owner told him it was the last remaining piece of a set that was over 170 years old. The soldier's uniform had long since faded in color, but the small bayonet it carried was still sharp as a tack. These pieces were her warrior's idols. Kathryn set them on the windowsill beside her small cauldron, her crystals and her glass bottles containing elements of earth, fire, water and air.

She spread her robe around her and knelt before the altar. Pulling the hood up over her head, she used a match to light three small candles: one white, one orange and one black. They flickered bright against the gray weather outside the window. Centering herself with a deep breath, Kathryn began her prayer.

"I am a servant of the light. I bring the light and share the light. I call on the guardians of north, south, east and west to bless my prayers this Samhain morn. This warrior asks for strength in battle and for courage in the direst of moments. I ask for the wisdom of my ancestors. I invite their spirits to come through on this day and celebrate the light along with me. We are one with the light. We make the light." Kathryn lowered her head and closed her eyes, the image of the dancing candle flames still bright behind her eyelids. She heard the fires crackling in the potbelly behind her and in the kitchen stove. Fire and light all around. She was ready.

In the darkness, Kathryn saw the eyes of her crow. It waited, watching and ready, sharing its energy with her. She connected her internal gaze to it and felt the immediate sensation of flight that always accompanied their joining. Kath knew she was still on the ground in the cabin living room, but her soul began to fly. She felt herself lifting out of her body and up through the roof, into the branches of the trees around the house.

When she looked down, she was inside the crow. Its wings were her wings; its huge black fan tail steered at her command. She flew over the cabin roof and up along the bend of Parker Drive, up to the compound where she hovered over Sonya's little house. A rill of pine smoke came from the fireplace chimney—Kath could smell it mingling with the cold wet air. She swooped down and circled the compound twice, sending blessings and light to Sonya.

Onward she flew over the trees to circle the roof of Jewel's little house. She went by the big windows in front twice, looking in to see her friend at the computer typing. Jewel glanced out the window as though she'd heard a noise but then Kathryn was gone, leaving her blessings for Jewel in the wake of her flapping wings.

She floated down the length of Sylvan Road and circled the rooftops of the Rhino and the Boulder Diner next door, where she and her brother would perform later that night. She felt the rain on her massive wings and fluttered her feathers to release its weight. Then she flew down into the village and toward Robbin Lake. The crow landed on top of Evan's roof. In her mind, she spoke this prayer:

> *My love, my partner, I bring you blessings on this day. Your strength sustains me; your love lets me fly. No road is too long between us. We shall never separate. Gray Wolf, I am yours. I love you. Blessed be today and always.*

Wings up, Kathryn flew over the three narrow streets to the roof of Henry Hunter's house. She landed, lowering her head to tap on the shingles with her gleaming beak. Three taps and then he was there. The stately snowy owl, spinning his head almost all the way around to see her. Their wild bird eyes met; the click of contact was audible. No words were needed here. The birds nodded in mutual reverence. They opened their wide wings to each other and flew up, up, then in opposite directions. The crow and the owl circled in the air, then returned to the roof of Henry's house together. Always together. Kathryn sent Henry a burst of blessing, love, and gratitude and then she lifted into the sky again.

Flying all around Bonny Lake, she returned to the roof of their cabin. She felt herself melt into the wood, through the shingles, stopping in Kellan's bedroom. He slept in a tangle of Ginny's quilts, but the gleaming, fierce red wolf with the emerald eyes sat on the edge of his bed, marking the crow. Kathryn opened her wings wide and held them out, drawing them gently inward to make a black feathered wall around her brother's bed.

The red wolf's head swiveled, warily watching all the huge crow's movements. It wasn't sure it should trust this giant beast it wasn't yet familiar with. Kathryn had only moved about in this form a few times before and she'd never visited her brother during. This was the first time the red wolf saw her like this. It had to learn this new presentation.

She held steady with her wings around the bed and the red wolf backed up to stretch out along Kellan's side, protecting from head to toe. In her mind, she spoke to the wolf.

> *We are the same; we protect the vessel. We are the same. Recognize me.*

Big ears twitching, green eyes piercing, the wolf raised its snout and barked once, then sent a howl up toward the sky. The crow raised its head and cawed, following the howl. Kathryn's crow eyes met the eyes of the red wolf. It lowered its massive head onto Kellan's sleeping shoulder and it closed its eyes.

Melting right through the floor, Kathryn's crow dissolved around her as she slipped back inside her body. She opened her eyes. The three small candles on her altar had a burn time of two and a half hours; they were nearly down to nubs. The color of the light outside had changed slightly as the sun moved behind the rain clouds. Kathryn brought her hands together in front of her, her muscles stiff from such a long stillness.

"On this Samhain morn, I add to the light. I am the light. I bring the light. I welcome my wise ancestors to come and bask in the light on this sacred day. Blessed be to all."

She left the three candles to finish burning and moved slowly to stand, stretching her legs to relieve the pins and needles as her circulation came back. Silently, she thanked the crow for the flight.

She'd brought her kit out to the island the night before in anticipation of her ritual. She took out an empty glass bottle with a cork stopper and went to the kitchen stove. Using the iron poker and a folded piece of newspaper, she carefully scraped out enough of the ash to fill the little bottle. She and Henry guessed they would only need a small amount for their banishment of the hag. Kath waited until the ash had cooled before replacing the stopper and tucking the bottle safely back into her kit.

"Blessed be," she said as she closed the little wooden drawer and returned The Magician and the Three of Swords to her deck.

From behind her at the stove, Ginny's voice was clear as day. "Blessed be, my black-winged angel."

Kathryn whirled around, but there was no image of Ginny. Only the palpable weight of her presence. Again, her grandmother's voice came, filling the space of the cabin's kitchen.

"You know you will be tested by this spirit, but you are strong. Your tribe is strong. You will prevail. I am with my grandchildren always. I will be at your side at the full moon. I love you, Kathryn."

The portal Ginny used to come and go would open at her will but remained so for varying amounts of time. When she visited them in full manifestation, she had an idea of how much time was available, but had to keep a careful eye on the opening. Getting trapped on this side would burn out her energy and rob her strength. The only time she didn't need to worry about that was when Kellan held the gateway open for her while she strengthened the protective wall around the cabin. The intense energy of a vessel could hold the opening forever if he chose to.

The laws of nature made it so Ginny was always coming in and going out; she couldn't simply remain there constantly. But she was always watching when her grandchildren were there; ready at a second's notice to come through. There was no sound in the kitchen just then but the snapping of the fires in the stoves. All was well and peaceful as the rain fell outside.

Kathryn spoke into the quiet room. "Thank you for stopping in, Grandma. See you soon."

Exhausted, she went back upstairs and put her robe back in the wardrobe. She crawled into bed and slept until Kellan woke her later for their sound check.

CHAPTER NINETEEN

AT THE BOULDER Diner, Kath and Kellan went over their set list with Brady, Matt and Mark. The owner, Tony Gillman, stalked around the venue barking at his laborers making sure all the preparations were to his liking. The tables were moved out to leave the floor open for the audience and a temporary bar was set up against the wall that sported Tony's many fishing trophies.

Evan had come with them to run a line of rock salt around the venue. The show would take place away from protected ground and he didn't want to take any chances. He'd told Tony that the salt was part of the props the band wanted for their Halloween show. Knowing this annual performance made up a huge chunk of his revenue, Tony extended the requested bit of leeway, but not without harrumphing about the mess.

The diner was next door to the Rhino and at 4:30, the crowd over there was light. While they rehearsed, Kath saw Sandie stroll out onto the Rhino's side terrace to take a smoke break. She grinned when she spotted Evan and leaned on the rail to enjoy watching him at his task.

Kath told the guys she'd be right back as she rested her guitar in a stand. "Looks like Evan needs his honor defended."

Kellan and Brady glanced out the window at the fascinated Sandie and chuckled at the sight. Kath went out to stand in front of the diner, grinning across the way. "Hey, girl!"

Sandie waved. "Sounds good in there. How's it goin'?"

"Thanks! We're just about ready for you all tonight." She walked to the edge of the diner's front patio and leaned out to see down the side of the building.

The sun had come out for a few hours between the rain storms. The late-day gold of it shown in Evan's blond hair. He had a gray plaid scarf wound around his neck for warmth, a tight black sweatshirt on over his form-fitting jeans and boots, and wherever there was a shred of sunlight, those black aviators were donned. He was indeed quite a dish out there bending and strutting as he worked. Kath was happy to join Sandie in her ogling.

Evan had a bag of road salt under his arm and a hoe from Jewel's gardening tool shed. He ran a line of the thick pellets down the side of the building and then pressed it close to the foundation with the hoe. This bag of salt had a pink tint to it that made it glitter in the low sun. Tony, a portly man in his late fifties with an odd affection for yellow Polo shirts, came out on the deck and glowered in the direction of the ladies' attention.

"That shit's bad for the paint," he grumbled. "You're gonna clean that up after the show, right MacTavish? Tonight?"

Evan straightened up, chin raised with a cocky smile. "Tonight might be hard since it's supposed to shit rain, but I'll do it as soon as it clears up. Scout's honor."

Tony muttered and shot a prickly glare at Kath before going back inside.

From across the way, Sandie said, "Not that I'm complaining about the view, darlin', but what *is* your man doing out here with all this bending and scraping?"

Evan waggled his brow at the compliment, but kept working.

Intending to keep the truth on the down low, Kath said, "The fans help us out with publicity by posting photos from the gigs on social media. We're doing the fun spooky thing for this show. We've got cobwebs and skeletons and dry ice to put around the stage. The salt outside is just another prop."

"So, you're not really warding off evil?" Sandie asked. "Because with you guys, it's good to check."

Kath nodded in agreement. "No, we're good. Just campin' it up for the audience."

Sandie grinned at Evan as he bent over again with the hoe. "MacTavish, stop it with that hot ass. You're hurtin' an old lady."

Evan laughed, leaning the hoe and bag of salt against the building. He took his cigarettes from his pocket and tapped one out, lighting it with his gleaming silver Zippo. Leaning on the railing below where Kathryn stood, he poked a thumb in Sandie's direction. "You wanna do somethin' about that? Woman's making me feel like meat."

Kath laughed hard. "You're the one who put all that hot on this morning, buddy. Don't whine." She leaned down, tapping her fingertip to her lips. "Sugar."

Evan kissed her, soft and sultry. "Get back in there and sing, would ya?" He winked and went back to his work.

Kath waved to Sandie as she started for the venue door. "We'll see you here in a few hours, yeah?"

"The whole Rhino crew is doing split shifts tonight so we can all catch part of it. Wouldn't miss your little bro's piano dance for a million bucks." Sandie winked and went back inside.

Back on the stage, Kellan and Brady were grinning through an acoustic rendition of AC/DCs *Whole Lotta Rosie*. They loved playing this when they were plugged in, but the song lost most of its guts without the amps. Kath chuckled as she sat back down with them.

"We're not playing that one tonight, boys. Let's focus." She picked up her copy of the set list to see what was up next. "Let's do *Hell's Bells*. I need to tune the cello."

The guys switched instruments; Kellan went to the piano and Brady picked up his twelve-string. As Kath went to the cello in the corner of the stage, she glanced out the window again. Evan's head bobbed up and down as he worked on the side of the building, but her eye was drawn across the way.

There were stairs at the end of the Rhino's side deck that led down to the parking lot behind the bar. Someone stood on the last stair; a bent old woman in filthy black rags. Her soulless murky eyes drilled into Kathryn through the window glass. The hag raised a bony hand and pointed at Evan, who was clearly unaware of her presence. That black-toothed mouth formed two words that Kath could clearly make out.

Cannon fodder.

The hag's wretched body shook with a cackle Kathryn couldn't hear but felt in her bones. And then it vanished into the last of the daylight.

"Kath?" Kellan said from the piano. "We playin'?"

She seethed at the two days she had to wait for the full moon. Every ounce of her being wanted to do the ritual that night right after the show, but she heard Ginny's voice in her head telling her not to be impatient. They needed the moon. She *must* wait for it. Kathryn hated few things more than being helpless, but for the next 48 hours she was.

"Yo, sissy."

Deciding not to waste any more precious energy on that monster until she had to, Kath took a deep, steadying breath. She brought the cello to the center of the stage where she'd placed a chair and sat down with the instrument positioned between her knees. She redirected her focus to how much she loved to play the cello, and to the sheet music of their creative arrangement of this song in front of her.

Fingers trembling with angry adrenalin, Kathryn positioned her bow. "Ready when you are."

✖

She told her brother and Evan what she'd seen as they sat down to the gorgeous meal Evan prepared for their Samhain night feast. It was their custom to use no electric light on Samhain night so candles glowed all through the cabin, dancing warmly on the island as they ate.

"Cannon fodder, eh?" Evan muttered as he took a bite of perfectly broiled steak. "Whatever."

Kellan topped off their glasses from the bottle of Merlot they were sharing. "Sabre rattling, right? Fuck her. Just forget about it."

Kath sat beside him in her black satin slip with her hair wound up in large rollers. She'd be going full out with the witch garb that night, complete with layers of black velvet and a flowing cape. She'd found a plain black witch hat at K-Mart when they did their errands before coming up the mountain, and planned to tease her hair out big underneath it with plastic spiders and fake cobwebs strategically woven in.

"I'm trying to forget about it, but she pisses me off." Kath stabbed a piece of sautéed asparagus with her fork. "I just want to bounce her and be done. At some point during our stay here, I'd like to be on vacation."

Evan smirked, sipping his wine. His slate-blue eyes danced beautifully in the candlelight, making her belly tingle when he winked at her. "I vote we put it out of all our minds for now. You guys have your biggest local show of the year in two hours; let's be cheerful and festive. Are the sheriffs here yet?"

In his plaid pajama pants and a t-shirt, Kellan leaned back in his stool to see out through the front door glass. "Looks like it; I see several pairs of tail lights across the road."

"Good. I'll bring the food out to them when we're done."

The addition of law enforcement had become necessary after their friend Brodie discovered multiple fan photos of the inside of the cabin taken through the windows while the band was out performing their Halloween show. The overcurious peepers were looking for evidence of the Samhain rituals the Brochs' wrote about on their website, and were thrilled to find all those spooky candles burning when no one was home.

While it had been good for their mysterious image, it freaked them both out that people would come so close to their sanctuary. Kellan found it appallingly disrespectful, but Kath found it dangerous. She'd asked local law enforcement for help and several of the deputies happily volunteered to assist the pretty local celebrity. Evan had been making them thank-you picnic baskets every year loaded down with sandwiches from Corsero's, Tilly Hunter's delicious fruit pies, and gourmet coffee in huge thermal mugs to keep them warm and awake.

"I have something for you for the show tonight," he said to Kath. "A little Samhain gift."

"Really?" she smiled, trying not to get too excited. "That's very sweet of you."

"I already gave Peach his." Evan and Kellan shared a wink across the table.

Kathryn shook her head. "I don't even want to know." She did, but knew it would do no good to ask.

After they'd finished and Evan brought the baskets out to the sheriffs, he returned with a large box he'd retrieved from his Jeep. It was wrapped in shiny silver paper and tied with a huge black satin bow. He handed it to Kath as she put away the last of the dinner dishes.

"My god, what is this?" She laughed as she set the huge box on the island.

"Open it, witchy-poo." He sat on a stool to wait for her, a playful grin lighting his eyes.

Kathryn hated how fast her heart was beating. Proposing to her on Samhain night would be most appropriate, and the romantic in him would surely enjoy hiding an engagement ring inside a massive box. It was lightweight so whatever was inside was either tiny or insubstantial. The ribbon slid off and she set it aside, then lifted off the lid. Black tissue paper was arranged neatly over the contents and she folded it back.

Inside was a witch's hat wrapped entirely in an elegant blue and brick red tartan and trimmed beautifully in layers of the same fabric cut in an artful ruffle. Excited, she held the hat up to the candlelight to better see the pattern.

Evan softly told her, "It's the MacTavish tartan. It was handmade for you in Glasgow."

Kathryn met his eyes in the flickering light. "You're giving me your clan tartan? Is this like hand-fasting, but with a hat?"

He chuckled. "Maybe. Do you like it?"

"I freakin' *love* it," she said, meaning it. She went around the island to hug and kiss him and then she tried vainly to place the hat on her head over the mountain of curlers. "That must mean it's time to take my hair down. Kell, look what I got!"

Rounding the corner into the bathroom, she saw her brother in front of the vanity mirror, shirtless and styling his hair with gel-covered fingers. The low-waisted leather pants he'd slipped into clung possessively to his lean hips, accentuating the faint trail of dark auburn hairs gleaming just beneath his navel. His costume plan for the evening was 'Jim Morrison, the devil', replete with a beaded necklace and impressively tall red vinyl goat horns.

She smirked. "We're gonna need paramedics for all the chicks passing out, dude."

He just winked.

"Look at my hat!"

"I've seen your hat, girl. Who do you think picked it up from the milliner's in Glasgow and shipped it here?"

Picturing the effort and clandestine arrangements that went into this gift made her smile so hard, her eyes watered. Kath quickly took the curlers out of her hair and loosened it with her fingers, then she balanced the tartan hat on top of her head proudly. "Perfect. I'm finally a proper Scots Witch."

Evan came in behind her, tilting the hat forward a bit rakishly. He was dressed as a pirate that night in tight black trousers, high leather boots and a blousy white shirt open to his navel. His feathered tricorn, fake parrot to clip to his shoulder, and his eye patch were waiting on the coffee table. He pressed in close, curling his fingers around her hips. In the candlelight, the blue fabric mirrored the hue of his eyes.

"Better than even I thought it would look," he purred.

"I love it," she said softly. "Thank you, babe."

"You're very welcome." Evan turned her around and kissed her, being careful not to tip the pointed hat too far back. He winked then went out to the living room to get the other pieces of his costume.

Kath adored the hat but would lie to say she wasn't a tiny bit disappointed. Her brother must have seen this in her reflection.

He rested his hand on hers and whispered. "You'll say yes, right? When he asks?"

Kathryn met his eyes in the mirror. "You know something I don't?"

Kellan laughed in the flickering light. "I know shit-tons you don't—and all of it's *awesome*." He leaned in and pressed a kiss to her cheek. "Happy Samhain night, sissy. We're gonna kill it out there."

"You know it." She kissed his forehead then reached for her make-up bag. It was time to put on a show.

CHAPTER TWENTY

SONYA HAD JUST finished sewing the wings she'd fashioned out of construction paper and coat hanger wire onto the dress she'd worn to her nephew's baptism. A little gold glitter paint she found at the general store made them sparkle nicely as she stood in front of the mirror in her guest room, struggling to do up the rear zipper. Henry's pick-up rattled onto the compound outside and she went to the door to greet him.

The rain hadn't yet started again but hard, chilling winds blew the dry leaves around her courtyard as Henry climbed out of the truck. He was head to toe in black—trench coat, jeans, polished cowboy boots and cowboy hat. They were all supposed to go to the Brochs' Halloween show in costume, but she couldn't begin to guess what the young shaman was dressed as.

"And a happy Samhain night to you, Lady Sonya!" he shouted over the wind as he came up the porch stairs. "An angel! How fitting."

"Ah, thank you." She lifted up on her toes to give him a hug; he put his large arms around her wings carefully. "If I can trouble you for your assistance with my zipper, this angel will be ready to fly."

"My pleasure. I shouted up to Jewel when I passed her place and told her we'd be right back for her."

Holding the wings out of the way so he could shimmy the long zipper up her back, Sonya had a flash of the first time she saw Henry Hunter and how utterly wrong her assumptions about him had been. She smiled thinking how much she'd already grown during their short acquaintance.

"Thank you. Does it work?" She turned in a slow circle to show him the flowing dress, and the curling gold and silver ribbons she'd run through her long hair. Her cheeks were dusted with glittery blush and she wore a pair of rhinestone star earrings she'd found in a box of clothes from the 1980s. She'd even tied some ribbons on her white fleece-lined boots that kept her feet warm and comfortable under the dress.

"Supremely angelic." Henry grinned. "But you'll make quite the contrast to your beau this evening. When I dropped them at the venue an hour ago, Kellan was a leather-clad devil."

"Well," she said. "He was halfway there already, wasn't he? And what have we got here with all this black, sir?"

Henry waggled his brow under his hat. "Johnny Cash."

Sonya laughed. "But of course! I love it. Just let me grab my bag and we can go." She made sure she had her keys, a collapsible umbrella and a flashlight, then laid her coat carefully over her shoulders and followed Henry out to his truck. She'd angled the wings to lie flat against her back when she sat down and was pleased that they worked as planned.

He scooped the edge of her dress into the cab before closing the door for her. She watched him walk around the front of the truck, holding his hat to keep it from blowing off in the wind. He suddenly stopped and looked toward the top of her driveway, frowning. Sonya's heart pounded. She'd been trying not to jump at shadows and just go about life normally, but she hadn't been having much luck. She feared what might happen with the hag. It had her horribly on edge.

She stared in the direction that caught his attention but saw nothing. Henry finally came around and got in behind the wheel. She anxiously asked what he'd seen.

"I didn't *see* anything, just thought I heard an animal out there. There was a grunting, growling noise, but it only happened once."

Sonya drew her arms around herself and stared into the darkness. "We do have coyotes, bears and mountain lions around here. I've seen them."

"Yep. And all the local critters are getting ready for winter, stocking up their cupboards. I'm sure it's nothing to worry about. Ready?"

She smiled, if a bit unsteadily. "Ready."

Henry started the engine. His radio came on to the colorful local weatherman telling them to expect a frigid, windy night with heavy rain after 8:00pm. Temps were expected to drop below freezing before dawn, which could bring snow flurries to areas as low as 6,000 feet. The town of Mount Iolite rested comfortably at 7,600 feet, with the elevations at the ski lodge reaching up to 13,000.

"Sounds like we'll be all white in the morning," she said as he piloted the truck down the narrow road toward Jewel's cabin. "I was hoping we'd have a little snow for my first retreat guests."

"That's next week, right? The 8th?"

"It is. My kitchen staff starts on the 6th."

"Exciting stuff. Do you feel prepared?"

"Yes," she said with mock enthusiasm, but then shook her head. "No, not at all."

Henry chuckled. "I'm sure you'll be just fine."

As they drove behind the Brochs' place, Sonya looked down at the house and became instantly alarmed. She knew Kathryn and

Kellan were already at the venue but there were two local sheriff's vehicles parked beside their property—one in the driveway of the uninhabited cabin next door and one across the street in front of their dock.

"Don't worry." Henry explained about the officers volunteering to keep watch after the incident with the nosy, picture-taking fans.

"Oh, wow." Sonya kept an eye on the place as they rounded the bend toward Jewel's. The curtains were all closed, but she could see a telltale flicker in all the rooms. "They left candles burning?"

"It's part of Kath's Samhain night ritual. No electric light from sundown to dawn. They don't want to come home to a dark house, though."

"I'm going to worry about that all night now."

"No need. Ginny's got it," he smiled. "Plus, the sheriffs are right outside."

Henry slowed the truck as he came up to Jewel's stone stairs. He tapped the horn and a moment later she appeared, waving down at them. Sonya almost didn't recognize her wrapped in a full-length brown felt robe with a large hood that flapped in the high wind. A rough braided rope was tied around her ample waist with bits of it crisscrossing her brown snow boots. Jewel brandished a stout clay jug with a cork stopper as Henry came around to open the door for her.

"Hello, dear," she said, climbing into the truck's rear passenger seat. She held up the jug with a merry grin. "Ale?"

Sonya cracked up. "Are we a drunk monk?"

"Close. Friar Tuck. I've worn this costume to the last four of the kids' Halloween shows. I think it's expected of me now."

"Excellent."

"Ale," Henry scoffed. "We all know it's really scotch."

"Oh, love," Jewel said in a purposefully terrible English accent. "I'll not be payin' Tony Gillman a single farthing to drink his watered-down booze."

They laughed and Henry turned up the heater as they started down the road toward town.

Sonya gaped at the lines of cars parked end to end down either side of the road behind the Boulder Diner. "Oh my god! Look at all these people!"

"The resorts and inns are all filled up every Halloween for this show," Jewel said. "The town gets its pockets lined when KKB is in residence."

"I didn't realize this many people would fit in Tony's diner."

Friar Tuck popped the cork out of her jug to take a swig of its contents. "He moves everything out—tables, chairs, pinball machines, everything. His capacity is about 650 then, as long as the fire marshal's feeling charitable."

"Luckily," Henry said. "Those of us with backstage passes have reserved parking." He had to wait for a large group of costumed revelers to pass before turning into the lot behind the Rhino. Two local firemen dressed in parkas and waving flare lights were directing traffic in the lot that usually held about eight cars. That night, they were stacking the cars in the opposite direction and parking them tandem to maximize the space.

One of the firemen recognized Henry and waved him through to an empty space right up against the diner. Two Mono County Police cars were situated on either side of the alley that usually went through from the main street in town to the parking lot. That night the alley was cordoned off and tented, and a large surly man stood at the opening with a clip board.

"Wow," Sonya said as they started out of the truck. "You'd think the president was visiting."

"Nah," Jewel muttered. "He's proven time and again that he couldn't get this much of a crowd."

Henry helped the ladies out of the truck and they all made their way through the icy night air into the tent. They showed the man with the clipboard the VIP tickets and passes Kellan had given them and he issued them wristbands, casting a suspicious glance at Jewel's clay jug.

"You're not supposed to bring in outside liquor," he grumped.

"It's part of my costume, dearie. Just a prop."

"Uh huh." He stood aside and let them all enter the make-shift backstage area.

Heaters were placed in the corners of the tent, string lights dangled from the canvas ceiling, and a card table covered with a white cloth served as the bar and nibbles zone. Sonya was amazed to find at least forty people crammed into the small space, all in gloriously creative costumes. Her instant favorite was the tall man dressed as Father Christmas in his flowing green velvet robe trimmed in ermine. Wizards, black cats, stormtroopers and French maids mingled joyfully with Michael Myers, Count Dracula and several interpretations of the Grinch. It was wonderful.

"How fun!" She clapped her hands and laughed and then someone handed her a frosty glass of vodka and tonic. Kellan stood before her with his lean chest lightly oiled and bare, his long legs wrapped deliciously in black leather, and the cutest set of devil horns she'd ever seen.

"Hello, beautiful angel," he purred, kissing her lips. He tasted of sweet red wine.

Heart pounding at the sight of him, she laughed girlishly. "Well, hello little devil. Have you come to take my soul?"

"Didn't I do that already?" Watching his amber eyes dance in the glow of the string lights, she couldn't stop thinking of him the other morning when Ginny finally let her see his vessel's aura.

He'd been so beautiful in that moment she'd almost fainted, but standing before her then he radiated a different light. This was the glow of his abundant sexual heat; the pulsing rock star emerging from the core of the gentle young man who loved to cuddle. Sonya kissed him, slow and soft, knowing she may not get another chance that night. In a matter of moments, he would be transformed by the footlights into the Rain King of M.T.I.

"I understand there's a dance on a piano bench I simply can't miss," she said in his ear.

Kellan laughed as his sister moved among their friends behind him, greeting everyone and thanking them for coming. Sonya watched Kathryn out of the corner of her eye, noting her beautiful black velvet gown and her most amazing witch's hat. Was it plaid? She couldn't really tell in the low light, but Kath was in front of her the next moment, hugging her tight and speaking excitedly.

"You look beautiful! This is the perfect costume!"

"Thank you," Sonya beamed. "Show me this hat!"

Kath handed Sonya her glass of red wine so she could slip the hat off and hold it up to the light. "Ev gave that to me about two hours ago. He had it made in Glasgow. It's the MacTavish tartan."

Sonya took in the delicate periwinkle and maroon pattern, run through with thin lines of gold and black. "Stunning. And how unbelievably romantic."

"I know!" Kath laughed as she set the hat back in place on her head. "He brought it in this enormous box tied with a satin bow and I thought …" She rolled her eyes and sighed, taking her glass back to sip from it. "You know what I thought."

"Were you disappointed?" Sonya said.

"I was. And I hate that. He may never ask me, you know. I have to prepare for that."

Sonya pressed a kiss into Kath's cheek, then gently wiped her sparkly angel lipstick off. "Don't concern yourself with that, my love. Where is he, by the way? I need to see his costume."

Kathryn pointed across the tent to Evan, engaged in a boisterous conversation with a laughing group of wildly attired guests. His feathered tricorn was tipped over his left eye and the fake parrot clipped to his shoulder bobbed ridiculously as he gestured. Sonya was sorry to see one of his beautiful blue eyes covered by that silly patch, but it was a costumed gathering after all. Evan's muscular chest was barely concealed by his wide-open shirt. Leaning in to Kath, she said, "Don't hate me, but I can't help noticing his golden chest hair."

"Oh, trust me"—Kath rolled her eyes—"he wants *everyone* to notice his chest hair." She laughed and then she and Kellan whispered something to each other. They checked the time, nodding that they should get going. Kath told her, "Tony has a small area next to the stage roped off for our guests. It's not all that comfortable because you're standing up, but hopefully you'll be dancing, anyway. Ev and HH will take you ladies out there."

"Have a great show, Witchy Woman." Sonya blew her a kiss as she slipped away toward the stage door.

Kellan kissed her and whispered, his silky whiskers tickling Sonya's neck. "Will you reform me later, angel?"

Playfully combing his body with her eyes, she said, "Not on your life."

He laughed brightly then was whisked away by one of their guest musicians. As he disappeared through the stage door, Sonya realized her cheeks were sore from smiling. She couldn't remember ever being so happy.

CHAPTER TWENTY-ONE

EARS STILL RINGING from the thundering music and shrieking crowd, Sonya and Jewel huddled under her umbrella and scurried through the pummeling rain to Henry's truck. They'd stayed for a bit of the after party, but when Jewel started yawning they decided to head out. The show had far exceeded the limitations Sonya expected from such a small town and small venue; KKB performed as though they commanded the stage of a concert arena.

Their guest guitarist, Brady King, wore a furry King Kong mask in the spirit of both his name and the occasion, while he lit the crowd on fire with one razor-sharp solo after another. The set was mostly seasonal covers to keep the crowd jumping, ranging from *Monster Mash* to *Werewolves of London* (during which Kellan did indeed howl and dance on the piano bench, wiggling his cute leather-covered butt).

There'd been an obscure old Eagles song the audience seemed to be greatly anticipating called *The Greeks Don't Want No Freaks*. The chorus was something about monsters, but Sonya couldn't quite make it out over the screaming revelers. Everyone danced and sang along, drinking and laughing in their wild costumes. It was obvious why this annual performance was such a popular local event; the kids put on a blistering hell of a show.

Her favorite moments were Kathryn's quiet but eerie renditions of *Rhiannon* and *Doll Parts*, but the best was the creepy arrangement of *Hell's Bells* slowed down and plinked on the piano by Kellan while Kathryn sang and caressed the cello strings with her bow. The arrangement turned the otherwise lively tune into a dirge; it was brilliant.

They brought the mood back up to finish with one of their up-tempo originals Sonya hadn't heard before. It was a little country rock and full of great harmonies; she loved it. But with the first strains of *Rain King*, the entire room erupted with ecstatic energy.

Kellan came to the front of the stage with only the mic while Kathryn and the band played behind him. The crowd sang with him except for the tight pack of young women pressed against the low stage. They all held up their phones to film him and jumped up on their toes to try to kiss him when he'd bend down to serenade. He beamed, glowing with perspiration and glitter, his red vinyl devil horns askance. He was magnificent.

Sighing at the memory of him like a swooning school girl, Sonya drew her coat around her as Henry waited for an opening to exit the crowded parking lot. Heavy wind and rain pelted the truck so hard it rocked from the force. On the dashboard display, the outside temperature read 21 degrees. It could snow any moment.

"Colder than a witch's tit out here!" A drunken Jewel exclaimed from the back seat, then laughed at her own remark. "No pun intended."

Henry chuckled as he finally got a window of opportunity and pulled out of the lot. "That was an epic show. One of their best."

"It was amazing." Sonya couldn't stop smiling as they left the street lights of town behind and turned into the darkness of Sylvan Road. The weather was relentless, even through the heavy tree cover. Leaves, twigs and pine cones flew across the road in splashes of rain before the headlights, all tumbling down to the shoreline of Bonny Lake. They were most definitely in for a cold and stormy night.

Henry borrowed Sonya's umbrella to get Jewel up her stone stairs and into her house. Sonya waited with the heater running full blast and the rain sheeting down the truck. She could barely see her friends through the fogged window, but was able to make out Jewel's figure waving down to her from the sitting room. She was safe inside. Sonya watched through the water bucketing down the passenger window for Henry to come out.

Something landed hard and heavy on the roof of the truck. Sonya was certain she'd heard the distinct sound of four feet hitting the metal. It sounded too heavy to be a coyote, and she'd seen several mountain lions near her property recently, skulking and soundless, camouflaged among the rocks and brush. Their stealth gave her the creeps, but they'd left her alone, at least so far.

The feet on the truck roof thudded as they moved across it, from the center where the beast had landed and then over to the driver's side. There was a growl so low and guttural, it turned her blood to ice. Sonya felt the rumble in her teeth and behind her eyelids. The growl came again followed by weighty footfalls, circling the roof, back and forth between the doors.

Frantic, Sonya turned toward the stairs to warn Henry before he came down, where he'd be blinded by the rain and her umbrella. The sheeting water made it impossible to see anything but a blurry glare from Jewel's porch light. No Henry. Not knowing what else to do, Sonya cracked the window a bit and shouted out the opening.

"Henry! There's an animal on the roof of your truck! Be careful!" The rain and wind screeched around the vehicle, blowing sharp bolts of water in through the open space. Squinting against the spray, Sonya tried to see the stone stairs and find Henry. All she saw was a smear of frozen water. Her cheeks burned from the cold, but she called out again. "Henry! There's an animal! Watch out!"

Claws scraped on the metal roof above the driver's side window, then raked the glass. She didn't see them, but the cringeworthy scrape was deafening. There was a hideous cracking and Sonya screamed, rolling up the window as fast as she could. She was terrified for Henry out there not knowing this thing was on his roof, but her own mortal fear paralyzed her from calling out again.

The driver's door flew open and Henry hurled himself in, slamming the door after him. He accidently poked her leg with the tip of the umbrella and started to apologize, but Sonya threw her arms around him.

"Whoa, there!" Henry held her, his trench coat drenched and his black hat shedding freezing water all over her. "Are you okay, Lady Sonya? I heard you shouting but I couldn't hear what you said over the weather. What happened?"

She was trembling so hard, all she could do was hold onto him for the moment. He let her compose herself, tucking her safe and solid against his large frame.

"It's all right, now," he said as the pounding rain hammered the truck on all sides like gunfire. "Tell me what happened?"

Finally able to speak, Sonya described what she'd heard and how she'd tried to warn him. "Did you see anything out there?" she stammered.

Henry shook his head, his big hands firm and gentle on her shoulders. "I didn't, but it was probably whatever I heard up at your place earlier. It's gone now. Jewel is safe inside; you and I are safe in here. Take it easy." He gave her a small reassuring smile as he put the truck in gear, frigid water still dripping from his hat. "Let's get you up top and out of the storm."

Sonya took a few deep breaths, wanting desperately to believe that had just been an animal and not something worse. The fact that Henry hadn't seen anything made no sense if there really was a huge living creature right on top of his car, but she tried not to focus on that. The Forest Service assured her none of the local animals were known man-eaters. Whatever had been out there was gone; no harm had been done.

The partially paved Parker Drive was muddy and slick, and bumpier than usual from new storm-created pot holes. Henry drove slowly passed the Brochs' cabin and Sonya saw the sheriffs were still there. Kath and Kellan would be out for a few more hours with after show festivities; Sonya was glad their cabin was being looked after, inside and out, during the storm.

At the top of the road, just before her driveway, she saw a light glinting out on the scrubby, steep hillside. It was a concentrated glow moving slowly like a flashlight; the color was a strange yellow-gold.

"Is that a flashlight?" She pointed for Henry. "Someone's walking out there in *this* weather?"

He stopped the truck just before her property line where the motion sensor lights would be triggered, and squinted through the windshield. All around was darkness and pounding rain, but the light out on the hillside continued to move slow and even, back and forth, as though whomever was out there was taking a leisurely stroll.

"Sure looks like it," he said. "But that's not a flashlight; it's a lantern." Henry rolled the truck forward and the compound lights came on, illuminating Sonya's courtyard.

Her heart was still pounding from the incident with the animal, but she kept her eye on that strange light. Henry pulled right up to her front porch and put the engine in neutral. Through the rain-soaked window, she watched the blur of golden light move back and forth, pause, then move again. It started coming toward the compound.

"Let's get you inside," Henry said. He took her umbrella and got out on the driver's side, asking her to slide across the bench seat and come out that way rather than running through the rain on the other side. Sonya was happy to do so, both to keep from getting drenched, and to be further from whatever was coming up the hill. She'd had about enough excitement for one night.

She stood inside the front door and Henry went to the edge of the porch. They both watched the light moving out on the hillside as the rain continued hammering down.

"Hello?" Henry called out. "Do you need some help out there?"

Wind whipped a tumbleweed across the driveway and off into the trees. Sonya watched that light get steadily closer until an image began to take form inside the glow. It was a long, black coat with a wide, bell-like drape that swayed through the illuminated sage and wild rose bushes. When the light was a few feet closer, she saw the outline of a black hood pulled up over the head of a tall, delicate-boned woman. The light she held was an old-fashioned iron oil lantern swinging on a wire handle. Emerald green eyes flashed bright through the pouring rain; Sonya saw the woman smile.

"Henry," she breathed. "It's Ginny!"

"It is?" He looked back at Sonya, confused, then back at the light. "I see the lantern, but I don't see Virginia."

"She's right there, just off the driveway. She's in a black coat like Mary Poppins with a hood over it. That lantern is—"

"An old kerosene one," he said. "That I can see. I cannot see the person holding it." He shook his head. "Then again, she's not here for me to see; she's here for you. She wants you to know she's keeping watch."

As Sonya stared, Ginny nodded once to confirm Henry's statement, and then she turned and started back across the hillside with her lantern lighting her way.

"The lantern is for you, too," Henry said. "She certainly wouldn't need it to see. She wants you to know where she is in case you need her. She knows you just had a bad fright."

Watching the lantern swing slow and steady out in the brush, Sonya felt the tense muscles in her shoulders relaxing. All at once, she realized how tired she was from the evening's rollercoaster of events.

Henry came to her in the doorway and placed his large hands on her shoulders. "You'll be all right, Lady Sonya. The Gatherer is on perimeter patrol." He smiled, tipped his hat out of the way and put a kiss on Sonya's forehead.

"So she is. Thank you for everything, Henry. Get yourself home." She lifted up and gave him a hug. "Text me when you get there so I know you're safe, okay?"

"Will do. Good night." He got back in the truck and turned it around in the courtyard. Sonya waved to him as he started down the driveway, even though she knew he couldn't see her through the rain. She went inside and locked the door.

She watched the light through the kitchen window for a long time before she went to change into her pajamas. It was steady in the driving rain, bright and true. Her text notification sounded; Henry was home safe and would talk to her tomorrow. She should feel free to call him if she needed him. Sonya smiled, feeling more protected than she ever had. She watched the lantern light through the window.

She pictured Virginia's lovely face as they sat across from each other at the cabin island, chatting away like old friends after a long separation. That was exactly how it had felt to Sonya—not like an introduction, but a reunion.

To the glowing lantern light, she whispered, "Good night, Ginny. Thank you for keeping watch."

Sonya went up to bed.

CHAPTER TWENTY-TWO

ON THE DAY of the full moon, Sonya woke beside Kellan in her bed. Her first thought wasn't about the complicated, frightening ritual to be done at the compound that very night, but of the way he'd looked at her while they made love the night before. He'd turned her over and put her on top of him, his gentle hands cradling her breasts. What he'd said brought tears to her eyes.

"Sonya, you honor me."

As he slept, she ran her fingertips ever so lightly over the back of his hand that rested on the pillow between them. The morning light whispered over his features through her filmy blue curtains, finding the many colors of auburn in his hair and lashes. Sonya touched those loosely parted lips; lips she'd kissed until he fell asleep in her arms only hours before. She was in love in a way she'd never experienced. She felt able to fly from the simple joy of it.

Leaving him to sleep, she went out to her studio for her morning practice. The light snow that had fallen in the last storm hadn't stuck on the ground, but decorated the peak of Mount Iolite with a crown of glistening white. The forecast that day was for crisp sunshine, and came with a strong suggestion to get out and see the last of the blazing fall colors before the next storm blew all the golden leaves away. That storm was due in two days.

She tried not to worry about the ritual as she moved through her poses. The view from the long studio windows was the hillside where Ginny had walked with her lantern in the pouring rain. Sonya meditated with that image in her mind, swelling with gratitude for being brought to that place and into the arms of these amazing people. She wanted more than anything to help them; to be worthy of them. As she worked the beads of her mala through her fingers, she prayed to be shown how best to do that.

Kellan was awake when she came back in, standing at the kitchen counter in his sweats and cutting up a ripe pear. He'd started a pot of coffee and got a fire going on the hearth. His hair stood up all around from sleeping like it always did; he was adorable.

"Hi." He smiled, slipping a slice of fruit into his mouth. "Did you have a good pretzel session?"

She laughed as she kissed him. "Yes, it was lovely, thanks. Would you like some cheese with that? I found a nice Vermont cheddar down in Mammoth."

"Sounds good." He took a plate down from her cupboard and arranged the fruit on it. "We have a lot of stuff to get for tonight," he said. "I'm going into Bridgeport with Ev and Jewel to hit the hardware store, and Kath and Henry are going to Mammoth for the apothecary and medical supplies."

"What can I do? Give me a task." Sonya handed him the block of cheese then leaned on the counter to admire him while he worked at the cutting board. She made no secret of her ogling and he grinned.

"Are you sure? We're already going to make a huge mess up here tonight."

"I'm not worried about that. Do you need any other supplies?"

Kellan cut a sliver of cheese and put it together with a piece of pear, gently feeding it to her. "You know that little shop down at Hematite Lake—the one near the pack station?"

"I've been in there a few times," she said, feeding him a bite of cheese and fruit and kissing him. Sonya loved to kiss him.

"There's a section in back by the fishing lures that has all this handmade jewelry. It's all done by Paiute women with locally sourced materials. We need a piece of sterling silver—it can be anything; a ring, earrings, a bracelet—it just has to be Mount Iolite silver and worked by a native person."

"Consider it done." Sonya was happy to contribute something beyond the use of her land.

They sat on the sofa in front of the fire with their coffee. Kellan balanced the plate of fruit and cheese on his lap, then put his arm around Sonya. Smiling into her eyes, he said he wanted to ask her something.

"Of course." Her heart sped up a bit, but she had no idea what his question might be.

"Will you come see me in EDI?" Kellan's amber eyes fixed her, tinged with something she'd never seen there before: vulnerability.

She sighed. "I've almost invited myself a hundred times, but I didn't want you to think I was being pushy—or assuming something that was out of step with your plans."

His smile was both relieved and pleased. "I'm not used to having plans in the first place," he laughed. "Other than when we're playing our next gig and when we're coming back here. But if I did have a plan with you, it would only be to spend as much time with you as I could."

She cupped his jaw in her hand, struggling not to cry. "I'd love to come see you and Kathryn in Scotland. Just tell me when you want me and I'll make it work."

He beamed, eyes lit from within. "I'm starting to want you all the time. I hope that's all right. I don't want to scare you, Sonya."

"You're not scaring me, Kellan. I'm far too busy scaring myself." She laughed a bit shyly. "But the truth is, you're bringing out wonderful things in me. Things I didn't know were there at all. I feel like you're introducing me to myself and I can't thank you enough for that."

Kellan drew her into a long, tight hug. Holding him against her, she let her tears fall. They were tears of joy and needed to be free.

When they parted that day to go in all different directions for supplies, Sonya was unspeakably happy. She decided her down canyon drive required some loud singing music and selected an old Tori Amos album. The circular refrain and lyrics to *Crazy* felt most poignant. She rolled the windows down and let her hair blow in the cool autumn breeze as she wound the Rover through the blazing gold aspen corridor just before Hematite Lake.

The low amber sun danced on the rushing waters of Reverse Creek as she passed. Some fisher folk worked the shoreline in waders and heavy jackets. Sonya drove slowly around the bend where the horseshoe road veered off to the parking lot of the Hematite community center. Campers and minivans lined the roads as people got in the last of the season's trout fishing.

Reverse Creek was so-named because its current went opposite the direction it should be flowing as it came down off the glacier. After last year's good snow season, the creek was still full and churning, playing peek-a-boo through the trees as Sonya drove.

She slowed when she saw a man walking alone on the side of the road because he was so familiar. In jeans, boots and a brown plaid flannel jacket, he wore exactly the same clothes Kellan had been wearing when he left her house not an hour ago. As she approached from behind, she saw the man's dark auburn hair blow in wind. Now only a few yards away, Sonya pulled over on the road. It *was* Kellan. It had to be.

But he was on his way to Bridgeport with Evan and Jewel. Sonya had seen them drive off.

The man was still walking ahead as she got out of the car and stood beside it on the road. She called out to him. "Kellan? Is that you?"

The man slowed and glanced back over his shoulder just long enough for her to see his features. Yes. It was Kellan; no doubt about it. He turned suddenly and went toward the shoreline of the rushing creek.

Sonya went after him, stopping at the spot where he'd disappeared in the golden rustling of the aspen trees. He stood on the shoreline facing her, features muted by the shadow of the sun behind the mountain. He smiled at her; that cunning, sexy smile she'd become addicted to.

"Kellan, what're you doing? I thought you were going to Bridgeport." Sonya walked toward him, thrilled to see him even if his presence there was confusing. Dead leaves and gravel crunched under her boots as she stepped down into the soft earth near the shoreline.

The creek roared behind him. He extended his hand to her, still smiling, but he didn't say anything. Not giving it a second thought, Sonya reached out and took that hand.

She heard the terrible cracking of glass, just like the sound the animal's claws made on Henry's truck roof. Next was the thunder of icy water all around her and the sight of her legs up over her head. The cold was unbearable and all-encompassing.

A flash of something small and white caught the edge of her vision before everything went black; her selenite stone had flown from the pocket of her jeans. In a flash of terrible realization, Sonya understood what was happening.

The monster in the woods beside her house, on her phone screen, and on the roof of Henry Hunter's truck had finally found a way to get in.

–To be continued

ACKNOWLEDGEMENTS

Extra special commendations go to my mom for staying by my side through every tiny moment of this journey. You are the world's greatest cheerleader. Huge thanks to my dad for supporting my writing and always protecting our mountain sanctuary. My remarkable stepsister and stepmom should give master classes on being pillars of encouragement. You are both blessings to me.

The publication of *Blackwing* brought out many old friends cheering on my behalf. To all who not only bought the book, but shared your thoughts with me as you read it, thank you. The photos of the paperbacks arriving in your homes brought tears to my eyes. I appreciate each and every one of you, but honorable mention must go to Victoria, Brenda, Deirdre, Cheri, Dion, Judith, Jean, Doug, Mia, Andie and Cindee, for rallying above and beyond the call.

To Shirley, the coolest neighbor in the world, who purchased ten copies of the *Blackwing* paperback to share with her family, you are simply a rock star. Thank you for your insightful attention to the story and its characters. I hope I've honored Chuck with my intrepid Jewel Early. She and I both raise a glass to him, and look forward to raising many more with you.

My 'day job' co-workers are excellent eggs, especially my kind, generous boss, John. Every day for the decade we've worked together, he has demonstrated the grace of the high road and how very difficult it is to stay on it.

Thanks to my editing and proofing team, Jinxie and CJ, for keeping everything tight and on track.

This book is for Erin, my best friend of forty years, and for my god-daughter, Emmi. I leave you both my love and gratitude in these pages. When the mountains call, I hear your voices.

December 29, 2017

Follow my blog at www.deannaczankich.com